SUDDENLY THE ROOM
WAS UNBEARABLY WARM

Awareness, like wildfire in dry summer grasses, sprang up between them, igniting their senses with a raging heat that consumed old misconceptions, former passions and old fears. Amanda felt Way's body grow hard against her abdomen, and without conscious thought she shifted her weight so that they fit together, like two pieces of the same puzzle.

Way's mouth took hers then, not in a sweet, tentative kiss of exploration, but in a scorching touch of lips that seared her emotions and her heart with the taste and feel of him.

"Mandy," he breathed, shaking his head as if he were having a hard time grasping what had just happened.

"I . . . I don't know what to say. . . ."

"Don't say anything." Way's husky voice bespoke his need. "You're quite a woman, Amanda Farrell, and I'd like to kiss you again."

ABOUT THE AUTHOR

Her husband, her three children, her
Thoroughbred horses and her writing career
hardly ever give Penny Richards a moment to
herself. When she does have some time to relax,
this multitalented resident of Haughton,
Louisiana, loves to paint, collect antiques and
putter around the kitchen. A down-to-earth
dreamer, Penny is an incurable romantic who is as
warm and loving as any of her heroines.
Unforgettable is her first Superromance.

Penny Richards
UNFORGETTABLE

Harlequin Books

TORONTO • NEW YORK • LONDON
AMSTERDAM • PARIS • SYDNEY • HAMBURG
STOCKHOLM • ATHENS • TOKYO • MILAN

Published September 1988

First printing July 1988

ISBN 0-373-70323-6

For Ken, with thanks for
uncomplainingly—mostly—
eating all the sandwiches,
for living in a sometimes
less than immaculate house,
and stoically bearing my
sometimes cranky moods while
I was writing this book.
Thanks especially for letting me have
the room to grow as a person
and for giving me
the freedom to try and grab
the brass ring.
Special thanks also
to Norm and Helen Harrop.

CHAPTER ONE

AMANDA FARRELL REGARDED the indisputably handsome specimen of the male sex sitting on the opposite side of her desk. With his curly blond hair, laughing blue eyes and Arnold Schwarzenegger build, Steve Harris, at nineteen, was the quintessential campus jock. He was the epitome of everything Amanda loathed.

Locking her hands together, she rested them on the worn top of the desk and met his smiling gaze with the violet coolness of her own. She might as well get this over with. "Look, Steve, we both know why you're here."

Steve spread his tanned fingers over his heart in a gesture of remorse that was as poor as it was phony. "Aw, Mandy. Do you mean you didn't call me in here because you wanted to see me alone?"

The fact that he was flirting with her again made only a marginal impression on Amanda, as did his use of the diminutive nickname. She'd given up trying to make him call her Ms Farrell months ago. Ignoring his question, she continued.

"I've begged you to study. I've cajoled. I've threatened. I've asked you to get a tutor." She spread her palms in a defeated gesture. "It's like talking to the wall. But this is it, Steve. Ultimatum time."

The tone of her voice and the steadiness of her gaze caused the smile on his handsome face to falter just the slightest bit. "What are you talking about?"

"I mean that if you don't get some help somehow, you're going to fail this class."

"You're not gonna pass me?" he asked incredulously.

Amanda's delicately arched brows lifted. "I can't pass you. Only you can do that."

Bewilderment replaced the laughter in Steve's eyes. "Coach said you had to pass me or..."

He stopped, aware that he was saying too much, but Amanda knew what he was alluding to. The powers that be had told her that regardless of his grades, she was to pass Steve Harris. Pass him—or else.

She and Steve were in a world of hurt here, unless she could pull off some kind of miracle. Her sardonic look was lost on him. "Believe it or not, Steve, there's more to life than seeing how many touchdowns and girls you can make in a season."

Her observation resurrected his confidence. He propped one elbow on her desk and leaned toward her in an intimate manner that most women—regardless of age—would find flattering. Infusing his voice with one thousand kilowatts of electrically charged sexuality, he said, "Yeah? So tell me, Mandy...what's more important than—" he offered her a wicked smile "—scoring?"

Amanda rubbed her throbbing temple with scarlet-tipped fingers. "Don't flirt with me, Steve. It won't work."

"Hey. We both know you're gonna pass me." He laughed. "It isn't like I really need school. I'm only here so some pro scout can sign me up."

Amanda shook her head at his naïveté. "Is that right? So what do you do if they don't sign you up?"

"They will."

"What if you get hurt?"

Surprise flickered in his eyes. "Hurt?"

"Yes. What if something happens and you can't play football? What happens to you then, if you don't get a college degree?"

Genuine distress crossed his features. Was it possible that the inherent invincibility of his youth had blinded him to the possibility that he might *not* play football?

His bravado returned in a matter of seconds. "No problem. I'll get a degree. The coach told me it's all been taken care of. It's the American way."

The band of tension around Amanda's head tightened. "Well, I'm sorry to have to break this to you, Steve, but it isn't my way."

"What do you mean?"

"I mean that I'm not passing you if you don't earn it."

His eyes widened. "B-but they'll fire you if you don't."

Amanda shrugged with a nonchalance she was far from feeling. "There are other jobs. But I'm not going to compromise my principles so you can run a football down the field."

Steve's gaze slid from hers. "Coach Hale will have a hemorrhage."

Amanda propped her chin in her palm. Ah . . . She'd rattled his cage. Since her job was on the line anyway, she might as well go for broke. "Frankly, Steve, I don't give a damn."

Shocked to silence, he gathered up his books. Framed in the doorway, he turned, his eyes filled with torment.

"What did I ever do to you to make you hate me so much?"

A tiny, wistful smile curved her mouth. "Oh, Steve," she said on a sigh, "I don't hate you. I'm doing this because I care about what happens to you. I care that you won't be able to get a good job without an education. And I don't want that on my conscience."

Steve stared at her, trying to absorb her meaning. Then he turned and left, swallowed up by the corridor.

Amanda buried her face in her palms. *Dammit!* Why couldn't he understand that she was doing this for his own good?

"It's the American way."

She slid open a drawer and grabbed her purse, slamming the drawer shut with a totally unnecessary, completely uncharacteristic and wonderfully satisfying *thud*.

Rising, she turned on the heel of her navy-and-white spectator pumps, tucked her purse beneath her arm and stalked out of her classroom into the blinding glare of the sassy Kansas City sun. The sweet breath of springtime blew the myriad scents of the season to her. Bird songs trilled sweetly from every branch, and an already overweight robin played tug-of-war with a worm hiding in the lush green of the tender shoots of grass. Unfortunately, the beauty of the Missouri April afternoon was lost as frustration joined forces with a fulminating anger.

What else could she have done? Amanda asked herself as she crossed the parking lot. She'd probably hate herself while out hunting for a new job, but the issue was too crucial. Passing some oversexed jock who wasn't making the grade just because he happened to be the best prospective running back to come through the school in the past decade wasn't a precedent she wanted to set.

"Hey, Ms Farrell!"

The cheerful greeting of one of her students broke the thread of her anger. Amanda waved, and her mouth—painted stylishly red—curved into an automatic smile. Her steps slowed and her breathing calmed to one notch above normal.

What was she going to do? Having come from an all-girls school three years before, she'd never encountered this particular problem. The decree to pass Steve went against the grain—especially since she wasn't crazy about athletics in the first place.

She supposed she should be thankful that this was the first time she'd been given a direct order to pass a failing pupil. Until now, she'd been able to persuade students to make some sort of effort, no matter how low the final grade might be. But Steve Harris was different. She'd realized early in the year that he wasn't going to do anything more than he had to.

Amanda unlocked the door of her ancient Volkswagen Rabbit and slid inside, the laughable memory of Steve making a move on her crossing her mind. What would Jeff think of that? Amanda wondered, starting the car and backing out of her parking space.

A genuine smile curved her mouth as her thoughts turned to Jeff, her own nineteen-year-old son, who was just finishing his freshman year at the University of Missouri. Indisputably masculine, he was still sensitive and dependable, not like so many of the guys—like Steve—who spent every spare moment in pursuit of a good time.

Jeff had never given her a minute's trouble, never done anything but what was expected of him since Deke Farrell had run out on them both when Jeff was only three. He'd left them without so much as a backward glance, ostensibly to give Arnold Palmer a run for his money, which, Amanda admitted to herself in a moment's honesty, was probably why she was so intolerant of anything to do with sports. Like the school's demand, her feelings weren't fair, but that's the way it was.

Thank goodness Jeff was nothing like Deke—or Steve. He was a son to be proud of.

AMANDA WAS STILL moderately aggravated when she pulled into her driveway and saw the afternoon sun glinting off the highly polished surface of the mint-condition '57 Chevy parked in the driveway of her modest suburban home. Why was Jeff home in the middle of the week?

The instant she opened the car door she was met by the mouth-watering smell of something cooking on the barbecue grill. The wrinkles in her forehead smoothed. Her maternal fears were somewhat allayed. If Jeff had started dinner, as he usually did when he got home first, could anything be too wrong?

She went into the house, sniffing the pleasantly mingled aromas of brewing coffee and apple pie. Her eyes scanned the country kitchen, going unerringly to the tall man/boy who stood at the kitchen sink.

Jeff, who wore low-riding, brightly colored jams, was drying his hands on a tea towel. He turned at the sound of the door closing and flashed her a quick, almost nervous smile. "Hi," he said in the deep voice that always reminded her of his father.

Amanda didn't smile back. "What are you doing here?" she asked. If it wasn't too ridiculous to consider, she could have sworn that Jeff's tanned complexion turned pink.

Shrugging and offering her an embarrassed, lopsided Jeff grin, he asked, "Would you believe I got homesick?"

Amanda relaxed. He hadn't been home in a month, and she'd missed him, too. "I believe it. But couldn't you have waited another two days?"

"No."

With a laugh, Amanda crossed the space separating them. Enveloped in a brief, fierce embrace, she was smothered for an instant in masculine scents, hard masculine arms and the sharp unexpected realization that Jeff was no longer her little boy. She felt the sting of tears beneath her eyelids at the thought and stepped away from him. They exchanged another gee-it's-great-to-see-you smile, and this smile seemed strange, too. Almost... worried. *Grades,* she reasoned.

"How's the chemistry?"

"Fair," he told her, moving to the coffeepot and pouring the fragrant brew into two mugs. "I should scrape by with a B for the semester."

"Not bad," Amanda said, accepting the coffee. "You know, Jeff, you really need to take that trig—"

"Don't start, Mom!"

Amanda's mouth snapped shut. He was right. Neither of them was ready for one of their continuing fights over his major, and his decisiveness was another reminder that he wasn't a child anymore. Jeff was pretty much on his own now and more than able to decide what he wanted to do with his life. The problem was that Amanda hadn't accepted this fact yet. She didn't feel his music major could ever be a dependable way to make a living—never mind that the field hardly scratched the surface of his potential.

"Go change your clothes," he commanded, softening the directive with a smile. "The steaks will be ready in a jiffy, and Mrs. Smith and I made Dutch apple pie for dessert." He held up the now empty box of a popular and tasty frozen dessert.

"I thought I smelled apples," she said, backing down with a half smile of defeat. She began to unfasten the small buttons of her polka-dot blouse. "I won't be but a minute."

Jeff didn't answer. She darted another questioning look toward him and, frowning, headed from the room. There was definitely something different about Jeff tonight, but she knew that he would tell her what was wrong when he was ready to tell her, and not a moment before.

"THAT WAS FIVE," Jeff said when she reentered the kitchen a few moments later, dressed in a summer-weight lavender sweater and pleated gray slacks.

"Five?"

"Minutes," he explained, setting the salad in the center of the small kitchen table and gesturing at her with a comical flourish to take a seat.

Smiling, Amanda sat down across from him. "I didn't know you were actually counting. What's the hurry?"

"I'm starving," he said, slicing through the foil of his baked potato and slathering it with huge chunks of butter.

"Jeff, the cholesterol!" Amanda cautioned, putting a small pat on each side of her own potato.

"Hey! Gimme a break, huh?"

Again, Amanda was stung by his sharpness. She shrugged. "It's your funeral."

Jeff threw back his head and looked up at the ceiling. A deep sigh issued from the depths of him; he lowered his head until their eyes met. "Look, I'm sorry." The expression in his eyes suggested something between apology and a very real sorrow.

"It's all right." After the day she'd experienced, Amanda was eager to ease the tension between them. Jeff was all she had, and she didn't like things out of kilter between them. She searched her mind for a safe topic of conversation. "I guess you're going to Heather's tonight."

The spoonful of sour cream he was putting on his potato stopped momentarily in midair before a big blob plopped onto the melting butter. "No. Not tonight."

Amanda said a little prayer. Heather Dalton was a nice girl, but she and Jeff had been going together for a long time now, and the last thing Amanda felt Jeff needed was a serious relationship. "This has to be a first," she said. "You two aren't having any trouble, are you?"

"No. Uh . . . her Dad got to fly in, and she wanted to spend some time with him." Jeff offered her a strained smile and forged ahead. "So how was your day? Are you glad the year is winding down?"

Amanda's answering smile was full-fledged and, to her son, heart-stoppingly beautiful. "Lousy and yes," she said in answer to both his questions.

"With finals coming up next month, I can relate to the last, but would you care to elaborate on the 'lousy' part?" he asked, eager to center the conversation on her.

"I was told from those in authority that I *would* give Steve Harris passing grades—or else."

"Or else, as in they'll fire you if you don't?"

Amanda's flash of lightheartedness fled. "It sounds that way, doesn't it?" She put down her fork, and leaning her elbow on the table, rested her chin in the palm of her hand.

"And there's no way he can pass?"

"With divine intervention...*maybe*," she assured him dryly.

"So what are you going to do?"

"I don't know. Getting fired doesn't bother me—much," she amended. "I feel that I could find another job. It's just that this sort of thing should be stopped. They should relegate sports to the bottom of their list of priorities, not the top. After all, school is a place to learn, not a place to kick and throw a ball around."

"That's a bit tough, isn't it?" Jeff asked. "Just because Dad left us to play golf doesn't make all sports bad...or the people who play them."

"Let's leave your father out of this, please," Amanda said. She smiled wryly. "My intellect tells me you're right, but my heart won't listen. I wonder why you never wanted to play sports?"

"I wanted to," Jeff confessed for the first time, "but I was always working after school and couldn't make the practices."

"Are you serious?"

Jeff's smile was wistful. "Yeah."

Amanda stared across the kitchen at a point Jeff couldn't see, a thoughtful expression on her classic features. "And thanks once again, Deke," she said sarcastically, lifting her tea glass in a mock salute. Her gaze moved back to Jeff's. "I'm sorry. I never realized when you were working that you would rather have been playing sports."

"Look, Mom. Don't get upset about it now. It isn't like I had a tremendous amount of potential or anything. I wasn't mean enough for football, tall enough for basketball or fast enough for baseball. That's why I took up music—so I wouldn't be a total nerd, and so I could be a part of that school spirit thing."

Amanda swallowed a thickness in her throat. She'd never dreamed that Jeff's old-fashioned and misplaced sense of duty about helping her out with money had kept him from doing something he wanted for himself.

"Hey, Mom. It's okay." He reached across the table and held out his hand. Amanda placed hers in it. "Forget it. It's no big deal. I'm happy."

"Are you?"

His eyes flickered from hers momentarily. "Yes."

"What about golf?"

He shrugged. "What about it?"

"Did you ever want to play golf?" she asked, her eyes twinkling.

"No," he told her seriously. "Never."

They shared a moment of laughter. Then, determined to turn the conversation to happier channels, she asked, "So Heather is spending the evening with her father?"

"Yeah," Jeff said, diving into his dinner with typical nineteen-year-old zeal.

"What is it he does?"

Jeff looked at her with disbelief. As it had so often this evening, his voice took on a defensive, almost angry tone. "He's first baseman for the Royals. I've been dating Heather for almost ten months now, and it seems like you could at least remember what her dad does for a living."

Amanda held her palm up as if to ward off any more angry words. "I'm sorry. And her mother was killed in a car accident, right?"

"You remembered," he said with a touch of sarcasm.

"Jeff—"

"Why do I always get the feeling that you ignore Heather and anything about her? It's like you think that if you don't acknowledge her, don't show any interest, she'll go away. Why? Don't you like her?"

The pounding in Amanda's head, which she'd tried to ignore for the past couple of hours, increased as he spoke. She wondered what had happened to her day and if there was some sort of conspiracy afoot to drive her completely crazy. And what on earth was the matter with Jeff?

Clenching her hands together in her lap, she said slowly and in what she hoped was a reasonable tone of voice, "I don't dislike Heather, Jeff. She seems very nice. It's just that you're so young and have so much school ahead of you that I hate to see you get too serious about any girl."

"You may as well get used to her, because I'm going to..." He paused, dropped his gaze from his mother's and took a deep breath. When his gaze met hers once more, his tobacco-brown eyes were filled with a sincerity that was hard to doubt, a sincerity that begged her to understand. "I love her."

"I know you think you love her, but—"

Jeff moved so quickly that the sound of his chair crashing to the floor was Amanda's only warning that she had overstepped some invisible boundary. She jumped at the sudden and unexpected action, blinked in surprise and swallowed back her shock.

Glaring at her, Jeff threw his napkin down. Placing his sensitive musician's hands on the tabletop, he leaned belligerently toward her. "I don't *think* I love her. I know I do. And if you were going to spout all those old platitudes about us growing apart and my finding someone else later, forget it, because it isn't going to happen."

"Jeff, I—"

"No! You listen." His brown eyes were intense and serious. "Heather is in my life to stay, Mom. You may as well accept it, because nothing that you or anyone else can say will change how I feel." Then, without even bothering to pick up the fallen chair, he stormed out of the room.

Total shock kept Amanda frozen in her chair. From somewhere on the other side of the house she heard a door slam. She laid her napkin beside her almost untouched plate, trying to comprehend the scene she'd just witnessed. Jeff's actions were totally unlike him, completely out of character. What was the matter? Why this sudden defensive attitude and these rapid mood changes? Drugs? She rejected the thought as soon as it entered her mind. No drugs. Not Jeff. Then what?

It must be the end-of-the-year-I've-had-it thing. That *must* be it. Everyone's nerves were stretched to the breaking point with finals looming on the horizon.

Amanda stood and rounded the table woodenly. Bending and gripping the finials on top of the chair's ladder back, she set it upright, staring at the door her only child had just exited. That was it. Like her, Jeff was just tired.

HEATHER DALTON LOOKED at her watch for the dozenth time in as many minutes. Where was her dad? It was almost nine, and he was later than he said he'd be. Normally she longed for the too-short, infrequent occasions that were all Way Dalton's career as a superstar baseball player and his two new restaurants, Wayfarers, allowed. Longed for—and needed them. But tonight was different. For once she was glad for the brief reprieve.

Heather crossed the living room to the area set apart for dining. The centerpiece was a milk-glass basket of fresh tulips, daisies and jonquils she'd bought at the supermarket. The flower motif was repeated in the casual china, a stark white with a bright red tulip hugging the rim. Yellow ceramic napkin rings held generous squares of spring-green linen. She hoped the setting looked cheerful, happy, positive—all the things she was far from feeling.

Suddenly, twin beams of light sliced through the darkness as her father's Blazer swept up the circular driveway. Her worried eyes found her reflection in the mirror across the room—a too-tall girl with a haunted expression stared back at her. A girl who looked as if she could use a smile to erase the frightened look from her eyes.

Making a sound of disgust, she tucked a swath of fine, shoulder-length blond hair behind her ear, knotted her hands together and pivoted toward the sound of a key turning in the lock. The door swung open, and a tall man strode into the large flagstone foyer off the living room with an easy, confident gait. Heather faced her father with a prayer in her heart, a queasy smile pasted on her lips. "Hi, Dad," she said in a soft, reedy voice.

Waylon "Way" Dalton, first baseman for the Kansas City Royals and, with any luck, within a good season of upsetting Hank Aaron's all-time home-run record, set his small bag on the floor and stared in disbelief at the beautiful picture his daughter made. It was a momentous moment, one he knew would be indelibly stamped in his mind.

He didn't know if it was because, if Carol had lived, they would be celebrating their eighteenth wedding anniversary in two days, or if it was just that he was feeling his forty years more and more lately, but Way thought that Heather had never looked more like her mother than she did at this moment, her streaky blond pageboy brushing her shoulders as she stared at him with dark, mysterious eyes.

She'd never looked more grown-up, Way thought, suddenly struck with the knowledge that, contrary to his belief that she would be his little girl forever, she would soon be grown...gone. Emotion tightened his throat. She would be graduating in another month. It seemed like just yesterday that he and Carol had walked Heather hand in hand to the school bus that had opened its yellow doors and swallowed her up—pigtails and all—and carried her off to kindergarten.

And wasn't it only last week that Heather had been all arms and legs with a long, silky ponytail hanging down her back and silver braces banding her teeth? Wasn't it only yesterday that she'd run to him and smothered him with kisses, giggled at his corny jokes and hung on to his every word? But this new, grown-up Heather just stood there, poised on the brink of womanhood, waiting.

Not surprisingly, she had grown taller and put on enough weight that the skinny was now a stylish slenderness. Her legs were still long, but graceful and feminine—just like the soft curve of her hips and the proud thrust of her small breasts. He swallowed back the obstruction in his throat. Where had all the years gone?

She's beautiful, Carol. You'd be so proud of her.

"You okay, Dad?" Heather's worried voice penetrated his thoughts, bringing his attention back from the past.

"I'm fine, baby," he said in a husky, betraying voice. He opened his arms. "Got a hug for your old dad?"

Heather forced a smile to her peach-glossed lips. "Sure."

For all her misgivings, she went to him, sliding her arms around his hard-muscled waist, holding him tightly. With her eyes closed, she pressed her cheek into his shirtfront and breathed in the spicy smell of his cologne, a scent that she'd branded "Dad's" from the time she was old enough to connect the masculine fragrance to him. Remembering those younger, carefree days brought the sting of tears to her eyes. If possible, she burrowed closer into his comforting embrace.

Way held her and wished he could turn back the clock, wished he'd spent more time on the playground with her after Carol had died and less time on a baseball diamond. His baby was grown-up, and he'd been too busy to be more than marginally aware of the fact. A treacherous lump rose in his throat again.

Heather lifted her head and looked up at him with sherry-hued eyes sparkling with unshed tears. "I love you, Daddy."

Way's smile lifted the corners of the luxuriant dark-blond mustache that swept boldly across his upper lip and bracketed the corners of his mouth. The mustache diminished the hawklike slice of his nose and accentuated the strong whiteness of his teeth. The smile scored creases into his lean, tanned cheeks and crinkled the corners of his usually laughing, warm brown eyes.

"I love you, too, baby," he said.

Heather smiled, a tremulous quirking of her lips.

"You've grown into a beautiful woman, Heather Dalton." Way lifted a hand and brushed his knuckles across the zenith of one blush-dusted cheek. "I'm proud of you . . . and so would your mother be, if she could see you."

Tears flooded Heather's already glistening eyes.

Then, because rough and tough Way Dalton felt like crying himself, he lifted his head and sniffed the air appreciatively. "What smells so good?"

Heather swallowed hard and brushed at her eyes, glad to push aside the tender feelings. His praise only made her feel worse.

"Muffy fixed roast, mashed potatoes and gravy, corn and asparagus," she told him, shortening the name of their housekeeper, Mrs. Moffett, to her affectionate nickname. "And I made you a peach cobbler for dessert."

"Hmm," Way said, releasing her and sliding his arm around her shoulders. "All my favorites. What is this? Are you trying to butter up old Dad?"

Her wide, startled eyes met his. "No," she said quickly.

"You didn't wreck your car or flunk chemistry, did you?" he teased.

"Daaad," she groaned.

Way laughed and dropped a kiss to the top of her head. "Let's go eat. I'm supposed to go to the restaurant and check some things out with Brent."

"The restaurant?" The light in Heather's eyes died a sudden death. "Do you have to? I mean...couldn't you stay here with me tonight?" she asked, trying to ignore the nervous churning of her stomach.

Way frowned. It wasn't like Heather to ask him to stay at home. Feelings of inadequacy and guilt rushed back with a vengeance. He should have spent more time with her, but maybe it wasn't too late. He smiled. "I'll call Brent and tell him I can't make it."

Heather's answering smile hovered between an expression of relief and anxiety, but Way didn't notice. He was already headed for the dining room. Heather followed, weighted down by suffocating dread.

As it turned out, the meal wasn't the ordeal she'd imagined it would be. She watched her dad devour his dinner and listened avidly as he related stories of spring training. She even laughed appropriately when he told her about the trick the team had played on one of the outfielders.

Heather answered Way's questions about school, gave him a report on her end-of-the-year activities and made him memorize the date of her graduation, but Way couldn't overlook the obvious: something was wrong.

He noted the circles beneath her eyes, which he'd overlooked earlier in his happiness to be home with her again. At second glance, her stylishly slender figure was too thin. He watched her pick at her food, rearranging it as she had when she was little so he would think she was eating more than she was. She made all the right responses to his questions about school, but her answers were abstracted, her attention obviously elsewhere.

"What's the matter, baby?" he asked, laying down his fork and looking at her with genuine concern.

Heather's gaze jumped from her plate to his. "N-nothing."

Way took a sip of his coffee, thinking. If school was all right, then she and Jeff must have had a fight. If they had, it was a shame. Jeff was a likable kid, and Way knew Heather was crazy about him. Still, even though she didn't think so, someone else would soon come along. He racked his mind for a way to broach the subject, but the best he could come up with was, "How's Jeff?"

Heather gave great attention to drizzling spoonfuls of melted ice cream over the top of her peaches. "He's... fine."

"The two of you aren't having trouble? You haven't broken up?"

She swallowed. "No." Her voice was a near whisper. She glanced at him from beneath her lashes and lifted a hand to cover her mouth.

"And the grades are—Heather! What is it?" The last question was asked on a note of anxiety when she pushed herself away from the table and fled from the dining room, down the hall.

Way followed, his concern escalating to an unaccustomed feeling of panic. His pursuit ended at the bathroom door. He lifted his hand to knock, but before his knuckles made contact, the unmistakable sounds of retching filtered through the wooden panel.

Perhaps it was because the memories of Carol were so strong, perhaps he had a suspicious mind, but whatever the reason, a feeling of déjà vu, unexpected and acute, washed over Way, sharpening his perception of the moment. Too many things were out of kilter here, and all of a sudden Heather's appearance and actions began to make sense. As clearly as if she were standing there, he saw Carol's pale, worried face.

"I'm pregnant, Way."

At the startling possibility that history might be repeating itself, the healthy color seeped from Way's face, leaving it white with shock. His hand, poised at the door, lowered to his side. He was trembling. He felt suddenly empty. Old. Drained. Leaning against the opposite wall for support, he scrubbed at his face with his hand, pulling his features downward in a gesture of supreme weariness. As if from the bottom of a deep, deep well he heard the sounds of flushing...water running... gargling....

The rattle of the doorknob turning focused his attention to the slowly widening aperture where Heather stood, looking pale and shaken. Her lips trembled in apprehension, and her eyes were wide and frightened as they searched his face for some sign of how he felt.

He felt hurt. Betrayed, even. And angry. His eyes flashed with all three emotions.

Heather saw only the anger and made an incoherent noise that sounded suspicously like a whimper. Way stood mutely looking at her. She was so much like Carol he could hardly bear it. The memory of his own mistake softened his heart and brought the sheen of tears to his eyes. He urged a wavering, understanding smile to his lips and held out his arms.

With a small, wounded cry, Heather hurtled into them and toward the comfort she knew waited for her there.

CHAPTER TWO

THE PERSISTENT RINGING invaded Amanda's sleep-fogged brain. She rolled to one side, her hand flailing the bedside table in search of the alarm clock. She pressed the button...to no avail. The ringing sounded again, shattering the stillness of the night.

The phone, she thought, pushing herself up on her elbow and groping for the bedside lamp. She flicked it on and glanced at the clock. *Five thirty-five!* She reached for the offending instrument, wondering irritably who on God's green earth could have the audacity to wake her after she'd worried about Jeff for half the night. Amanda put the receiver to her ear and sank back against the pillow.

"Hello?"

"Mrs. Farrell?"

The voice questioning her was attractive and masculine, she noted drowsily. He called her by name, so it wasn't a wrong number. "Yes?" she answered in a sleep-husky tone.

"This is Way Dalton," he said, marveling at the unbearably sexy sound of her voice.

While Amanda was searching her mind for a clue as to who Way Dalton was, he spoke again.

"Way Dalton. Heather's father."

Of course, Amanda thought. *Heather's father.*

"Mrs. Farrell? Are you awake?"

"Barely," she said, frowning as she began to wonder just why Heather's father would be calling at such an ungodly hour.

"Well, get up," he said in a no-nonsense tone, "and put on some coffee. We're coming over there."

His aggressiveness sliced through Amanda's sleepy state with razor sharpness. Spurred awake by anger, Amanda snapped, "Look here, Mr. Dalton, just who do you think you are?"

"I think, Mrs. Farrell," he said in voice laden with unutterable weariness, "that I am the father of a seventeen-year-old girl who's gone and got herself pregnant—by your son."

"What?" Amanda screeched, vaulting into a sitting position, while her mind rejected his statement.

"Heather is pregnant," he repeated. "She told me Jeff was supposed to tell you last night."

Heather. Pregnant. Jeff...supposed to tell her. Amanda's mind whirled. Her head hurt and her stomach lurched. Even so, the words and the way Jeff had acted the night before began to mesh in her mind. His behavior made perfect sense when superimposed on what Heather's father had just told her.

"Mrs. Farrell? Are you all right?"

The calm tenor of his voice grated on Amanda's screaming nerves. All right? No, she wasn't all right. She might never be all right again. She made a concerted effort to collect herself. "I-I'm fine," she stammered.

"Look, I'm sorry I broke it to you like this," Waylon Dalton said, the apology in his voice overriding the anger he kept carefully leashed. "I should have waited, but I..." He paused. "I guess the truth is, I'm pretty damn mad at Jeff over this."

He was mad at *Jeff*? Amanda thought in disbelief. Her world and Jeff's was smashed into a million pieces, and this . . . baseball player was mad at *Jeff*? Amanda began a slow boil. The nerve of him! If he'd accepted the part of a father and stayed at home to give Heather the support she needed during these troubled teenage years, instead of going off for months on end to hit a ball in front of thousands of people—like a kid who needed to hear the crowd's verbal adulation—this might not have happened. And when he got here, she planned on telling him so!

"Mrs. Farrell?"

Amanda dragged her thoughts back from the precipice of her deepening anger. "Yes?"

"We'll be there in about thirty minutes."

Thirty minutes. Not enough time to tell Jeff and make him understand. Not nearly enough time to make him see the right course he should take with his life.

"Fine."

To Way, the word sounded cool, even cold. When he spoke, he sounded considerably less amenable. "We'll see you then."

He hung up, one side of his mustache lifting in a snarl. He mimed a flip, sarcastic "Fine" at the telephone receiver. Then, rubbing the back of his neck, he rose naked from the bed, shaking his head at the remembrance of Amanda Farrell's frigid attitude.

He headed for the shower and turned on the spray, his mind recollecting bits and snatches of what Heather had told him about Jeff's mother. Prim and proper and very protective of Jeff, since she'd raised him alone. He could see Ms College English Professor now—tall, mannish, dressed in tweeds, sensible brogans and self-righteousness, complete with glasses and a mustache that

was the result of some sort of female hormonal imbalance. As for the sexy sound of her voice...well, he'd
awoken her, and more than likely it was nothing but the
remnants of sleep that had made her sound so appeal-
ing. He knew the type, and it was a wonder poor Jeff
had turned out as well as he had, a wonder the old crow
hadn't emasculated him with her domination.

Way sighed and stepped into the welcome warmth of
the shower. He dreaded the upcoming meeting more
than he'd dreaded the '85 Series against the Cardinals.
It had been a long night; it promised to be an even longer
day.

AMANDA STARED at the phone briefly, then rose and
pulled on the robe that matched the seersucker shorty
pajamas she wore. Her sole goal at the moment was to
confront Jeff with Way Dalton's accusation, even
though her heart knew that what Heather's father had
said was true. Opting for glasses instead of her contacts
for the sake of time, she shoved the large, round, out-of-
style frames onto the bridge of her nose and, without
bothering to brush her hair, went to Jeff's room.

She found him sleeping peacefully, innocently, one
arm flung over his head, the other resting across his
chest. It was the way he'd slept since he was a little boy.
Amanda's eyes clouded with tears. The breadth of his
chest and the soft cloud of hair sprawling across it attested to the fact that he wasn't her innocent little boy
anymore. He was a man. And he'd got a girl pregnant.
Oh, Jeff, how could you do this to me? To yourself?

She reached out and grasped his shoulder, shaking
him awake. ''Jeff, wake up.''

He moaned and lifted his lashes slowly. The first thing
he saw was his mother's tear-filled eyes staring down at

him through the owlish lenses of her glasses, their depths holding a strange mixture of condemnation and sorrow. Without knowing how, he knew that she knew about Heather. Raising himself on one elbow, he blinked and asked, "Who told you?"

He didn't even bother to deny it, Amanda thought as her heart broke into a million irreparable pieces. "Heather's father called a few minutes ago. He thought you'd already told me."

Jeff sat up and rested his elbows on his knees. He dropped his head in his hands, his fingers plowing through his dark hair. "I tried to tell you," he said in a low voice, "but I couldn't." He lifted his head and met her eyes once more. "I wasn't sure I could handle your disappointment."

Disappointment. Yes, she was disappointed. And hurt. And furious. Amanda clamped her teeth down on her bottom lip and nodded, her own failures snapping at the heels of her memory. "Get dressed. The Daltons are on their way over."

She was through the door when Jeff's voice stopped her. "Mom!"

Amanda turned back to her son. This time there was a faint shimmer of tears in his eyes, tears and a bleakness Amanda felt in her very soul.

"I'm sorry."

Pain for the carefree youth he'd let slip away with such thoughtlessness by his temporary sojourn into the world of adulthood saturated her heart. He'd made a choice by sleeping with Heather Dalton—a choice that narrowed all future options. As her grandma used to say, Jeff had danced, now he had to pay the fiddler.

Her words revealed the ache growing in her heart. "So am I, Jeff."

"I LOVE HER, dammit!"

Jeff's voice raised in anger was the first sound Way heard as he stepped from his car. He glanced at Heather, who looked worried, and gave his daughter what he hoped was an encouraging smile. He held out his hand, and they started toward the place that seemed to be the origin of the argument, the back of the Farrell house.

"You don't know the meaning of love!"

Together, Way and Heather rounded the corner of the house and stepped onto the patio. Sliding glass doors gave them an unobliterated view of the kitchen and its occupants. Surprise gripped Way as he tried to reconcile his picture of Amanda Farrell with the woman pacing the kitchen. Some part of his mind told him he'd only been right about one thing: she wore glasses. Large, round-lensed glasses that overwhelmed the dainty features of her face and gave her the appearance of a very young, very innocent owl.

Every other aspect of the mental picture he'd manufactured of her was as wrong as wrong could be. This woman looked more like Jeff's sister than his mother and nothing like any English professor he'd ever seen. She didn't have a mustache; her skin was creamy white, unblemished by so much as a freckle. She wasn't wearing tweeds and brogans; she was barefoot, her body barely covered by a short cotton robe sprinkled with tiny purple flowers. She wasn't tall and mannish as he had imagined; the real Amanda Farrell was short, petite even, and everything about her—especially her shapely legs and softly curving body—was excruciatingly feminine, despite the shortness of her hair, which looked as if it would curl given half a chance... or half an inch.

Before Way could do anything more than register the disparities in his mind, she whirled around and saw them standing in the doorway. He took advantage of her momentary surprise to ask, "Mrs. Farrell? May we come in?"

Jeff turned toward them, a smile of welcome replacing his angry scowl. "Sure," he said, answering for her. "Come on in."

To cover her embarrassment at being caught in her pajamas and screaming like a fishwife, Amanda redirected her fury toward the newcomers, who were being ushered in by her traitorous offspring. She crossed her arms and threw her one hundred pounds to one hip, raking Heather's father with a jaded eye. Good grief! If it wasn't an older version of Steve Harris!

Way Dalton was well over six feet and, despite his age, which she guessed was near her own, he looked to be in peak physical condition. The breadth of his shoulders, the dimensions of his biceps and the narrowness of his waist had to come from hours in a weight room, hours that should have been spent with his daughter. His hair—blond, naturally—was like the color of ripened wheat and laced with sun-kissed, almost platinum streaks. Of course it was curly—if only enough to curl over his collar—and well past needing a trim, as was the drooping mustache that failed to hide the sensual shape of his upper lip. What was it anyway? she wondered. Did God have a mold in various but similar shapes for athletes—not to mention their personalities and egos?

Jeff's voice registered his nervousness as he said, "Mr. Dalton, this is my mother, Amanda Farrell. Mom, Heather's dad, Way Dalton."

"Mr. Dalton," Amanda said, managing to assume a semiregal aura despite her clothes—or lack of them.

"Mrs. Farrell," Way answered with a polite nod, determined to be civil. Acting immature and screaming the way Jeff and his mother had been a few moments before would accomplish nothing. Way understood her anger, but anger wasn't the way to work things out.

Amanda offered him a saccharine smile. "Ms," she corrected.

"*Ms* Farrell," he acknowledged with another nod, which was only a tiny bit exaggerated.

Chauvinist! Amanda turned to Heather, her expression softening. After all, this wasn't the poor child's fault. She should have had better training at home. "Hello, Heather. How are you?"

Heather shifted from one foot to the other. "Fine," she squeaked, glancing at Jeff as if for support.

Grabbing a chair, Jeff pulled it out for her and said, "Why don't we all sit down? I'll pour the coffee."

Her nerves screaming in frustration and fury, Amanda said, "If you'll excuse me for just a moment, I'll go get dressed." Without waiting for an answer, she left the room, storming through the house, her mind replaying the sardonic lift of Way Dalton's mustache and damning the whiteness of his smile.

She reentered the kitchen five minutes later, reassured by the fact that while her sharply creased slacks and blouse were casual enough for the occasion, they still projected an aura of no-nonsense professionalism. She stepped through the door in time to hear Way say, "The whole thing shouldn't take more than three or four days."

"What shouldn't take more than three or four days?" she asked the trio seated at the table while she helped herself to a cup of coffee and some warm cinnamon rolls dripping powdered-sugar glaze.

"Getting a license and blood test."

Amanda's saucer clattered to the countertop at Jeff's matter-of-fact announcement. She'd known it would come to this, of course, but she couldn't accept the assumed fait accompli calmly. Turning to face them, she said softly, "I forbid it."

"Forbid it?"

"Mom!"

"Oh!"

The reactions came simultaneously from Way, Jeff and Heather.

Amanda's gaze moved from one person to the next, lighting finally on Way. Her eyes said that she would fight a marriage between the two teenagers to the bitter end.

"Jeff has to get his education. He can't support a family by going to school and working part-time at a fast-food chain."

"I can drop out of school for a while," Jeff said, before Way had a chance to respond. "Just until we get on our feet."

Amanda shook her head. "Once you get tied down with a wife and child, you'll have a full-time job and full-time responsibilities. It might be years before you'll be able to go back."

"So what? I'll finish somehow, Mom. College is always there for me," he said in an attempt to reason with her.

Amanda leaned against the cabinets. "That's what everyone says, but few ever do go back. I want better for you, Jeff."

"You want something better for him than marriage to my daughter?" The question—out before Way could stop it—was delivered in a tone bare millimeters from full-fledged fury. So much for calm rationalization.

Amanda raised her coffee cup to her lips with a nonchalance that set his teeth on edge, and looked him directly and unrelentingly in the eye. "Better than marriage, Mr. Dalton—to anyone."

"You have something against marriage?" he bit out, pushing back the plate bearing the remains of cinnamon-and-brown-sugar rolls. He rose and went to where she stood by the coffeepot, staring down at her for a moment in an act of unstudied aggression. Amanda looked up into his probing brown eyes. It was almost, she thought, as if he were trying to see what made her tick. After several searching seconds, he reached past her and refilled his cup. Then he turned and went back to the table, raising the cup to his lips and staring at her over its rim.

The look that passed between them told him that she didn't like the liberty he'd taken by making himself at home. Way's expression said he didn't give a damn. Both had forgotten that Jeff and Heather were in the room. The confrontation had somehow become something personal and private.

"Is it correct to assume, then, *Ms* Farrell, that you aren't enamored of the wedded state?"

"You might say that, Mr. Dalton," Amanda replied in arctic tones.

"Why?"

Her eyes widened. "I beg your pardon?"

"What do you have against marriage?"

"Look, Mr. Dalton," she said, "I hardly think that's any of your business."

"The hell it isn't!" he snapped. "We're talking about my daughter's reputation here...her future! Anything that stands in the way of her happiness *is* my business."

"*Her* happiness!" Amanda shrieked. "What about Jeff's happiness?"

"He'll be happy with Heather!" Way shouted. "They love each other."

"They *think* they love each other! What they call love is sex! And what happens to that love when she's nine months pregnant and there's no money? What happens to that love when there's nothing but hospital bills and a colicky baby to look forward to?" As she posed each question, the memory of Amanda's own situation with Deke took on a sharp new focus.

"Why paint such a grim picture?" Way countered. "It doesn't have to be that way."

"Oh, you're one hundred percent right about that, Mr. Dalton. It doesn't have to be that way. There's always adoption or—"

Way leaped to his feet and leaned across the table with a quiet menace that silenced Amanda in the span of a heartbeat. "Don't say it, Amanda," he warned, using her first name without realizing it. "Remember that you're talking about my grandchild. Your grandchild."

Surprise softened the edge of her anger and her voice. "I wasn't going to suggest abortion, but there are alternatives to marriage. They made a mistake. Why compound it with another? Two wrongs don't make a right."

"Maybe you're right, Ms Farrell," Heather said, speaking for the first time since she'd said hello. Her eyes found Jeff's, and two tears slid down her cheeks. "I want to do the best thing for all of us."

"Heather!" Jeff's voice held disbelief, which changed to disgust when he turned toward Amanda. "I hope to hell you're happy. And if you were as negative when you were married to Dad as you are now, it's no wonder he walked out on you!"

Amanda gasped, unable to believe that Jeff had mentioned Deke's desertion in front of strangers. But there were a lot of things she couldn't believe about Jeff lately. Hoping to salvage the moment, she said, "Your father's desertion of us is one reason I want you to be very certain that what you're doing is right. Don't rule out adoption, or the possibility of Heather raising the baby alone."

Way Dalton's snort of anger shifted everyone's attention to him. His mustache lifted in a mockery of a smile. "You know, lady, you're a real gem." He turned to Heather and held out his hand. "Come on, baby. Let's get out of here."

"Wait!" Jeff cried. He looked his mother straight in the eye and asked, "You loved Dad when you married him, didn't you?"

Amanda frowned. What was he getting at?

"Come on, Mom! Let's have some of that honesty you're always touting!" Jeff urged. "When you got pregnant with me, you loved him, didn't you?"

Amanda's heart plummeted to her toes, and another soft gasp escaped her lips. He knew? How?

Jeff smiled. It was a young-old, bittersweet-sorrowful smile. "I was valedictorian of my class last year, Mom. I had straight A's in all my biology classes."

Amanda's gaze moved from one face to the other; her eyes held sorrow and shame. She pushed herself away from the cabinets, her actions slow and heavy as she once again scanned the faces in the room, this time without really seeing anyone. When she spoke it was to everyone and no one.

"Excuse me." Without another word, she left the room.

IT MUST HAVE BEEN NOON when Amanda opened her eyes. After she'd called in sick to school, she'd taken two aspirin and gone back to bed in search of a few hours' respite from memories of the tension-fraught scene in the kitchen. She needed to escape, needed to forget her own mistakes—especially the fact that Jeff knew he'd been conceived outside of marriage.

Now Jeff had fallen into the same trap with Heather that she herself had once fallen into with Deke. She'd dreaded it happening, prayed he would have more sense, hoped she would never have to confess her own mistake to him. But her prayers and hopes had been for nothing.

Remembering the compassion she'd seen on her son's face when he'd confronted her, she began to cry. She couldn't remember when she'd cried last. Was it when the divorce became final, some fifteen years ago? It had been too long, surely. But she hadn't had time to cry. She'd taken whatever job was necessary to provide for Jeff and to get where she was today, and she'd worked hard. She hadn't had much time for crying.

Softly at first, then with increasing volume, the tears and sobs flowed, releasing feelings that should have been vented years before. She cried for the impetuosity of youth. She cried because Jeff had never known a father. For the past. And for the future.

Amanda didn't hear Jeff come into the room, but she felt his weight on the side of the bed.

"Sh.... It's going to be all right," he murmured, pulling her up and into his arms, using the same words to comfort his mother that she had used to ease the pain during his growing-up years. "I'm sorry I said anything in front of the Daltons. I shouldn't have."

Amanda lifted her lashes and looked at him through a veil of tears. "Why didn't you say something before now?"

"What could I say? I couldn't change things. I was angry at first, because you always preached 'be good' to me, but after a while I began to realize that parents only want what's best for their kids, and if they've made a mistake, they'll try extra hard to keep their kids from making the same one."

Amanda pushed herself up to a sitting position and reached for another tissue from the bedside table. She wiped at her eyes and blew her nose. "That's pretty adult thinking."

"Maybe because I am an adult," Jeff said.

She attempted to smile. "Maybe."

"*Did* you love him?"

The question came out of the blue and picked up the conversation that had been abandoned in the kitchen. Amanda saw the question in Jeff's eyes. Saw the sincerity, the worry...the fear.

"Yes, I loved him. I loved him for a long time after the divorce. And then I got mad, and then bitter, I think."

"What happened?"

"Just what I was trying to make you see this morning. Deke couldn't finish college, and he wanted to play golf, but even with the scholarship he got, there was just no way. Our parents couldn't help us, we didn't have any insurance, and there were so many bills. I think he felt trapped—I know at times I did. He started to drink, and there was another woman for a while...maybe more than one." Amanda heaved a deep sigh and glanced at Jeff to gauge his reaction.

"Go on," he encouraged.

"The more he gave up, the harder I tried. I took a job at a Laundromat at night, doing washing for other people. I did baby-sitting at home during the day. I stuffed envelopes..." Amanda stared at some spot across the room. When she spoke again it was the barest thread of sound. "One day he left and didn't come home. I was worried sick. He called the next day and told me he wouldn't be back, that I was nothing but a drudge and that he was suing for divorce as soon as he could scrape up the money."

"That's all?"

"That's all. I didn't fight it. And I've only seen him twice since then. Both times he came asking for money."

"You gave it to him?" Jeff asked incredulously.

"No. But I wanted to see him. I wanted to see how he'd done for himself since he'd left us behind."

"And?"

"He was still drinking. He never made it big on the golf tours. He didn't have a steady job. He sort of moved from place to place, working as a golf pro."

"And how did you feel about him? Still bitter?"

She looked up into her son's eyes and shook her head. "I felt sorry for him. He could have had so much." She reached out and clutched one of Jeff's hands in both of her own. "But he has nothing. Nothing."

Jeff reached out with his free hand and touched the solitary tear slipping down her cheek. His heart was both lighter and heavier. She was a strong woman. A fighter. She'd been mother, father, friend. She'd given him the best of herself and never asked for anything in return. He understood better now. It wasn't that she didn't want him to marry Heather; it was just that she was afraid that he would eventually come to feel the way his father had. Trapped. Cheated. Robbed of the best that life could offer.

Jeff knew that would never happen. He loved Heather and she loved him. They would make it work. He was too much like his mother. Too much of a fighter. All he had to do was convince her of that.

WAY STALKED the perimeter of the large swimming pool behind his Tudor-style home, a can of Miller in one hand, the other hooked at his waist. Downing a huge mouthful of beer, he stared unseeingly at the profusion of flowers bordering the house, his mind filled with the memory of Amanda Farrell's shapely legs. He swore. Better to remember her acidic personality.

In compliance, his mind dredged up her extremely plausible reasons why Jeff shouldn't marry Heather, and Way's blood began to boil. She'd painted a very convincing picture of why Jeff should remain single and in school.

Maybe his mental picture of her appearance had been wrong, but his psychological rendering wasn't far off base. That soft feminine exterior of hers was just a guise...a ruse to lull a man into thinking she was helpless and dependent, a fallacy that couldn't be farther from the truth. The truth was that the woman was as tough as nails. Way scowled at the day. He'd give odds that if someone traced her ancestry back far enough they'd find she was a direct descendant of Attila the Hun.

Way finished the beer, his emotions seesawing. On the one hand he wanted to throttle Amanda for her stubborn attitude, and on the other he felt a grudging admiration for her. Her own experience had enabled her to see the potential dangers in store for Jeff and Heather that Way's own happiness in the same situation had blinded him to. Amanda Farrell loved her son and was trying to protect his best interests the same way he himself was trying to protect Heather's. In all fairness, Way supposed that someone should point out the pitfalls of a marriage between two kids.

"I want something better for Jeff...."

The words and the look on her face bolted through his mind.

"Better than marriage... to anyone!"

The empty can caved in beneath his crushing grip as his mood swung toward fury once more.

"Excuse me."

Another picture, this one of the sorrow and shame on her face after Jeff had announced that he knew of his conception, elbowed its way into Way's thoughts. His anger dissipated like morning mist. She hadn't been tough and hard then. She'd been hurt, vulnerable and unable to face any more pain. Her full bottom lip, the kind of bottom lip designed solely to drive a man to distraction, had quivered as she struggled to hold on to her composure.

Way cursed for even daring to find her attractive. She was nothing like the kind of woman who usually snagged his attention. Nonetheless, when he'd looked into those challenging eyes of hers, he felt the same exhilaration swelling inside him that he experienced when he approached the plate, the same, I've-gotta-get-this-one feeling that pushed him to excel year after year.

The feeling was ridiculous under the present circumstances; it didn't even deserve further exploration. Amanda Farrell was worse than out of his league. She wasn't even interested in playing the game.

Relentlessly the pictures paraded onto the screen of his mind. He swore again. It was no use. The diverse images of her were irreconcilable, but they were there. Amanda haughty. Amanda shocked. Disdainful. Hurting. Hard. All soft, warm woman. Unforgettable. Way sighed and lifted his troubled gaze to the cloudless, azure sky.

CHAPTER THREE

THE FOLLOWING EVENING, Amanda was still trying to impress the gravity of their situation on Jeff and Heather. Looking into their faces, she wasn't at all certain that she was getting her message through to them. Jeff's face, while not showing anger, displayed a definite lack of interest in what she was saying; Heather's wore a shell-shocked appearance, as if the surfeit of emotions she'd been subjected to the past few days had left her numb.

At some time during the sleepless night while she'd burned with embarrassment for the fact that not only her son, but the Daltons knew that she'd been pregnant when she'd married Deke, Amanda had come to the realization that that very knowledge might be the tool to use to stop a marriage between Jeff and Heather.

"It's because I do know firsthand what problems can come up that I'm begging you to consider every aspect of this situation," she said for perhaps the tenth time.

Jeff reached for Heather's hand. "Look, Mom, we'll think about it. I promise."

"And what exactly does that mean?"

"It means that when I take Heather home tonight, we won't skip out and drive to Oklahoma to get married. It means that I'm going to take this long weekend, then go back to school as if I don't have a problem in the world—okay?"

Amanda recognized the signs of stubbornness in Jeff's eyes. Combined with the blatant sarcasm in his voice, she knew she'd done all she could for the moment. Her own weariness manifested itself in a soft sigh. "That's all I ask. Just give it some time before you make the final decision."

"We will." Jeff stood and pulled Heather to her feet. "I'll be home by midnight," he said, heading for the front door.

Amanda watched them go. Midnight? She glanced at her watch. It was only six. Where were they going? And what were they going to do? Her mind filled with pictures of Jeff making love to Heather. She couldn't imagine it, couldn't bear it.

Numbly, she made her way to the kitchen and rummaged around in the cabinet for a bottle of whiskey someone had left when she'd had a Christmas get-together for some of the faculty. She made herself a stiff drink with tap water and downed a large mouthful. Choking and sputtering, she made a futile attempt to wipe away the moisture that kept flooding her eyes. Swearing with unAmandalike fervor, she dumped the rest of the drink and the remains of the bottle down the drain. Then she succumbed to the misery invading every molecule of her being and sought solace in her solitary bed.

But even that escape was denied her when her fitful sleep was invaded by erotic dreams that mirrored her concern for Jeff and Heather. Strangely, it wasn't Jeff making love to Heather that Amanda pictured, it was herself being kissed and caressed . . . by Way Dalton. Secure in the arms of sleep, she moaned in protest—or was it pleasure?—as Way's mouth possessed the straining peaks of her breasts. And, at the exact moment he moved to take her in total possession, she came to complete wakefulness, lurching to a sitting position and staring at the darkened room with wide, frightened eyes.

Real. It had seemed, no, *felt* so real. She struggled to calm her ragged breathing, and her trembling hands moved without conscious consent to cover her throbbing breasts. It was foolishness to dream of Way Dalton in such a way. She didn't even like the man. So why had she dreamed of him? Worse—why had she dreamed of him making love to her?

It's been a long time, Amanda. Too long.

She closed her eyes and her teeth clamped down on her bottom lip, willing the unwanted sexual longings away. But it was a long time before her heartbeats slowed to normal and even longer before the restlessness turning her inside out allowed her to fall into another uneasy sleep.

WAY STEPPED OUT of a hot shower. The water had only partially diminished the lingering weariness after a grueling practice. He blew his hair dry and wrapped a towel around his lean hips, wondering how Heather was doing and if Jeff had managed, in the two days since Way had been gone, to talk any sense into his stubborn-as-a-Missouri-mule mother.

Going to the hotel bedroom, he raked the sheet back and, sitting on the edge of the bed, dialed his home number. Heather answered on the third ring.

"Hi, baby," he said, a smile softening his firm lips.

"Daddy! Hi!"

"How's it going?"

The enthusiasm in Heather's voice dropped a degree. "Everything's the same. Jeff promised his mother we wouldn't rush into anything."

Way stifled his anger, telling himself that Amanda would have to give in sooner or later. "So how are you feeling?"

"I'm okay. I'm sleepy a lot."

Way smiled again. "Your mother was the same way when she was carrying you."

"Really?"

"Really. Have you seen a doctor yet?"

"No. I'm afraid to go. It was bad enough buying the home pregnancy test."

"There's nothing to be afraid of," Way said soothingly.

"I know, but . . . it's just so . . . personal."

Way heard the quaver in her voice. Dammit, she was scared to death. And why not? Her whole life was in a turmoil, and there wasn't any end in sight. "Yeah, I guess it is. Why don't you ask Mrs. Moffett to go with you?"

"Oh, Daddy, I can't! I'm afraid of what Muffy will say when she finds out."

"I told her before I left," Way said, his voice gruff with emotion. "She was hurt, of course, but she still loves you, Heather. You don't stop loving someone just because they make a mistake."

"It didn't seem like a mistake at the time," Heather said. "It seemed so right. I love Jeff, Daddy. Making love with him was just another way to show him how much I cared."

"Oh, God, Way, I love you so much . . . so much. . . ."

Carol's voice, along with a time-blurred image of them making love, flitted through his mind. Had it really been eleven years since he'd made love to a woman out of a need to show how much he cared instead of immediate self-gratification?

"I know, baby," he said gruffly. "I remember."

"I love you, Daddy."

Heather's voice was hardly more than a whisper, and Way could tell that tears were imminent. "I love you, too," he told her. "I'll talk to Jeff and see what we can come up with, okay?"

He heard her sniff. "Okay."

"You take care and I'll call you soon."

"All right."

"Bye, baby."

"Goodbye."

Way cradled the phone and sat staring at it for long moments, aching for Heather's pain and wishing Carol was there to help him through this. Heather needed someone who understood. Someone who could relate to what she was feeling. He was a man, and he had nothing but a secondhand idea of what she could expect from a visit to the doctor as well as what questions and problems might arise during the coming months. She needed a woman, but if not Muffy, then who?

Amanda. His mind whispered the name and rejected it almost simultaneously. But, then again—why not Amanda? If Jeff's observation was true—and it obviously was—then Amanda Farrell knew exactly what Heather was going through. And like it or not, this baby was as much her grandchild as it was his. It seemed only fitting that if she wouldn't sanction a marriage between their two kids, she should at least shoulder some of the **rest of the problem. With the fire of determination** lighting his eyes, Way dialed Information.

AMANDA STOOD at the side of the bed, her hands on her hips, her teeth worrying her bottom lip as she regarded the two dresses with a curious mixture of pleasure and dismay. One was a simple white-on-white A-line, daintily adorned with a combination of smocking, embroidery, lace and ribbon; the other was petal pink, a profusion of double ruffles on the short skirt and sleeves.

Both were suitable for a female three months old.

Amanda didn't know what had got into her. One moment she was looking at blouses, and the next thing she knew she'd noticed the display of baby dresses hanging on the wall across the way. Before she realized what she was doing, she'd found herself trying to decide which color to get. If the baby was blond like Heather, the pink would be adorable, and if she had Jeff's coloring, the white would be a good choice. Amanda had finally chosen the traditional pink, but then had been unable to keep from buying the old-fashioned-looking white dress, too.

She shook her head in disgust. It wasn't like her to be so impulsive. Thought and careful planning had got her where she was today, and buying two dresses for a baby who'd be disrupting so many lives was certainly out of character. Was she already assuming—hoping?—that this baby would be a girl, because she'd always secretly wanted a prissy little girl of her own? Ridiculous! Gathering both of the dresses, she started to thrust them back into the plastic shopping bag, but the phone rang, shattering the stillness of the room and halting her movements in midair.

Placing the small garments on the bed, Amanda pulled off the button earring she wore and lifted the receiver. "Hello."

"Hi. This is Way."

Shock at the sound of the deep masculine voice rumbling in her ear rendered Amanda speechless. Memories of her dreams—sharp and unexpectedly stimulating—rushed through her, causing her breath to come in shallow, unsatisfying bursts.

"Amanda? Are you there?"

She cleared her throat and placed her fingers against her throat. Her pulse was racing. "Yes."

"I called to ask a favor," he said without preamble.

"A favor?" she echoed, the mundane statement effectively calming her. What kind of favor could Way Dalton possibly want from her?

"I talked to Heather a little while ago and she's pretty nervous about going to the doctor by herself the first time. I'd like you to go with her."

That's asking? Amanda thought with a frown. *More like telling.*

"Well?" he prompted when she didn't answer. "I know it's a lot to ask, but this is an area I don't feel qualified to deal with. You've been there. You understand better than I ever could what she's going through."

Amanda couldn't believe her ears. He was actually thick-skinned enough to refer to Jeff's confession. "You're right, Mr. Dalton," she said with icy calm. "I've been pregnant and unmarried. I know exactly what she's going through."

Way's mouth fell open in surprise. What had he said now? He suddenly realized what he'd done. "That isn't what I mean, dammit!" he exploded, tired of the way she misinterpreted everything. "I mean that you're a woman, and you can relate to morning sickness and being afraid of your first visit to an obstetrician the way no man ever could."

Amanda felt the flush of embarrassment warm her cheeks. Okay. She'd made an honest mistake. He *wasn't* rubbing in the knowledge of her prenuptial pregnancy.

And, he had a point. She did understand what Heather was going through. She remembered with a bittersweet pang how her own mother had stood by her. He was right. Heather needed a woman now.

"Look, even if you are dead set against marriage between our kids—"

"I'll go," she interrupted.

"—it seems to me that you'd at least be willing to shoulder some of the responsibility for a child who's going to be your grandchild," he finished.

"I said I'll go with her," Amanda reiterated softly. "You're right. It's the least I can do."

Way wanted to tell her—and not nicely—that she was damn right it was the least she could do, but he thought better of it. The situation called for strategy and tact, not anger. He expelled a deep breath. "Look, I know you'd rather this hadn't happened. We all do. But it has, and I think it's time you started accustoming yourself to the fact that this situation is real."

She could hear the carefully checked anger in his voice. "Believe me, Mr. Dalton, I'm very aware of how real it is."

Way struggled to hold on to his frayed temper. His voice was as cool as hers had been before. "If you know it's real, Mandy, why don't you start trying to accept it?"

Amanda's first reaction was to the hated name—Mandy—Deke's name for her. Her second reaction was to the question, valid but unwanted. She was to accept the fact that Jeff was going to be a father? That she was going to be a grandmother? That her son had got a girl pregnant? Though she'd played ostrich for the past couple of days, she knew he was right...again. She had to accept it. The question was...how?

"I'm doing my very best, Mr. Dalton," she assured him. "I really am."

"YOU DON'T KNOW how much I appreciate you asking Heather over for the day," Jeff told Amanda as he filled two glasses with cola.

"It's no big deal, Jeff. Just hamburgers on the grill," Amanda said, as uncomfortable with his thanks as she had been when she'd asked Heather to spend Saturday with them.

"I know you're trying to come to terms with all this, and I'm glad."

Amanda finished slicing a tomato and looked at Jeff. He was standing close by, a bag of potato chips in his hands, a look of pleading on his face.

"I know you'll love her, too, if you only give her a chance. She's really a good girl, Mom, in spite of this."

Under the circumstances, Amanda couldn't take issue with his statement. She offered Jeff a faint smile, the best she could do at the moment. "I'm sure she is."

Bolstered a bit by her smile, Jeff said, "Actually, Heather reminds me a lot of you."

"She does?"

"Yeah. She's very goal oriented, and a really hard worker."

Amanda dried her hands. *We'll see.* "That's a plus." She handed Jeff the platter of sliced pickles, tomatoes and onions. "Cover these with some foil and put them in the fridge, please."

Jeff took the platter, covering her hands with his. Amanda looked into his eyes. "Thanks, Mom."

Her gaze wavered beneath the tenderness in his. "There's nothing to thank me for."

Jeff only smiled and, leaning across the plate, kissed her cheek. He put the vegetables away and picked up the two glasses of soft drink, the first hint of happiness she'd seen in a long time glimmering in his eyes. "I'll take these in and then I'll come back and put the hamburgers on."

When he left the room, Amanda sat down at the kitchen table, her hand curling around her sweating glass of iced tea. She was making the effort. After Way's call, she'd hardly slept at all. He was right, even though it galled her to admit it. Marriage or no marriage, she and Jeff did owe something to Heather.

Way's daughter was carrying her grandchild, a thought that came to her at the strangest times, catching her off balance and filling her with unexpectedly tender longings. There was so much she could do for a grandchild she'd never been able to do for Jeff, so much she could *give*. Time, as well as things. Due to all the odd jobs she'd been forced to take, the time she'd spent with Jeff was precious little, a fact that had always caused her tremendous pain. She'd gone out of her way to make sure that the time they did have was what the psychologists were now calling "quality" time and, without meaning to be defensive, Jeff didn't appear to have suffered. He was smart, well adjusted, hardworking and loving. She prayed this new child would be, too.

Amanda had also realized that it would be better for them all if this unplanned pregnancy could be faced with a certain equanimity. So, while she was still light-years away from approving a marriage, she had decided to straddle the fence. She would be as helpful as she could be to Heather. It was the best she could do.

"Ready to cook the burgers?"

The sound of Jeff's voice snapped Amanda out of her thoughts. She turned to see him and Heather in the kitchen doorway. "Past ready," she said, forcing a smile to her lips. She got the patties out of the refrigerator and turned them over to Jeff. "Make sure mine's well-done," she cautioned.

Jeff rolled his eyes. "She means cremated," he told Heather in an audible aside.

Heather's lips curved slightly, and she gave Amanda a shy look from beneath her lashes. "I like mine well-done, too," she confided.

Jeff made a noise that sounded suspiciously like a snort. "All I need to do with mine is knock the horns off and get out the moo."

"That's disgusting, Jeff," Heather told him with a grimace.

Jeff pulled her close with his free arm and dropped a kiss to her forehead. "I guess I'm just a disgusting guy."

Nostalgia, pungent and sharp, knifed through Amanda as she watched the tender byplay. She'd forgotten the happiness that came with new love. Barely recalled how sweet those gentle kisses and touches were. Couldn't remember at all the thrill of just holding hands or feeling the heart-bursting fulfillment of the whispered words, "I love you." Watching Heather and Jeff brought back those memories. It also brought a sense of loss for not having those things in her life anymore, for not finding them again in all these years.

She wasn't aware of the naked longing clouding her eyes, wasn't aware that Jeff saw it. She wasn't even aware that he still stood there until he spoke.

"Why don't you come outside and keep us company while I cook?"

Amanda's faraway gaze snapped to his, then moved to Heather. "Oh, I don't know...."

"Please," Heather said. "I saw some shrubs the other day that I'd like to ask you about." At the surprised look on Amanda's face, she continued. "Mrs. Moffett, our housekeeper, loves anything green. I thought if you didn't mind, I'd take her some cuttings."

The word *thoughtful* came to mind. Smiling slightly, Amanda pushed herself to her feet. "I don't mind at all."

While Jeff cooked, Amanda made cuttings of her shrubs as well as her rosebushes, while Heather labeled them with pieces of paper. They were almost finished when Amanda decided to mention Way's call. She placed three branches into the basket Heather carried. "Your father phoned."

"He did?"

Amanda nodded. "He asked me if I'd go with you to the doctor."

Blushing to the roots of her blond hair, Heather murmured, "I can't believe he asked you!"

Amanda felt the younger woman's embarrassment and, for the first time, she realized with a sharp awareness just how alone Heather was and how hard it must be for her to be going through this without a mother's comforting, guiding hand. Reaching out, she covered the younger woman's hand with hers. "Who better?"

Unshed tears flooded Heather's eyes. "I know you don't like me because of all this, Mrs. Farrell, but thanks."

"Oh, Heather," Amanda said on a sigh, tightening her grip on Heather's hands. "I don't dislike you. I don't even know you. I just hate that this has happened for both your sakes." She sighed again. "But you know how I feel, so we won't go into that. We won't look back. Is there any particular doctor you want to see?"

Heather shook her head. "I don't even know a gynecologist."

"Would you like for me to make an appointment for you with mine?"

"It doesn't matter."

Amanda stifled a feeling of frustration. Heather wasn't the easiest person to talk to. Amanda chalked the girl's quietness up to youth and inexperience and decided to forge ahead. "Fine. I'll call first thing Monday morning and see when we can get you in."

Heather nodded.

Amanda reached for the basket. "I'll take these in and put them in some water while you hurry Jeff up, okay?"

Heather nodded again and Amanda watched her walk toward Jeff. Then, wearing a worried frown, she turned and went into the kitchen. Maybe once they got to know each other better...

AMANDA, WHO HAD INSISTED that she would clean up the lunch dishes without any help, was just wiping off the kitchen cabinets when Jeff stuck his head through the door and announced, "Hurry up. The game's about to start."

"Game? What game?"

"The Royals. Mr. Dalton's team."

Amanda offered Jeff a tolerant smile and shook her head. "Thanks, but no thanks. I think I'll grade papers."

Jeff's own smile faltered a little. "C'mon, Mom. Baseball's a really fast game, and Heather's dad is great. Besides, how can you ever get to know her if you don't spend time with her?"

Amanda felt her resolve melting in the face of Jeff's eager need to see harmony between her and Heather. While she was beginning to believe that Heather truly was a nice girl, one afternoon spent in her company wasn't going to change Amanda's stand on their marriage. But Jeff didn't know that, and because she hated any friction with her only child, Amanda found herself agreeing to something she knew she wouldn't enjoy at all.

"Okay. I'll watch this time," she told him, smoothing the dishrag over the sink's divider.

"Great!" Jeff disappeared and Amanda stared out the closed door, wondering what she'd let herself in for.

A few minutes later, she was seated in a wing chair, a glass of iced tea on the table beside her, watching the pregame program, which focused on how the players of each team spent their leisure time. She saw players boating, skiing, playing Scrabble with their families and helping their kids learn to ride bicycles. She saw them at the car races, the horse races, the dog races. She saw married players, single players, divorced players with their kids. And she saw Way Dalton and his friend, Jose Delgato, the Royals' pitcher, out on the town.

The segment on Way started with a breakdown of how he spent his day. He got up at five-thirty—a fact that drew a groan from Jeff—to run three days a week and to work out at the gym three days, a fact that drew an I-thought-so smile from Amanda.

Her smile faltered as Way appeared on the screen, shirtless and in baggy shorts that exposed his well-muscled legs, working out on the Nautilus equipment. Perspiration darkened the blond hair that fell across his forehead and beaded his tanned, hair-dusted chest. A half-remembered feeling from her dream of what his flesh felt like surfaced from her subconscious. She knew exactly how his skin felt, exactly how the play of muscles felt beneath her palm. She chided herself for the ridiculous thoughts, since dreamstuff was notorious for its lack of real substance. Yet, when he flashed a smile toward the camera, Amanda's heart—a heart hardened from years of conscious denial—sprinted to a faster pace. A pace she sought to slow by taking another sip of tea.

The camera rolled on, following Way through practice, through several sensational—if the reaction of the crowd was anything to go by—plays, and on to show him getting ready for a night on the town. The heavy metal music that accompanied the brief documentary changed to Z.Z. Top's hard-driving song "Sharp Dressed Man" as the camera showed Way and his friend Jose, resplendent in black tuxedos. They were seated in a classy restaurant with two women who had, Amanda noted with vexation and just a hint of jealousy, bodies to kill for. As fans flocked to the table for autographs and Way signed everything from napkins to creamy flesh spilling from a strapless gown, Amanda began to think that everyone, as the song suggested, *was* crazy about sharp-dressed men.

She set her drink onto the table with unnecessary force, unable to separate her disgust for the blatant way the man was cashing in on his popularity and good looks from her disgust at the undeniable way she had reacted.

Jeff shot her a questioning look; Heather was smiling at the image of her handsome father. "I'm going to get more tea," Amanda said to Jeff. "Want some?"

"Yeah. Sure." He turned to Heather. "How about it, Heather? Tea?"

She looked up, the smile still firmly in place. "No, thanks."

Amanda escaped to the kitchen. She wondered why, out of all the men she'd come into contact with since Deke had deserted her, this one man, who was the ultimate example of everything she hated, had the power to elicit a response from a libido she'd thought had gone into hiding years ago. Her sexual encounters since her divorce were almost nonexistent and, while pleasant enough, they had never threatened her in any way. But this man, this perfect symbol of all she'd sworn to steer clear of, could raise her blood pressure just by smiling into a camera.

Amanda filled up the glasses and carried them back to the living room. If, she thought grimly, she was having this kind of reaction to a man like Way Dalton, it could mean only one thing: her deprived body was clamoring for fulfillment. Maybe it was time she took Dale Patterson, the drama teacher, up on his offer of dinner and uninvolved sex.

Just as she reached the living room, the announcer was introducing the team's players. When each man's name and position was called out, he doffed his cap and waved it to the crowd. Amanda noticed that a drooping mustache like Way Dalton's seemed to be par for most of the players, as was a bulge of something in their jaw. What that something was, came to her in a moment of blinding clarity when a Hispanic player waved, nodded and spat.

"Tobacco!" she said in an affronted tone.

Heather and Jeff turned to look at her simultaneously.

"They're chewing tobacco. And spitting. On national television." The last was noted in a disbelieving tone and accompanied by a delicate shudder that summed up her feelings. Her gaze was drawn hypnotically back to the television just as Way strode forward, waved his cap and blew a huge bubble before he stepped back into the line.

"Some of them chew tobacco. Most of them—like my dad—chew bubble gum," Heather said, eager to explain away any negative aspects of her father's behavior and completely unaware that Amanda's mouth had dropped open when she saw him blowing the bubble.

Eyes wide, Amanda looked back at Heather. "Bubble gum?"

Heather gave Jeff an uncomfortable glance. "Yes."

"Your father chews bubble gum?"

Heather nodded. Obviously Mrs. Farrell wasn't impressed with baseball or her father... so far.

"If he's chewing bubble gum, why is he spitting?" Amanda asked, her questioning gaze shifting from Heather to Jeff, who was having a hard time stifling a smile.

Jeff knew his mother like a book. Prim and proper Amanda Farrell was appalled by the most basic of baseball customs. "Spitting is to baseball what verbs are to sentence structure, Mom," he told her with pseudoseriousness. "You can't have one without the other."

"I see," Amanda said, but Jeff doubted it. She was horrified at the players' behavior, she didn't understand a thing about it, and it seemed ridiculous for grown men to be playing a child's game. However, because she had agreed to watch with Jeff and Heather, she did.

Two hours or so later, the game was over and Way's friend, Jose, was declared the winning pitcher. According to Jeff, Way had played a great game. Dedicated to stay until the entire thing was over, Amanda watched the postgame locker-room interviews, a farcical episode that consisted of half-naked men whooping and hollering, making victory signs and smiling like imbeciles into the camera. They were also pouring water over one another's heads and, in general, acting less than adult.

When congratulated on his win, Jose Delgato graciously gave credit to Way for his outstanding efforts at first base. The microphone was thrust into Way's face, and he was asked about his amazing triple play. He only shrugged and smiled another of those lazy, devastating smiles.

"Just lucky," he said laconically.

"Rumor has it that your fortieth birthday is coming up," the reporter said. "Is there any truth to that?"

His brilliant white smile flashed. "One hundred percent truth."

"That's the age most players start really slowing down, but from the looks of things today, that isn't the case with you. You're obviously as fit today as you were when you started. What's your secret?"

Way scrubbed a hand through his sweat-dampened hair and, grinning, winked into the camera. "Hard work. Hard play."

The reporter tilted the microphone back toward himself. "Any women in your life right now?"

"Heather. My daughter." Way looked directly into the camera and said, "Hi, baby."

Amanda looked at Heather, who was blushing again. Jeff was smiling indulgently.

"Is it safe to say, then, that since you're approaching forty and your daughter is the only woman in your life, the pleasure-seeking Way Dalton we've come to know is a thing of the past?"

"Yeah," Way said. "You could say that."

"You could say that."

Could.

Somehow Amanda doubted it. Way Dalton was too handsome, too confident...too athletic! He was *too much* as her surging hormones attested. And knowing the cloth he was cut from, she had little faith that he was different from the rest of the jocks in the world. She sighed and picked up her empty glass. Her wanting libido and raging hormones would just have to be conquered. Way Dalton was too much like Deke Farrell to suit her.

CHAPTER FOUR

MONDAY MORNING found Amanda praying that her life would resume its normal tenor now that the traumatic week was past. Once Jeff had taken Heather home and pulled out of the driveway to head back to school, she could almost believe that it would. Almost. Except that this morning, she had to call her doctor and make an appointment for Heather. And then, at one o'clock, Steve Harris strolled into her classroom.

Amanda had looked up when the first group of students sauntered in, Steve in their midst. She knew her surprise was evident, but when he hadn't shown up at all on Friday, she'd assumed that he'd dropped the class.

As he took a seat at the back of the room, he was careful not to meet her gaze, and, though she wondered what would happen next, she went on with the class as if nothing were out of the ordinary. To her added puzzlement, Steve was attentive, and she saw him scribbling in his notebook on several occasions.

When the class was over, the students, like lemmings drawn to the sea, filed out of the room. Amanda was **rummaging around in her desk, gathering her things up** to go home for the day, when she heard a familiar, masculine voice say, "Excuse me, Ms Farrell."

Lifting her head, she saw Steve standing on the opposite side of her desk, his hands plunged into the pockets of the light windbreaker he wore, an uncomfortable look on his handsome face. *What now?* she wondered, straightening and sitting back in her chair. "Hello, Steve," she said, careful not to let her unease show. "What can I do for you?"

He took a deep breath and rolled his eyes toward the ceiling. "I want you to help me," he blurted.

Help him? Shock rendered Amanda temporarily speechless. She could only stare up into his embarrassed blue eyes and try to figure out whether or not he was sincere. He was. Her heart turned over in sympathy. She had an idea of what this must be costing him in terms of his ego. "Sit down," she offered, indicating a chair next to the desk.

Steve sat down, but his actions were nervous, jumpy.

"What brought all this about?" Amanda asked.

He stared at the floor, almost as if he were afraid she might see weakness in his eyes. "I've been thinking about what you said, and you're right." He cleared his throat and forced himself to meet her gaze. "I was doing it for them."

"Who?" Amanda asked, not understanding.

"My parents." He shrugged. "Well, my dad, anyway. My mother hardly knows I'm alive."

She was beginning to get the picture. It was a very common one.

"They're divorced," Steve said by way of explanation, even though the comment didn't clear up a thing for Amanda.

"So am I," she offered for no reason she could put her finger on.

"You don't look divorced."

She couldn't help the small smile that tugged at her lips. "What do divorced people look like?"

A look of comprehension crossed Steve's face. He gave her back a brief grin. "Yeah. I see what you mean. Do you have kids?"

"A son, Jeff. He's a freshman at the University of Missouri."

"Do you get along?"

"Yes, very well. Usually," she tacked on, recalling the weekend.

"My mother is . . . uh—" Steve stared up at the ceiling and cleared his throat again. "I guess you could say she's wrapped up in her own life. She's still young and pretty, and . . . she, uh, likes to have a good time, you know?" He looked Amanda directly in the eye. "I don't think she wants anyone to know she has a kid my age."

Amanda knew the type of woman well, and her understanding of Steve grew a little more.

"Does your son get along with your ex-husband?"

"He's never seen him," she confided, the sadness of that fact hitting her for the first time. Until now, she'd always been glad that Jeff hadn't had to deal with his father's failures. "He deserted us when Jeff was three."

Steve looked appalled. "Gee, Ms Farrell, I'm sorry, but, hey, it might be for the best."

Amanda sensed that Steve was working his way around to the crux of his problem, if she only had the patience to wait.

"My dad was a first-round draft pick for the Green Bay Packers when he graduated from college."

The statement, seemingly unrelated to the conversation, nevertheless spoke volumes to Amanda. "And he wanted you to follow in his footsteps."

There was anguish in Steve's eyes, and a hint of guilt. "Yeah. It was almost expected. But I wanted to play, too," he hastened to add.

Amanda propped her chin in her hand. "Well, you're obviously very good, or you wouldn't be here on an athletic scholarship."

"I am good," he said. The statement, though made with confidence, held none of the boastfulness she usually expected of him. "But it isn't enough."

Amanda pretended not to notice the suspicious sparkle in his eyes. "It isn't enough for what?" she probed.

"To make him care. I've tried all my life to please him, just to hear him say, 'Great, Stevie.'" He rose and began to pace the room, talking as much to himself as to Amanda. Now that the Pandora's box of his emotions was open, the hurt, the pain and the feelings of self-doubt spilled like a torrent from him.

"My mom never cared what happened to me, and when I went to live with him, I wanted to be the best for him, you know?"

There was a seriousness on Steve's face that Amanda found almost pitiful. She wanted to go out, hunt down and confront Steve's father—whoever he was—and give him a good dressing down.

"A boy needs a father, Ms Farrell," Steve said with a brief, bitter laugh. "I used to lie in bed at night and pray for him to love me." He stopped prowling the room and looked at her. "I even learned to shoot a gun and forced myself to kill an elk, even though I hated hunting. But did he appreciate it? Hell, no. He chewed me out because it wasn't a clean kill. The elk suffered."

Amanda searched her mind for something to say that would ease his obvious and very raw pain.

"Excelling in football was the only way I managed to get his attention, the only thing I could do to earn his love."

Amanda found her voice, but to her surprise it was as pain filled as his. "You don't earn love, Steve. Real love comes without strings."

He nodded. "You're right. But I only found that out this weekend."

Amanda leaned her elbows on the top of her desk and laced her fingers together. "What happened?" she asked again.

"After I had the fight with you, I was madder than hell, but when I got back to the fraternity house I started thinking about what you said." He ran his fingers through his curly blond hair.

"I don't know, there was something in your eyes that told me you were telling the truth, that you weren't giving in to the system just to get back at me, but because you did care. And then I got to thinking about my dad. I realized that he gets off on his own ego, and that no matter how many girls I have, they would never be as many or as pretty as the ones he'd had, and that *if* I ever ran as far or for as many touchdowns as he had, they would have been against lesser teams, or flukes of luck."

Amanda saw the new maturity and the instant "old" in Steve's eyes, scars of his inner battle. She swallowed back the lump of emotion in her throat and wondered why growing up invariably had to be so painful.

"I figured out that—through no fault of my own—I can't compete with him. No one could. And if I try, I'll only eat myself up."

"That's very mature thinking, Steve. And you're right," Amanda told him. "So where do you go from here?"

Steve looked her squarely in the eye. "For starters, I want to pass your course. For myself. Because if you're right, and I think you are, I'd like to have something to fall back on. I'm not stupid or anything, and I think I can do it."

Amanda smiled. "Of course you aren't stupid. I never thought you were. Conceited, maybe," she added dryly.

Steve smiled back. "Yeah. I think I had the market cornered."

"It's going to mean a lot of studying," she warned.

"I know."

"I'll have to give you some make-up work, and you'll have to make an A on the final to pull it off."

He whistled. "That bad?"

"That bad," she said with a nod.

"Will you tutor me, Ms Farrell? On the weekends?"

Amanda smiled at his naïveté. College professors didn't tutor. "I usually have some of my better students do the tutoring, Steve."

"Please. I don't want the guys on the team to find out. I promise I'll work really hard."

There was a pleading quality in his blue eyes that Amanda found hard to resist. Coupled with her new-found knowledge about his bid for love, how could she deny him this one small thing?

"All right." She reached for a notepad and scribbled down her address. "Be at my house next Saturday about one."

Steve took the paper and smiled broadly, the same smile that always captured feminine hearts. This time it even managed to touch Amanda's. "You won't be sorry, Ms Farrell," he said, heading out the door with a bounce to his step. "I promise."

Amanda sighed. She hoped he was right.

"YOU'RE A NERVOUS WRECK, young lady," Amanda's doctor, Grant Palmer, said to Heather. He'd just given her a thorough checkup. "You've got to settle down for the baby's sake."

Heather, who was still battling embarrassment over her first gynecological exam, glanced at Amanda, who was sitting beside her.

Amanda looked at the doctor, her concern apparent. "She's all right, isn't she? The baby's all right?"

"She's Rh-negative, a little anemic, and to be frank, Amanda, her nerves are shot," he said. "On the other hand, she has the resilience of youth on her side, and that'll take care of everything but the Rh factor."

"Is that a problem in this day and age?" Amanda asked.

The doctor shook his white head. "Not the way it used to be, and there's usually no problem with a first baby. We do need to get Jeff in for a blood test, though. If he's positive, we'll just give Heather the shot after the baby is born, and that takes care of problems with future pregnancies." He looked at Heather over the top of his glasses. "I'm prescribing the usual prenatal vitamins, plus an iron tablet. See that you take them."

Heather nodded, her white teeth clamped over her lower lip.

"It isn't advisable to give anything for the nervousness at this point, so a lot is going to depend on you. I want you to come in from school and go to bed for an hour or so. I see a dozen teen pregnancies every month. You're not the first it's happened to, and you won't be the last, so try to relax, and don't worry so much."

He scribbled on a pad, ripped the pages off and handed them to Heather. "I'd like to have a word with Amanda, Heather. Why don't you wait for her outside?"

Heather rose obediently and started for the door. "I'll be in the waiting room," she said shyly.

"Fine," Amanda said.

The door closed behind Heather, and Amanda faced the doctor who had delivered Jeff nineteen years before.

"I just wanted to reassure you that she's really in pretty good shape and that she'll settle down a lot once they're married," Dr. Palmer said when he was certain Heather was out of earshot.

"I'm trying to talk them out of marriage," Amanda told him. "I'm not certain that's a good idea."

"What!" Grant Palmer frowned at Amanda in a way that, even after twenty years, she still found intimidating. "Why the hell not?"

Amanda leaned back in the chair. Grant knew the circumstances behind Deke's desertion, knew what hell she'd been through, but he was as conservative and old-fashioned as they came. She sighed. It was going to be another one of those harrowing discussions, and she wasn't sure she was up to it.

"SHE'S FINE, Jeff. Really," Amanda said several hours later as she tried, via the telephone, to calm her worried son.

"I've heard of the Rh factor," he said, the fear in his voice evident.

"Then you know that it's no great problem these days," Amanda said soothingly.

"What about her anemia? Is that why she's so pale, why she feels faint so much?"

"Yes. But she's taking iron for that."

"And what about her nervousness?" he asked for the tenth time. Then, before she could answer, he blurted out, "Mom, I'm worried."

Amanda sighed. She was worried, too. About a lot of things. "I know you are, Jeff, but believe me, she'll be fine. Look, I've been thinking. The next time I talk to Heather's father, I'll tell him that I'll take care of all her medical expenses. That will get rid of one of your headaches. Finals are coming up, and I don't want you to have all this worry hanging over your head."

Jeff's comment about what she and the university could do with finals was short and graphic.

"Finals are the last thing on my mind. We're talking about my *baby* and the woman I love. What about Heather and all she has hanging over her head?"

Amanda flinched at the hostility in his voice. Why was it that everything she did or said was met with resentment? Why couldn't Jeff see that she was trying—hard—to accept the situation and help him? At the moment she was doing so in the only way she could.

"I need to talk to Mr. Dalton," Jeff said suddenly.

A feeling of betrayal, so strong she felt herself sway, swept through Amanda at the thought of Jeff turning to anyone but her for help. She gripped the telephone receiver tightly and willed her voice to normalcy. "He can't tell you anything to do for Heather," she told him, unable to hide the hurt in her voice.

"Maybe not, but it's nice to have a man to talk to. You wouldn't understand."

Amanda battled the green-eyed monster growing within her.

"I love her, Mom," he said quietly. "And I want to get married. Soon."

Amanda heard the unwavering conviction in his voice. Like Heather, he was under a lot of pressure and wasn't thinking beyond the moment. She felt the same pain she heard in his voice and, for the first time, she couldn't find it in her heart to try to change his mind.

"Look, Jeff, it's been a long week," she said. "Dr. Palmer is very competent, and he'll take excellent care of Heather. Why don't you go to bed and try to get some sleep?"

She heard him breathe a deep sigh. "Yeah. You're right."

"Mothers usually are," she said, smiling, offering one of the lines that he usually had a comeback to. But this time there was no quip, no cocksure answer.

"Yeah. I guess so."

The same feeling she'd felt on Monday when she'd seen the "old" look in Steve's eyes came hauntingly back. Jeff was growing up—fast. She couldn't mediate his life anymore, or keep harm from him. She couldn't kiss him and make it all better. Ready or not, Jeff had taken charge of his life, and somewhere along the way, he'd realized that she didn't have all the answers. Now he was looking to Way Dalton for answers, and for Amanda, trying to accept that was excruciatingly painful.

"I'll call you if I hear anything else," she said, blinking back the moisture gathering in her eyes.

"Okay," he said. "I'll talk to you later. Bye, Mom."

"Goodbye," Amanda replied. She started to hang up the phone but heard Jeff call her name. "What?" she asked.

"Thanks for taking Heather to the doctor. I appreciate it."

"It's all right."

"Will you take care of her, Mom?" he asked. "She needs someone right now."

There was hesitation in his voice. Hesitation and...fear. Did he really think she wouldn't do what he asked? Amanda wondered.

Jeff, Jeff...

"Of course I will. If she needs me, all she has to do is call."

Jeff offered her his undying thanks, and Amanda hung the receiver up and crawled into bed. It was early, but she was exhausted. And try as she might, she couldn't push aside the fact that Jeff needed to talk to Way.

"A boy needs a father."

Steve Harris's statement on Monday wandered through her mind. Did Jeff? Could Deke have given Jeff anything she hadn't? Wasn't it enough that she had given him everything in her, that she had even sacrificed relationships because he hadn't seemed to have rapport with the men she was dating? What more could she have done? she asked herself, punching the pillow and turning restlessly to her side.

Nothing.

The answer came to her in a sudden and almost peaceful realization. The tenseness left her body, and she felt the tension knotting her muscles loosen its hold. She had done all she could. She had loved Jeff more than herself, and he loved her. The fact that he was now seeking out someone else's advice didn't lessen that love, and it didn't make Way Dalton a threat to what she and Jeff had.

"This is an area I don't really feel qualified to deal with. You understand better than I ever could what she's going through."

Without warning, the memory of Way's plea for her to accompany Heather to the doctor's flashed through her mind, and with it a feeling of shame that both Steve and Way should have singled out such a basic need before she became aware of it. They were both right. Boys did need a man to talk to... just as girls craved a woman's understanding.

"She needs someone right now."

Jeff needed a man to talk to for the same reasons that no one could understand Heather's innermost feelings the way another woman could.

Amanda was mulling over her newfound realization when the doorbell rang. A quick glance at the clock at her bedside showed that it wasn't quite ten. She frowned, wondering who could possibly be dropping by at this time of night. Flicking on the brass lamp beside her bed, Amanda rose and reached for her robe. She turned on the hall light and started through the house, drawn by the doorbell's insistent ringing.

"I'm coming!" she called, turning on the porch light and peeking through the peephole to see a uniformed policeman standing beside a bedraggled-looking Heather.

An urgency she couldn't describe fought with a sinking feeling for control. What had happened that Heather was with a policeman? Amanda fumbled with the night bolt, her fingers clumsy with apprehension. She finally shot the bolt back and flung open the door.

The policeman touched the bill of his hat. "Ms Farrell?"

"Yes." Her eyes flicked from the officer to Heather, whose eyes were red and swollen from crying.

"I'm Sergeant Bowers. Miss Dalton here was in an accident and asked that we bring her here."

"An accident!" Amanda echoed. Her troubled eyes made a cursory investigation of Heather's features. "Are you all right?"

Heather nodded.

"What happened?"

"She must have fainted and lost control. She hit a mailbox and ruined her right front fender. It was a good thing she wasn't going very fast."

"Has she seen a doctor?"

"Yes, ma'am. She's fine. Just has a nasty bump on her forehead. I took her by the emergency room myself after I found out she was Way Dalton's daughter."

Thank goodness Way's name had some power in the city, Amanda thought. "Is there anything else to do?" she asked.

"No, ma'am," he said. "All the reports have been taken care of. I'd just see to it that this young lady gets a good night's rest."

"Thank you. I will."

Amanda put her arm around Heather and ushered her through the door while the policeman got in his car and backed out of the driveway. Inside, she reached up and cradled Heather's tear-stained face in her palms. "Are you all right?"

Heather's bottom lip trembled and her eyes filled. She nodded.

Amanda could almost see the girl's determination not to break down and cry again. She admired her bid for control. Smiling, she said, "Come on in, and I'll fix us some hot chocolate."

"I really appreciate this, Ms Farrell," Heather said, her voice sounding less weepy by the second. "I hope I didn't wake you."

Amanda flipped on the kitchen light. "I wasn't asleep." Seeing the doubt in Heather's eyes, she smiled. "Weeell, not *quite* asleep."

"Can I help with anything?"

"No, thanks," Amanda said. "Just sit. Or you might want to go get a cool cloth for your forehead."

"That's a good idea."

"You know where the bathroom is. Just make yourself at home."

Heather left the room, and Amanda started the hot chocolate, anxious to hear Heather's account of the accident.

"Marshmallows?" she asked when Heather returned a couple of minutes later. Heather nodded and Amanda added a few to the cup. "Have you called Mrs. Moffett to let her know you're here?"

"She went to see her daughter for a few days."

"And left you alone?" Amanda asked, setting two steaming mugs of fragrant hot chocolate on the table. She seated herself across from the seventeen-year-old girl carrying her grandchild.

Heather smiled. "You sound like my dad. He still about croaks every time Muffy leaves me alone, but I've been staying by myself at night for a couple of years now. Sometimes I have a friend stay over."

Jeff? The errant thought was squelched by a rush of guilt. Amanda sipped her cocoa. "What happened?"

"I don't know," Heather said, knowing that Amanda meant the wreck. "I was just out riding around, killing time. I ate at Burger King and stopped by the Rack and Snack for a while. No one was there, so I started home. I remember being cool, so I turned on the heater. Then I got too hot. I rolled down the window because I was feeling light-headed, but I don't remember fainting.

When I woke up, there was a man standing over me, asking if I was all right.''

Amanda looked thoughtful.

"I was dizzy a lot when I was pregnant with Jeff.''

"Really? How long does it last?''

"I don't remember. Have you been sleepy?''

"Oh, yeah,'' Heather said with a smile. "I can hardly hold my eyes open by midafternoon.''

Amanda was thinking how pretty Heather was when the girl's next question created a mild sense of panic.

"Did I faint because something's wrong, Ms Farrell?'' Heather asked, a frown etched into her usually smooth forehead.

Amanda reached out and covered Heather's hand with her own. "I wouldn't worry if I were you. Grant Palmer is a good doctor. The Rh factor isn't the problem it used to be.''

"Thanks for going with me today,'' Heather said shyly. "I appreciate it.''

"No problem.''

Almost an hour later, Amanda was making sure that Heather had everything she needed for the night when the telephone rang. She stifled a feeling of irritation—it was probably Jeff wanting to know where Heather was—and went into her bedroom to answer it.

"Hello,'' she said wearily.

"What the hell took you so long to answer the phone?'' Way Dalton's angry voice crackled through the phone lines.

"Did anyone ever tell you that your telephone manners are abominable, Mr. Dalton?'' Amanda asked with false sweetness, recalling her two previous telephone conversations with him.

There was a lengthy pause, as if her sharp answer had taken him aback. Then she heard him chuckle, a low laugh that sent a jolt of awareness vibrating through her. "They're about on par with my patience, aren't they? You could be magnanimous just this once and chalk it off to worry."

"I could," she agreed. "And I could also ease your worry by telling you that Heather is spending the night here with me."

"What's the matter? I talked to Jeff earlier, and he was worried about the doctor's report. Is Heather all right?"

"If you'll stop talking long enough for me to get a word in edgeways, I'll tell you," Amanda said.

"I'm sorry, but Heather's all I have." He cleared his throat. "I guess you understand that better than most."

For some reason Amanda's heart went out to him. She did understand. Deliberately hardening her heart against too great a degree of thawing where Way Dalton was concerned, she recounted the doctor's findings and assured Way that Heather was fine. But when she told him about her accident, he flew to pieces and demanded to speak to her. Amanda had no choice but to rouse a sleepy Heather, who was then instructed to give him a blow-by-blow account of the accident.

By the time Heather turned the phone back over to Amanda, it was eleven-thirty, and they were both feeling the effects of the long day.

"Are you sure she's okay?" Way asked after Heather had returned to bed.

"Way," Amanda said, unaware that she'd called him by his first name, "the policeman took her by the emergency room. She's fine." She moved the phone to her other ear and turned back the covers of her bed. "I admit I was concerned at the doctor's report, but she's okay. Really."

"I hope so."

"What worries me is her being so young and missing out on so much," Amanda said, having been that route herself.

"Maybe she won't miss as much as we think."

"What do you mean?"

"She told me the other night that all she's ever wanted was someone around her to love and to love her back," Way confided. "I guess Jeff gave her something I failed to."

Despite the feelings she'd had along those same lines, Amanda couldn't bear hearing the sadness and insecurity in Way Dalton's voice. "That isn't necessarily so," she told him. "Everyone does what seems right at the moment, and sometimes life demands instant decisions. You've done the best you could, what you thought was right, the same way I have. And I just realized today that that's all any of us can do. I can't help but believe that if someone really loves his kids, they can't go too far wrong."

"Even now?"

"Even now. As Dr. Palmer says, teen pregnancies happen. That doesn't make it right for our kids, any more than it was for me. It just makes it . . . happen."

Way listened to the woman he'd compared to Attila the Hun and felt the burden he'd been carrying for almost a week lighten. Every now and then Amanda Farrell surprised him with a show of tenderness, a glimpse of the woman she might have once been and could maybe become again—if she ever lowered her guard long enough to let some emotion into her well-ordered existence.

As he had on other occasions, Way wondered suddenly, and for no reason, what her mouth tasted like, how it would feel to hold her slender body in his arms and love her far into the night...to make her become soft and yielding and giving. As soon as the thought entered his mind, he banished it.

"Thanks," he told her, his voice holding a leftover softness.

"For what?" Amanda asked.

"The pep talk. I needed it. I've been feeling pretty low since Heather told me that, even though I know she didn't mean to hurt me when she said it."

"Jeff has said some pretty hurtful things to me, too," Amanda confessed. Her bitter laugh caught on a sob. "And I think he meant all of them."

Way heard the threat of tears in her voice, and he already knew Amanda Farrell well enough to know that if he saw any crack in her demeanor, it would completely demoralize her. He injected a deliberate lightness into his voice. "I doubt that. Jeff's a good kid. I wouldn't put too much stock in anything he says right now. We're all under a lot of strain."

"I guess you're right."

"Speaking of which, I've got to let you get some sleep. I didn't realize it was so late."

Amanda glanced at the clock. Almost midnight.

"Look, Amanda, I appreciate you taking care of **Heather this way. I feel better knowing she's with you.**" The seriousness of their situation was back in his voice, she noted.

"I don't mind," she said, and knew she meant it.

"Thanks anyway. I'll talk to you soon. Good night."

"Good night."

Way heard the receiver click and cradled his own. He drew a deep breath, and, resting his head in his hands, propped his elbows on his knees. What was the matter with him? Had he suddenly turned into a masochist? Amanda Farrell wouldn't give him the time of day, so why this sudden, irrational longing to taste the passion he somehow knew she was capable of? Why her, when there were hundreds of women out there who would be more than happy if he showed them some attention?

Way rose and swept back the covers on the bed, sliding between the sheets and folding his arms beneath his head. For a long time after Carol, there hadn't been anyone. Dating seemed tantamount to betrayal. But after a while, his hormones had got the best of his good intentions, and he'd found someone who, like him, had no interest in anything more than a good time. And for the past ten years, that's the way he'd kept it. He wasn't looking for anyone to take Carol's place. No one could.

So how did he explain his interest in Amanda? An interest that had been piqued from the first time he'd heard her voice over the phone and had grown when he'd seen her pacing her kitchen in her shorty pajamas and robe. Interest he couldn't deny, even though she could infuriate him with a look and had a tongue as unexpectedly cutting as the pampas grass bordering his driveway. No doubt about it, Amanda Farrell could use a good shaking, or a good— Way drew his thoughts up sharply. Maybe she did need someone to make love to her until her head swam, but that person wasn't him. She wasn't the kind of woman out looking for a one-night stand or a season's fling, and he wasn't in the market for anything other than that.

By nature, he respected anyone who met a challenge head-on, whether they conquered it or not. And

Amanda Farrell had done both. Earlier that evening, Jeff had explained his father's desertion and how his mother had coped with it. She hadn't let circumstances dictate her life; she had taken those circumstances and molded them to suit her. As Way's mother had often told him, life either makes you or breaks you, and it had been Amanda's making. He admired her, that's all.

Then why do you want to take her to bed, Dalton? he chided himself.

It was the challenge, he thought, turning to his side. Like the game, Amanda Farrell challenged him both physically and mentally. It would be exhilarating to try to conquer her, and, like the game, it would be a never-ending quest.

He grunted as a pain pierced his shoulder. Today's game had been a tough one, and despite his physical condition, the years were telling. He grinned in the darkness. What was the old saying? He was in pretty good shape for the shape he was in? But no matter what shape he was in, he was in no condition to take on a woman like Amanda—if he ever had the inclination.

"Forget it." Way spoke aloud, hoping the forcefulness of his voice would rid his mind of its wayward longings. It did, but only temporarily. He dreamed of Carol, and she was young and pretty as he remembered. He was happy in the dream, but then, without warning, Carol brought him a covered bird cage. When he lifted the covering, he found himself staring at an owl that looked as if it wore large, round-lensed glasses. He knew he was dreaming, and knew the dream didn't make any sense at all. He was shaving the following morning when he remembered what was so strange about the dream. The gray owl's eyes were a deep, dark violet.

CHAPTER FIVE

BY THE FOLLOWING WEEKEND, things did seem to have calmed down. Once Heather began to take the vitamins and iron, she started feeling better. Jeff's attitude improved after his talk with Way, and he didn't plan on coming home for the weekend. Amanda told herself that her life had returned to a semblance of normalcy, though it seemed there was a waiting, brooding quality to the glorious spring days.

On Saturday, Steve arrived promptly a few minutes before one, and they sat down at the kitchen table and got to work. To his credit, he caught on fairly easily, but Amanda was amazed to see how negligible his knowledge was in some areas.

"Time for a break," she told him when they'd been hard at work for more than an hour.

Steve stretched. "Sounds great to me," he said with a smile. "Do you mind if I turn on the television and catch a little of the baseball game? The Royals are playing the Orioles here today."

"Not at all," Amanda said. "What would you like to drink?"

"Coke's fine, if you have it," Steve called over his shoulder, already headed toward the living room.

Amanda joined him a few minutes later, carrying a cola for him and a glass of tea for herself. Handing him the drink, she settled into a corner of the sofa and mentally prepared herself to once more watch a game she didn't understand at all. Even as the thought crossed her mind, one batter swung at a ball that, to her untrained eye, looked impossible to hit. Nonetheless, he did hit it and the ball went sailing up. Still, the batter didn't have a chance against the perfect catch made by the center fielder, who caught the ball and threw it to the second baseman.

"Okay!" Steve said.

"Okay? Aren't you rooting for the Royals?"

"Yeah, sure, but the bases are loaded and Davies' sacrifice will put Way Dalton up to bat."

"What difference does it make?"

"Davies is a great fielder, but his batting has been way off so far this season. When he hit the fly to center field, the runner at third tagged and scored. The runner at second tagged and went to third. The runner at first stayed. Dalton is a power hitter. He could hit a homer, which would bring the other two guys in making it a three-run home run and giving the Royals a 4–0 lead in the third inning," Steve explained.

"Oh," Amanda said, nodding and turning her attention back to the television screen where Way Dalton stood, scuffing his shoes in the dirt near home plate. He took a couple of practice swings and stood expectantly. The pitcher wound up for the pitch, stepping forward and letting the ball fly in what looked to Amanda like a perfect ball to strike at. Way let it pass.

"Ball one," the sportscaster said. "Outside."

Amanda looked at Steve.

"The balls have to be thrown within certain parameters," he explained. "They have to go directly over home plate and between the shoulder blades and knees. That ball was too far to the outside of the plate, so Way didn't swing at it.''

While Amanda watched, Way hit two balls that went foul, something else Steve explained. With two strikes and one ball and a runner at first and third, Way stepped away from the batter's box and, calling time, banged the dirt off his cleats.

"What's he doing?"

"Trying to break the pitcher's concentration."

"Why?"

"To knock his pitching off form."

Amanda was amazed. Did anyone ever just go up there and try to hit the ball, or was every move calculated to produce a certain effect? "It sounds as if baseball's more a mind game than anything."

"A lot of it is," Steve agreed, "but you have to be in top-notch physical condition, too."

Way stepped back toward the plate and the pitcher wound up and threw the ball, the force of his entire body behind the pitch. Way swung and, like the pitcher, put all the force he could into the forward motion of the bat. The whack of the wood hitting the ball was clearly audible.

"The bat broke!"

But Amanda had eyes only for the ball that went up, up, up, hanging for interminable seconds before falling into the mass of screaming, groping spectators, while a disgruntled outfielder reached the end of the field and stood helplessly as the ball flew out of the stadium.

"All right!"

"What does this mean?"

"Dalton hit a home run, just like they hoped he could."

While the unseen announcer and his protégé extolled Way Dalton's luck, his RBIs and his incredibly consistent ability to knock the ball out of the park—almost any park—Amanda watched the runners go from base to base, bringing the Royals to a 4–0 lead.

Despite her views on athletics, Amanda felt a grudging admiration for the strategy involved in playing the game. As she was learning from Steve, there was a lot more to the game than grown men hitting a ball with a stick. She became so wrapped up in his play-by-play commentary that Amanda forgot she was supposed to be tutoring English.

Soon, in spite of the runs hit in by Way, it was the Orioles' turn at bat, and the Royals were sent to the field.

"What position does Way Dalton play?" she asked, unable for the life of her to remember what Jeff had told her.

"First base," Steve said.

"Oh. My son, Jeff, goes with his daughter."

Steve's eyes brightened. "Really? I guess you've met him, then?"

Amanda nodded. "Once," she said, in what she hoped was a casual tone. "And we've spoken over the phone a few times."

"Man oh man! I'd give my eye teeth to meet him," Steve said, shaking his head. "And your son dates his daughter. Small world, huh, Ms Farrell?"

Even Amanda couldn't fail to see that Steve was star struck. She smiled. "Yes, Steve, it's a small world. Maybe you'll get to meet him sometime."

"That'd be great."

A roar from the televised crowd drew their attention back to the screen. One of the Orioles had hit a ground ball directly toward Jose Delgato, the Royals' starting pitcher. It had somehow escaped him, hurtling along the ground toward the shortstop, who dove for it, scooped it into his glove, got up and threw it with lightning speed back toward Way, who was standing with one foot on first base and stretching to reach the ball. Amanda would have been hard-pressed to say which got to him first—the ball or the runner, but according to the base umpire, the man was safe.

Way shrugged and threw the ball back to Delgato with nonchalance. "Way doesn't look upset," Amanda noted with some surprise.

"He doesn't rattle easily," Steve informed her. "That's why he's such a good player. He keeps his mind on his business."

As the next batter came out of the dugout, the catcher came out to the mound to say something to Jose, who wiped his perspiring face on the shoulder of his uniform and nodded.

"He's probably telling Jose what kind of pitches to throw this guy," Steve said.

Amanda didn't answer. She was busy watching as the camera shot Way at first base, and the commentators speculated on the very thing that she and Steve had just been talking about—Way's unflappability. The camera moved in for a medium close-up, and, unaware that he was the focus of the camera, Way blew a huge bubble.

"Now that's what I call laid-back," the announcer said with a laugh, which was joined by another.

Amanda hardly noticed. She was too busy studying the alertness in the warm brown of Way's eyes and the sweep of blond mustache that grew over his upper lip and bracketed his mouth—his very sensuously shaped mouth. The camera pulled back, and Amanda noticed the way the uniform shirt made his broad shoulders look even broader and his waist more narrow. His tush was very nice, too, she thought randomly. The firm, masculine roundness went very nicely with the strong length of his legs. Realizing the direction of her thoughts, she shot a glance at Steve to see if he'd noticed. Thankfully, his gaze was glued to the television screen.

Control yourself, Amanda.

The harsh reprimand somehow brought her to her senses, and Amanda realized that, like some teenager, she was all but drooling over a famous ball player. But she wasn't a teenager, she reminded herself. She was a woman who'd been divorced for sixteen years who should know better—especially after what Deke had put her through.

"I hate to drag you away from all this," Amanda said abruptly, rising and picking up her glass, "but we do have English waiting for us in the kitchen."

Steve looked up, embarrassment on his face. "Yeah. Right. I'm sorry."

She turned off the television. "No problem. But we'd better get after it. We have a long way to go."

STEVE LEFT AN HOUR LATER, and Amanda fixed a pot of coffee in hopes that it would revive her. Tutoring him was reminiscent of helping Jeff with his homework, something that had always been draining. They had made inroads on Steve's make-up work, though, and he did seem to grasp some things better. He was a long way from being out of the woods, but at least Amanda could give him something for trying.

While the coffee perked, she went back to the living room and turned on the television, wondering—just because Way was Heather's father, of course—if the game was still on. She tuned in just in time to see another vic-

tory celebration in the dressing room, where the sportscasters were quizzing Jose Delgato. Way, his hair damp
with perspiration, shirtless, and with a towel hanging
around his neck, was standing with a group of players
when the microphone was thrust under his nose and he
was asked about a "spectacular" double play in the fifth
inning.

Amanda didn't hear his answer. She was too wrapped
up in cataloging the play of muscles in his shoulders and
biceps, the rock hardness of his stomach, and the alluring way the golden hair grew over it and the muscular
planes of his chest. When was the last time she'd seen a
chest so broad, so muscular? Had she ever? She felt a
tickling of desire deep within her and despised herself for
feeling it.

"After that homer in the third inning, what do you
think your chances are of reaching your goal of shattering Aaron's record this season?"

Goal? His ambition in life was to hit more home runs
than someone else? Amanda's newfound respect, triggered by Way's skill at playing the game, plummeted to
a new low with the news that his aspiration was to break
someone's home-run record. Disappointment, sharp and
unexpected, knifed through her. She didn't know why
she felt so let down. Had she hoped there was more to
him than she really expected? She should have known
that anyone as physically attractive as Way Dalton, *and*
someone who was involved in athletics, would have
considerably lower goals than the rest of the world.

In answer to the question, Way crossed his arms over
his chest and laughed. "I wouldn't say breaking records
is a goal. I've been lucky, and it's certainly within the
realm of possibility, but who knows what tomorrow will
bring? It would be nice to bring the record down, but

I'm not playing ball to shatter records. I just take it one game at a time. If it happens, it happens.''

The reporter nodded his understanding. ''I hear you're very involved in an antidrug campaign,'' he said, changing the tone of the impromptu interview.

''That's right,'' Way said, his serious tone matching the sobriety suddenly apparent in his eyes. ''I think the commercials start airing this weekend, as a matter of fact.''

''Any particular reason for taking up this cause over a dozen others?''

Way shrugged. ''Not really, other than we've slanted it toward kids, and I have a daughter.'' He smiled into the camera and said, ''Hi, Heather and Jeff. Hi, Mandy.''

Mandy! Surely he didn't mean her—did he?

''I'd hate to think my daughter would ever become involved with drugs,'' he continued, ''and I'd like to think that maybe some kid out there thinks enough of me, or baseball players in general, that they'll think twice before using them.''

The announcer commented on Way's statement and thanked him, ending the postgame interviews.

Strongly opposed to drugs herself, his announcement moved Way back up a notch or two on Amanda's opinion scale. That grudging respect was smothered by feelings of guilt for making a snap judgment about him. And it was no consolation that her snap judgments were rooted more in her own bitterness and lack of trust in male athletes than on any sound reasoning.

In coming to her and asking for help, Steve had made a lie of part of the myth about jocks, and that one small fact fueled her hope that maybe, just maybe, she was wrong about Way, too. With her mind filled with the

game and the interview, Amanda rose and turned off the
television set. She didn't ask herself why it mattered
whether or not Way redeemed himself. She didn't have
the courage to face the probable answer.

WAY SCRUBBED at his face and paced the living room,
eyeing the telephone with trepidation. Should he call her
or not? Since last weekend, he hadn't been able to keep
Amanda Farrell off his mind for ten consecutive minutes, except for the time he was playing ball. At some
point near the end of the week, he'd stopped trying to
fool himself and admitted that he was interested in getting to know her better. Much better. He knew it was
stupid and that under the circumstances he would get
nowhere, but that didn't change his feelings.

She intrigued him. He wanted to find out if there was
a warm flesh-and-blood woman beneath her cool, controlled exterior. Anyone as feminine as Amanda looked
had to be warm and caring, didn't she? Surely there was
some law of science that dictated that much. And besides the fact that she was attractive to him physically,
she'd brought up a decent child. Jeff was down-to-earth,
solid as a rock, a hard worker. If Amanda had helped
shape him, could she be the hard person she seemed?
Look at what she'd done with her life.

Amanda sent out conflicting signals that ranged from
a heart-wrenching vulnerability to a daunting strong-
willed independence that had enabled her to shape her
destiny.

She... intrigued him. That was the only word for it.
She'd reached goals as a single parent that few women
had reached with support and help. He admired her independence, but at the same time he could see how that
independence could be a stumbling block to any man

interested enough to try to reach her heart. She was different from the kind of woman who usually interested him, but then he'd hardly looked beyond a woman's face and figure in the past few years. Why now—of all times and with this woman—was he feeling a need to look deeper?

You're getting older, Dalton, that's why. You're getting older and one way or the other, Heather's going to be gone. Your baseball days are numbered, and that scares you. Worse than that, the thought of growing old alone scares you to death.

Way sank onto the sofa and, resting his elbows on his knees, buried his face in his hands. *What am I going to do, Carol? Our baby's pregnant, I'm alone in this, and... oh, God, I miss you so much....*

Way leaned against the sofa back and stared dry-eyed at the ceiling. He did miss her. Still. But it wasn't a devastating, destroying kind of sorrow; it was more like having a good friend move away. His heart ached sometimes with memories of things they'd shared and hurt for the things they hadn't.

He knew that their life, though good, hadn't been perfect. And, with the statistics on divorce that came out every few months, he realized that even though they had been perfect for each other then, if they met today, the man he had become might not interest her at all, just as he knew that the girl she'd been wouldn't interest him now. If she'd lived, they might not even be together. Captured in the innocence of the time, they had adored each other, and that adoration hadn't diminished until the day she died... but it might have.

What you're saying is that you loved her, but a different kind of woman appeals to the man you are now.

Way sat up, a little surprised at the turn of his thoughts. Yes. That was it. He didn't need total adoration anymore after not having it for so long. Unlike the young Way Dalton, he didn't need someone who agreed with his every idea, who hung on his every word. Maturity had changed his taste. He liked the idea of pursuing a woman who would stimulate him mentally as well as physically. A woman who would give him a surprise or two along the way. A woman like...

Amanda Farrell.

Hell, Dalton, call her. It's what you want to do.

Way turned his head and looked at the phone. Should he? She wasn't interested in him. Was his ego up to the beating it would take at her ruthless hands? How would he even go about starting a relationship with her under the circumstances? It would be hard enough if they *weren't* tied together by the kids' problem.

The kids' problem.

That was it. That was the only thing they had in common at this point, so why not use it to his best advantage? Wasn't that the way you played the game? And didn't the use of strategy determine the outcome? A smile curved Way's lips, lifting the corners of his luxuriant mustache. Watch out, Amanda Farrell! He might be a baseball player, but he was about to show her a blitz!

VISIONS OF A COMFORTABLE GOWN, a bowl of popcorn and a night watching a movie on HBO dissipated when the doorbell rang just past seven. Amanda, drying herself with a fluffy aqua-tinted towel, groaned in dismay and wondered who on earth could be visiting.

Struggling to pull a pair of shorts up her still-damp legs, she bellowed an irritated "I'm coming!" Then, snapping and zipping the shorts, she grabbed a sleeve-less knit shirt on her way out of the bedroom, pulling it over her wet head and settling it over her hips just as she reached the door. Standing on tiptoe, she peered out the peephole.

Shock widened her eyes and set her heels to the floor. Way Dalton! Unexpected feelings of nervous excite-ment—the likes of which she hadn't felt since her high-school days—rushed through her, bringing an irregular rhythm to her heart and a blush to her cheeks. With no makeup on, wearing old shorts and with her hair still wet from her shower, she looked like the wrath of God. Amanda groaned and covered her hot cheeks with her palms, rising on tiptoe and looking again.

Way stood there, his hands—palms out—in his back pockets, facing the street and looking, she thought with a sinking heart, like a million dollars in a pair of form-fitting Levi's. He turned, and she saw that the soft pas-tel-plaid shirt he was wearing was unbuttoned at least three buttons, enough to reveal a bit of his bronzed chest and sun-bleached hair.

The doorbell rang again, and Amanda frantically finger combed her damp hair, swearing in futility when she realized she was fighting a losing battle. Her innate pride came to her rescue, reminding her that it didn't really matter what she looked like. Heather's father meant nothing to her. She swung open the door, her chin high and a look of composure she was far from feeling on her face.

Way turned at the sound of the door opening, a smile of greeting curving his mouth. Then the smile faded and his breath hung in his throat for a brief second. All the nervousness and uncertainty he'd battled with before he'd left the house returned with a vengeance. He took

a deep, calming breath, and his plan to use the kids'
problem to infiltrate her life now made him feel like a
lowlife. This wasn't the controlled, hard-hearted woman
whose slacks had creases so sharp they'd cut you. This
wasn't the woman he'd tangled with before. This was the
same Amanda he'd glimpsed in the short gown and robe.
An Amanda who was innocent looking and incredibly
beautiful. Like a love-struck teenager, all he could do
was stand and look at her, from the cap of dark hair that
clung in damp spikes to her shapely head to her bare feet
with the crimson-tipped toenails.

She had just got out of the shower. Her face, scrubbed
free of makeup, glowed with a healthy tint that made her
look much younger than she was. Her eyes, devoid of
the added glamour of eye shadow and mascara and
without the aid of either contacts or glasses, were filled
with a soft myopic wonder. Eyes that might have belonged to a fifteen-year-old. Her legs were slender and
shapely, just the way he remembered and—he swallowed—if the pebble hardness of her nipples pushing
impudently against the fabric of her white tank top was
any indication, she wasn't wearing a bra.

Desire, hot and strong, roused from its dormant state
to instant, hungry awareness. Way couldn't remember
the last time he'd felt such an overwhelming need to taste
a woman's mouth, to see how her breasts would feel
against his palms. He ran his tongue over his dry lips and
offered her a half smile.

"Hi."

"Hi." Amanda sounded breathless.

"I hope I'm not disturbing anything."

She shook her head and raised a self-conscious hand
to her wet hair. "I was just getting out of the shower. I
hope I didn't keep you waiting too long."

"No." *Way to go, Dalton. Dazzle her with your erudite conversation.*

"Jeff isn't here," Amanda said apologetically. "He stayed at school this weekend."

"I didn't come to see Jeff."

Surprise flickered in the depths of her amethyst-hued eyes.

"I came to thank you for having Heather over the night of the accident."

"No problem," Amanda said with a small shrug. Then, because she felt awkward standing in the open doorway, she asked, "Would you like to come in?"

"Thanks."

She stood aside for him to enter and led the way into the living room, wishing suddenly that she'd gone ahead and bought the new sofa she'd looked at the month before. What she considered a homey room probably looked shabby and worn to a man like Way Dalton. Her eyes never left his face as he looked around the room with unconcealed interest, taking in the warmth of the country decor—a hodgepodge of craft-type items and secondhand and antique "finds."

"Nice room," he said, plunging his hands back into his rear pockets.

"Thank you." For no reason that was immediately apparent, it occurred to Amanda that he wasn't sitting because she hadn't. Was it possible that Way Dalton was a little old-fashioned, despite his reputation? "Please, sit down," she offered, perching on the edge of a cane chair.

Feet spread apart, Way sat down on the traditional-style sofa, stretching his arms across the low back. "You don't know how much better I feel knowing that you're helping Heather take care of things."

Amanda tried not to stare at the way the wash-softened denim pulled across the bulge of his masculinity. "I haven't really done anything."

"You've been here to support her. I think that's important to her since she doesn't have a mother to help her get through this. I understand that it's probably hard for you, knowing the way you feel about things, and I really appreciate it."

How did she feel about things? Amanda wondered. While it was true that nothing had changed, she could honestly say that there was little animosity in her at the moment. For some unknown reason, a strange combination of acceptance and anticipation now filled the void left by her anger.

She met his gaze squarely. "Heather is very easy to like," she said honestly. "It's been a pleasure to do things for her."

There was a considering quality in Way's eyes as he looked deeply into hers, almost as if he couldn't believe that she would make such an admission. In truth, it surprised Amanda almost as much as it had him. And more of a surprise, the statement left her heart feeling lighter than it had in days.

"Would you like something to drink?" she asked, as much to break the silence growing between them as because she realized her manners were remiss.

Way was knocked off guard by her openness and unexpected goodwill. Wanting to take advantage of her apparent softening, he felt the need to get Amanda on neutral territory. He always felt at a distinct disadvantage when he wasn't on home turf.

"No, thanks," he said. "Have you had dinner? We could go somewhere and talk about . . . things."

"I had a sandwich earlier," she said.

One corner of his mustache lifted in a half smile. "Well, then, would you like to come along while I get something? You could have coffee and dessert."

Should I? Amanda wondered. And close on the heels of that thought came another: why was she even considering going with him? Her heart was pounding ninety-to-nothing as she said, "I'm not dressed."

Way indicated his casual attire. "Hey. Look at me. I'm not talking about dinner and dancing here. I'm talking more like Pizza Hut. If you're interested, just dry your hair and put on something casual." He smiled, a dazzling smile that revealed his even white teeth and gouged deep creases in his cheeks. It was a smile that didn't play fair, a hit-'em-below-the-belt sort of smile that destroyed the last lingering bit of animosity.

Amanda forgot that she and Way Dalton didn't agree on the "things" they had to talk about, forgot that she hated his kind of man. Discounting the rapid beating of her heart, she reasoned that she was going to be in contact with him a lot in the future. There was no sense in making him an enemy. She offered him a tentative smile. "That sounds...nice, if you don't mind waiting. Do you think Heather would like to go?" she asked.

"Heather has gone to spend the weekend with her aunt in Saint Louis, so I'm sort of at loose ends. And I don't mind waiting at all. Take your time."

"I won't be but a minute," she promised. "Make yourself at home."

"Thanks. And there's no hurry."

Amanda carried a picture of his slow smile with her to the bedroom, where she flung open the closet door and made a quick perusal of her wardrobe. Suddenly everything she owned seemed too dressy—even her slacks. There was something about the prospect of an evening with Way Dalton that called for jeans, sweatshirts and tennis shoes. The kind of outfit that hadn't had a place in her wardrobe since she got her degree. In the end she settled for a long denim skirt and a red, short-sleeve summer sweater with a scoop neck, dragging them from their hangers and over her head in record time.

When she reentered the living room, Way was standing at the window, watching a trio of hummingbirds fight over the sugared water in the feeder. He turned when he heard her steps in the hall, and Amanda could have sworn she saw a flicker of pleasure light his eyes.

"Ready?" he asked.

She nodded. "Let me get my purse."

They walked out into the spring dusk toward the car sitting at the curb—a blue 1957 Chevrolet convertible complete with a rolled-and-pleated dash—direct from Mexico.

They reached the car, and Amanda smoothed her palm over the fender, turning to him with a smile of pleasure on her face. "Jeff needs to see this. He's car crazy."

Way opened the passenger door and smiled back. "He has."

"Really?" she asked as the door slammed shut.

"Yeah." Way walked around the hood to his side and got in. He cranked the engine and pulled away from the curb. "After he showed the proper amount of awe and deference, I decided I liked the kid."

Amanda laughed, a light gurgling of sound that seemed totally out of character. Way felt a frisson of desire scampering down his spine.

"Where did you get it?" she asked, her eyes taking in the details of restoration.

"The junkyard. I worked on it in my garage for three winters, and the money I've spent on restoring it could make serious inroads on the national debt."

Amanda laughed again. She could imagine. She knew how hard Jeff had worked on his car and had an inkling of what it cost, even with her mechanic father doing a major portion of the restorative work. She settled into the corner and stretched her arms across the back of the seat and the car door so that she would have a better view of Way, who, at that moment, was searching for a radio station whose decibel level wouldn't curdle their brains.

He controlled the car easily as they drove along, and Amanda was soon lost in thoughts of him. His sense of humor was the biggest surprise, as surprising as how easy he was to talk to. And who would ever have thought he would be interested in old cars? Was it not only possible but probable that there was more to him than met the eye?

She pondered the question while the wind riffled his hair into careless disarray and the last rays of the evening sun gilded it with gold. The radio, tuned to a station specializing in oldies but goodies, blared out "Duke of Earl," while Amanda tried to visualize Way at seventeen. He would have been much the same then, she thought—handsome and confident. She'd bet next week's paycheck that the girls had flocked to him in absolute droves. And if she'd known him then, she probably wouldn't have been an exception.

Way turned and caught her staring at him. He smiled, that slow, gorgeous smile that invariably set her heart to pounding and made her mouth dry. She smiled back. Tentatively. Almost fearfully.

There was something happening here that she didn't want, didn't need, but knowing it didn't stop the throb of desire deep inside her. An undeniable excitement held her in its grip, and a million butterflies were doing jumping jacks in her stomach. What was the matter with her? She was just going for coffee, for goodness' sake! It wasn't as if it were a real date.

But it felt like a real date. She felt sixteen again. Sixteen and innocent, with all the same fears and insecurities she'd felt back then. She and Way had nothing in common. Once they'd talked about Heather and Jeff, what would she say to him? After the kind of woman he was used to, how could she possibly hold his interest? Way Dalton was a national celebrity. A famous baseball player. And way out of her league.

CHAPTER SIX

WAY DROVE THEM to the Sonic Drive-In, perhaps the last bastion of that anachronism, the carhop. The girls, all pretty teenagers with great legs, skated to and fro from the cars to the building, serving up the orders on trays that hooked over partially rolled up windows. The feeling of déjà vu that had struck Amanda when she'd first got into the car grew stronger. How many times had she gone out with a boy who'd taken her to get a hamburger at just such a place?

She watched with a half smile as Way ordered a burger, some onion rings and a chocolate malt. She'd decided on just a Coke, but Way overrode her objections and told the girl to bring her a chocolate milk shake. Amanda gave in graciously. She loved chocolate shakes and hardly ever indulged her craving because she seemed to be forever conscious of her eating habits. Just one wouldn't hurt, would it?

"So," Way said, once the order had gone to the grill, "what's Jeff doing this weekend?"

Amanda crossed her legs nervously. Now that they had arrived and the ordering had been done, there was nothing left to do but talk. Her butterflies returned with a vengeance. "I don't know. He said something about having a gig at a new club."

Way leaned against the door and faced Amanda. "You don't sound pleased."

Amanda sighed. "You may as well know that I'm not crazy about Jeff's music major."

"Why?"

"What can he do with it besides teach?"

"What's wrong with that? You teach."

"There's nothing *wrong* with it, but Jeff is capable of so much more. He's a whiz at math. He could be an engineer, or an architect." Her voice was laced with the frustration she faced every time she thought about the subject.

"What does he want to be?"

She looked askance at him, her eyes holding the unlikely combination of disgust and wry humor. "The next Van Halen."

Way laughed.

"Don't laugh," she begged. "This is serious. He has a minor in business, which still doesn't tap into his potential as far as I'm concerned."

"Look, Mandy," Way told her, "there's no use losing any sleep over this. He'll do what he wants, and all your worrying won't change things."

"Please, don't," she said.

A frown furrowed his brow. "Don't what?"

"Call me Mandy."

"Why not?"

Amanda stared thoughtfully at a spot behind his left shoulder. Because Mandy was another man's name for her. It belonged to another lifetime, to a girl who was captain of the cheerleaders, head of the drama club. Mandy, the straight-A student. Mandy, who had the lightest laughter and the highest cheerleading jumps.

Amanda was the grown-up, serious woman who'd left everything youthful behind. Amanda was the mother, the dutiful daughter, the teacher, the person who'd paid for her mistake and was still paying. There was no Mandy left inside her, no matter how much she might wish there was.

She dragged her gaze back to Way's. "Deke called me Mandy."

Way nodded his understanding. "I'll try to remember, but I'm not making any promises. You look like a Mandy to me." Then, as if the conversation hadn't been interrupted by the small altercation over her name, he steered them back to their original topic. "My mother nearly went into cardiac arrest when I started playing baseball. She didn't think it was a real job and was convinced that we'd starve to death."

We'd starve to death? Who was *"we"*?

Way must have seen the question in her eyes, because he shifted his gaze from hers. When he faced her again there was a sort of determination on his face.

"Carol and Heather and I."

Before Amanda's brain could arrive at any conclusions, Way settled the matter once and for all. The look in his eyes was kind, his smile bittersweet. "You didn't corner the market on getting pregnant out of wedlock, Mandy. There were a lot of us who got caught in the same trap."

Amanda didn't even notice that he'd called her Mandy. The only thing she heard was his confession. "You and Carol?"

He nodded. "Yeah. The only difference is that for us, it worked... until she died, anyway."

"What happened?" It never occurred to Amanda that her question might not be appreciated, that he might not want to talk about it. There was a sort of intimacy to the moment that superseded any unspoken code of conduct and good manners. Somehow she intuitively knew that it was all right to ask.

There was a lost expression in Way's eyes, as if the memory brought back all the pain and heartache. "She was killed in a car accident not a mile from the house, pulling out of the parking lot of the grocery store."

"I'm sorry," Amanda whispered, lacing her hands together tightly.

He looked at her and saw the empathy on her face. "So am I, when I think about it." His eyes held a keen awareness as he asked, "What about you?"

"What do you mean?"

"Do you miss Deke when you think about it?"

"No." Her voice was as emphatic as the shake of her head. "Not anymore. I loved him for a long time after he left, but when the love was gone, it was gone for good. I've only seen him twice since he moved out."

"Did he come to see Jeff?"

Amanda laughed, a short, harsh sound that seemed out of character with her recent softness. "No. He came to ask me for money."

"Wow," he said, shaking his head in disbelief. "He didn't want to see Jeff at all?"

"He never asked to, and if he had, I doubt I would have let him."

Way straightened in his seat and looked at her again. "When I first saw you, I wondered what could have happened to give you such a bad taste in your mouth about marriage. I knew it had to be something pretty terrible, because anyone who looks like you do could have found someone else a hundred times over."

Amanda's eyes clung to his and her heartbeat sped up at the knowledge that he found her attractive. She deliberately made her tone light. "I haven't been looking," she said. "What about you? If your marriage was so good, why haven't you taken the plunge a second time?"

Amanda held her breath while Way gave the question careful consideration. Was there a woman in his life?

"I guess because it was so good," he said at last. "And because I saw so many marriages around me failing. I think I was afraid I'd never get lucky enough to find that kind of happiness a second time."

"The same way I was afraid I'd find misery the second time," she said, understanding fully what he meant.

There was acceptance in his eyes. "At least I understand now why you don't want the kids to get married."

Her mouth curved in a smile. "And I see why you do."

He smiled back, the action deepening the crow's-feet at the corners of his eyes. It was, she thought later, one of those rare and inexplicable moments of complete rapport. For one brief second they had glimpsed the secrets of each other's hearts, and she knew exactly what Way Dalton was all about. The fact that there was more to him than she might have expected wasn't as big a surprise as it might have been a few weeks ago.

"Look, Amanda, they made the decision to have sex before they were married, and they'll have to make the decision to marry or not, too," he told her, breaking the brief silence.

Amanda stared at her hands. She sighed. "I know."

"If we try to sway them either way and anything happens, they'll hold us responsible."

She lifted her gaze to his. "You're right. I know you're right, Way, it's just that it's so hard. They don't have any idea how hard it's going to be."

"No, they don't. But they say they love each other, and I don't feel like I'm in any position to say that what they feel isn't real, do you?"

"No," she admitted. "But if they do . . . decide to get married, I don't know how Jeff thinks he can support her and the baby working at a fast-food chain by day and playing and singing at two-bit clubs by night."

"He'll manage. The same way we both did. Jeff's a good kid and a hard worker, Amanda. You've instilled a lot of good qualities in him. If they decide to get married, he'll be okay. It's Heather I worry about."

Amanda frowned. "Why?"

"I'm not sure I've done as good a job with her as you have with Jeff. Heather is spoiled. I'm afraid she might not adjust to a limited income too easily."

Amanda could see the pain his admission caused. She imagined that it had been easy for him to assuage his guilty conscience for not spending time with Heather by buying her things. Somehow the realization brought a sense of sadness instead of the pleasure it might have a couple of weeks ago. Unexpectedly, Amanda wanted to ease the hurt she knew he was feeling. "She seems to have her head on pretty straight. I wouldn't worry about Heather."

"Here you go!"

The breezy voice of the carhop temporarily ended the conversation. Amanda watched as the waitress hooked the tray over the window and handed Way the ticket.

"Excuse me," he said, leaning across the seat and pushing the button of the glove compartment. For the span of a few brief heartbeats, his arm was pressed against her as he reached inside and pulled out his billfold. Amanda was acutely aware of the strength in his forearm, the masculine, peppery scent of his cologne and the heady effect of his nearness. Then he moved away and the moment was gone, leaving only a breathless anticipation that was accompanied by the reckless surging of her blood through her veins.

She wasn't aware that she was staring at him with wide, mystified eyes or that Way was trying to deal with his own awareness of her. Only when the girl left and he turned, offering her the milk shake, did she rouse herself and force herself to act normally.

"Thanks," she said, taking the cold container and willing her fingers to stillness when they accidentally brushed his.

Way picked up an onion ring. "This place makes the best onion rings in town," he proclaimed, offering it to Amanda. "Here. Try one."

"It's fried. I don't eat fried food," she said, saying the first thing that came to mind.

"You don't eat fried food?" he repeated.

"Very seldom," she said with a shake of her head. "I'm not dogmatic about it. I started out with a concern about cholesterol, and now it's habit more than anything."

Way stared into her amethyst-tinted eyes for a moment. "Habit, huh? Well, I can certainly introduce you to a few of the less desirable ones."

I'll bet you could. Breathlessly, Amanda wondered which ones he meant.

He held out the onion ring again. "Humor me?" he asked in a teasing voice, the creases in his cheeks appearing along with his smile.

How could she refuse him without seeming churlish? There was something about Way Dalton that was hard to resist. And she was becoming increasingly aware that she wasn't certain she wanted to.

A feeling of rebellion swept through her. Why shouldn't she eat fried food if she wanted to once in a while? She felt a giggle rising at the ridiculous thought that eating an onion ring signified rebellion. If that was rebellion, she had definitely become staid and stuffy.

"I shouldn't," she said, "but I will."

"I WILL."

Jeff uttered the words with a fervency that drove all the lingering doubts from Heather's mind. As she smiled, the tension and worry etched on her face were erased and the sherry tints in her brown eyes lit up. Jeff was promising to take care of her in sickness and health, until death parted them. He loved her. He really did. And he was marrying her despite his mother's objections and fears. How had she ever imagined that he was only marrying her because of the baby?

Her smile faltered when she thought of what his mother would say when she found out—though Heather had learned that Amanda Farrell wasn't the ogre she'd seemed at first. Jeff's mother could be warm and caring, and Heather was beginning to see that Amanda was, in a sense, right. Even though she and Jeff loved each other, there would be some tough times ahead.

The sound of the justice of the peace's voice became a faraway drone as Heather stared at her hands, held tightly in Jeff's. The plain gold band he had just put on her finger glittered under the overhead lights. He hadn't been able to afford an engagement ring, but that didn't seem so bad considering that she hadn't even been able to buy him a wedding band. All her allowance had been spent on the dress she was wearing. She and Jeff had agreed not to tell anyone they were married until after her graduation, almost a month away, and she'd been afraid to ask her dad for any more money for fear she would rouse his suspicions. She hated being devious, hated lying, but Jeff had convinced her that it was the right thing to do.

The strangest thing was, Heather thought, that she was beginning to understand why Amanda felt the way she did. She was already dreaming about the baby she carried, wondering what it would look like, how it would act and what kind of a person it would grow up to be. Womanlike, motherlike, she already wanted only the best for her child.

"I now pronounce you man and wife," the justice of the peace said. "You may kiss your bride."

The pronouncement brought Heather's thoughts back to the present and drew her gaze from their entwined hands to Jeff's face. He smiled, and she found herself hoping that the baby would have a smile just like his. He moved his hands to her waist and pulled her nearer, lowering his head and taking her lips in a gentle, loving kiss. Heather clung to him, and all too soon he pulled away, looking down at her with love and the glimmer of tears in his warm brown eyes.

He swallowed hard. "I love you, Heather Farrell."

Heather Farrell. It was real. She was Jeff's wife. And she was going to have his baby. She smiled up at him, a smile so radiant and glowing it took his breath away.

"I love you," she whispered.

Jeff thought the three words sounded like another promise. They signed the necessary papers, paid the JP and thanked his wife, who had acted as a witness. Finally Heather was handed the wedding certificate to put in her purse. Then Jeff put his arms around her shoulders, and they walked out into the spring evening and the beginning of a new life together.

Once they were in the car, he pulled her close and kissed her, a long, heated kiss that quickly got out of hand while Jeff caressed her breasts through the fabric of her dress. Heather pressed closer, offering the very thing he wanted so badly.

Abruptly, Jeff pulled away, resting his forehead against hers while they struggled to gain control of their breathing. "I wish we could spend the night together."

"Me, too," Heather said, "but Aunt Jill is expecting me early in the morning, and—"

"And we're going to have to drive all night to get you there. I know."

The frustration in his voice matched what Heather was feeling. "I'm sorry," she whispered.

Jeff released her and scooted down in the seat, resting his dark head against the back. "It's not your fault," he said to the car's roof. He turned to look at her. "But it's been so long since—"

"I know."

Jeff laughed. "I don't know why we decided to abstain *after* we found out you were pregnant. It was kind of late to be careful then, wasn't it?"

Heather knew what he was talking about. By silent mutual agreement, he hadn't touched her since she told him she was carrying his baby. Somehow, it had seemed the thing to do. "It might seem silly, Jeff, but it was right. I know it was."

He sighed and smiled. "Yeah, I know. But it's almost a month until you graduate and we tell them." He reached out and skimmed his palm over her breast and down her stomach. "And I probably won't even get to see you three times during that month, let alone touch you."

Heather's breath caught in her throat at the intimacy of his touch. Her eyelashes drifted shut. "Jeff," she murmured softly.

"Yeah?"

She opened her closed lids and looked at him. With the twinkle of lighthearted mischief in her eyes, she looked uncannily like her father. "How do you feel about quickies?"

"Quickies?" Jeff asked with a frown. "What do you know about quickies?"

She smiled, a smile as old as time, as alluring as a siren's song. "Find us a nice country road," she said, "and I'll show you."

MAY DREW TO A CLOSE along with the school year, grinding to a standstill as the days grew warmer, and leaving everyone with a sense of wanting to get the last term over with. The college finals were over, and nothing stood in the way of summer vacation but the high school graduation ceremony.

Thanks to a lot of hard work on both Steve and Amanda's part, he had passed the year with a low C, which settled the issue of whether she would give him the grade or not, as she'd been directed to do. It didn't settle the basic issue, though. She'd managed to pull it off this time without compromising her principles, but what about next year or the year after that? Amanda decided that she wouldn't worry anymore. Not until she had to.

Heather had settled down and was feeling better now that she was on a regular regimen of rest and medication. Her blood count was up, and she looked much better to Amanda, who often found herself wondering just what was going to happen. No one mentioned marriage anymore—not Way or Jeff or Heather. She supposed everyone was doing as she suggested and thinking through the options, but her woman's intuition told her that everything hinged on Heather getting out of school. She didn't know what would happen after that, she only knew something would.

And, Amanda thought, blowing her hair dry, the wait was almost over. Heather's graduation ceremony was in a few hours. There had been a panicky moment or two when Amanda had received the formal invitation in the mail, and she'd wondered how she would feel about Way when she saw him next. Would she still feel that naive nervousness that she thought she'd finished with when she'd entered adulthood? Had she imagined the interest she'd seen in his eyes almost a month ago?

A month. Where had the time gone? As it had too frequently since the night she'd gone with Way to the Sonic, her mind replayed the evening from the moment she'd opened the door until two hours later when he'd left her standing beneath the golden glow of her front porch light.

Way had been surprisingly easy to talk to, and they really did have a lot in common. At first she'd felt young and gauche and insecure, but the longer they'd talked, comparing their own marriages, and later, when they'd laughed over some of the songs they heard on the "oldies" station, she had relaxed and really enjoyed the evening. She'd actually had fun, something she couldn't remember happening with a man in years. There was no denying that Way Dalton elicited a response from her, even though that response was given grudgingly.

Own up to it, Amanda. Despite what and who the man is, despite the damnable circumstances that brought you together, you're attracted to him. Physically attracted to him. Say it.

"All right," she said loudly, over the humming of the hand-held hair dryer. "I'm attracted to him." She glared at her mirror image. "There. I said it. Are you satisfied?"

Are you?

She heaved a sigh that lifted her breasts beneath the deep rose satin of the robe she wore. No. She wasn't satisfied. As a matter of fact, she didn't know when she'd been so on edge. Her body had never given her any trouble before—in fact, she'd never felt she just *had* to have a man during the years she'd been single—but the thought of Way Dalton touching her... making love to her, made her ache with need. She didn't know how many nights she'd awakened from a dream in which his body possessed hers, to find herself trembling, her breasts hurting for a touch she'd never known, and smothered by a soul-deep embarrassment for not having more control over her emotions.

You have the hots for him, Amanda.

"Okay," she cried loudly. "I admit it. You're right. I do."

"What?"

The single word called from Jeff's room put a stop to her introspection. She turned off the hair dryer and yelled back. "What?"

"What did you want?" he called.

Amanda frowned. "What do you mean? I didn't want anything."

"Then why were you yelling?" Jeff called irritably.

"I wasn't yelling!"

"Yes, you were."

Amanda thought about her conversation with herself. A blush crept up over her cheeks. "I guess I was just thinking out loud," she said. "Sorry."

She turned the dryer back on, drowning out his answer. She'd better get hold of herself before she came face-to-face with Way, or no telling what kind of fool she would make of herself. *Concentrate on one thing at a time, Amanda. Get ready, and worry about how you're going to act when you get there. First finish your hair.*

Taking her own advice, she switched the brush to her left hand, lamenting the condition of her hair. She needed a haircut. She usually had one every five or six weeks, and it had been almost two months now. It seemed as if there was always something that prevented her from taking time out to visit the hairdresser.

Amanda sighed and brushed the sides back, spraying them in place and spritzing the top, which now wanted to curl over her forehead. Feathery tendrils curled at her nape. The look was too carefree, she thought, too young looking and not at all in keeping with her usual appearance. It was too... soft. Her hair was a pain and a nuisance, she decided, setting the spray down with a bang. And she was going to call tomorrow and get an appointment to have it whacked off.

Going to the closet, Amanda donned the dress she'd bought for Heather's graduation. The saleswoman had raved about the way it looked on her, and she'd known that wearing the garment with her black, ridiculously high heels and her pearl accessories, she could hold her own in any crowd. She hoped she was right. She sprayed cloudlike puffs of Anaïs to her wrists and put a glaze of clear lip moisturizer over lips painted a carmine red. Then she stood back and surveyed her handiwork.

Amanda was pleased with the results. The deep purple hue of the silk shirtwaist brought out the translucence of her ivory complexion and the violet of her eyes, and the wide belt accentuated the smallness of her waist.

Not bad for a woman staring grandmotherhood in the face, she thought with a half smile. Not bad at all. A ripple of excitement shimmered through her as she wondered if Way would share her sentiments.

"WHAT ARE YOU so nervous about, Daddy?" Heather asked as Way stood impatiently while she turned the collar of his pale yellow dress shirt over his contrasting tie.

Way thought of Amanda and the fact that he hadn't seen her in nearly a month—partly due to his schedule, and partly due to a conscious effort on his part not to call her when he was in town. After all, if he was going to use Jeff and Heather as excuses to have contact with her, his meeting with her the first of the month had effectively ended that ruse. By talking Amanda into agreeing to let Jeff and Heather make their own decision, he had put an end to any logical reason to meet with her. His lips twisted wryly. He was hoist with his own petard. Caught in an impasse of his own making. But he would see her tonight. Finally. And this time without any flimsy excuses.

"I'm nervous because I don't have a daughter who graduates every day." Way adjusted the knot of his tie and turned. "How do I look?"

Locking her hands behind her back, she cocked her head to one side and pretended to give his question serious consideration. "Hmm," she said, lifting herself to her toes, then lowering her heels to the floor in a considering manner. "Wonderful. Handsome. Dare I say sexy?"

Way grinned. "You may." He turned back to the mirror, and Heather slid her arms around his waist from behind. She breathed in the masculine cologne that he always wore and peeked around his arm in order to meet his gaze in the mirror.

"Are you sure about the sexy?" he queried with lifted brows. "Don't forget I'm going to be a grandfather. Are grandfathers sexy?"

Heather smiled, her pert nose wrinkling attractively. "Men don't get old, they just get better."

"You're sure?"

"Look at Ricardo Montalban...Paul Newman...Charles Bronson."

"They're sexy?"

"They're sexy. Trust me on this, Daddy. I'm a woman. I know about these things. I know sexy when I see it. And I'm looking at it right now."

"Okay, if you're sure."

Heather released her hold on him and said, "What is this? Insecurity from the celebrity ball player? Who are you trying to impress, anyway? We won't see anyone but Jeff and his moth..."

A sudden thought came to her. "Daddy, you aren't...I mean, you don't think Jeff's mother... Are you interested in her?"

"I just don't want to give her any reason to think we aren't good enough for her son," Way said, unable to meet her gaze.

"Fine," Heather said with a nod. "I can relate to that. But Daddy, what does that have to do with whether or not you're handsome and sexy?"

Way glanced at the gold Rolex nestled against the hair of his wrist. "Would you look at the time? Are you ready, baby? We're going to be late."

Heather shook her head. She knew he was putting her off. She let him hustle her outside and into the Chevy. But she didn't forget his evasiveness.

CHAPTER SEVEN

BY THE TIME Amanda and Jeff arrived at the auditorium, there were no close parking spaces and the huge room was packed. Jeff looked around in vain for Way, who had promised to hold them seats, and in the end they settled for some places almost three-quarters of the way back. Amanda wasn't certain whether she was relieved or disappointed when Jeff gave up the quest for Way and took the available seats.

Thankfully her feelings disappeared once the ceremony—lengthy, with over two hundred graduates—and the announcement of scholarships, began. It was over at nine-thirty, and Amanda, who hadn't taken time to eat before they left, had forgotten her nervousness over the possibility of seeing Way. She was longing for a cup of coffee and at least something sweet to revive her.

Holding on to Jeff's hand for dear life and murmuring breathless apologies when she accidentally bumped into someone, Amanda allowed him to drag her through the throng in hopes of finding Heather before she left with Way. As Amanda expected, the hall outside was a crush, too, and she didn't know how Jeff ever hoped to find Heather.

She hadn't counted on his advantageous height.

He spied Heather across the way and called her name, releasing Amanda's hand to wave. "Over here!"

At the same time that Jeff waved in order to get Heather's attention, Amanda sidestepped a quarterback-looking type with a flattop, who was pushing his way toward the outside door. When she looked back, Jeff had somehow disappeared. A feeling of dismay swept through her as she scanned the nearby faces. It would take her ages to find him in this throng. She was considering the possibility of waiting outside until the crowd began to thin out, when she was bumped from behind—straight into a hard chest. Her hands reached for something solid; at the same time strong hands gripped her shoulders, and her senses were assaulted by a familiar pepper-and-spice scent.

"Excuse me," she said, pushing herself away and noting that the chest was covered with a pale yellow shirt and a pearl-gray suit coat. She tipped her head back to see whom she had almost mowed down and found herself looking up into warm brown eyes with laugh lines at the corners. Familiar, warm brown eyes. Way's eyes.

"You're excused," he replied, "Are you okay?"

"Fine," she said, staring up at him while her heart raced beneath the purple silk.

"Some guy who looked like he weighed about three hundred pounds bumped you from behind," he explained.

"Oh." Amanda couldn't think of anything else to say. In the crush of the crowd he was too close, and it didn't help that because of the noise he had bent lower to hear her responses. "What happened to Jeff?" she asked, saying the first thing that came to mind.

"He and Heather have gone."

"Gone? Where?" she asked as panic set in.

"Settle down, Mandy," Way said soothingly. Sliding his arm around her shoulders, he headed toward the double doors leading outside. "Let's get out of this madhouse and I'll tell you."

As she had only moments before with Jeff, Amanda let Way lead her through the crowd to the comparative calm of the spring evening. After the closeness of the crowded corridor and the mingled odors of perfumes and colognes, the night air was fresh and cool. Way released her, plunging his hands into his slacks pockets in a way that splayed the fabric over his manhood in a provocative and disturbing manner. His eyes raked her with a thorough, composure-shattering perusal that any woman but Amanda would have recognized as hungry, as if he'd missed her and was trying to get his fill of the sight of her.

"Your hair is longer," he said at last.

His voice was low and husky. The sound shimmied up her spine, leaving behind a breathless excitement. Automatically, Amanda touched a lock of dark hair curling against the side of her neck. "It's a mess."

"I like it."

"You do?"

His smile was slow, and like his voice, very seductive. His gaze meshed with hers, and Way removed his right hand from his pocket and tugged at a ribbon of hair that lay in a loose spiral against the zenith of her cheekbone. The silky black curl slid through his fingers and bounced back into place.

"I do like it," he said with a slow nod, "very much."

"Thank you."

"And the color of that dress is perfect. You look...great."

Amanda's heart swelled with a feeling she couldn't put a name to. "So do you."

"Yeah?" he said, tugging at the knot of his tie. "Well, too bad. You know the old magician's trick—now you see it, now you don't!"

With the same economy of motion she'd seen him put to effect on the baseball field, he pulled the tie off and stuffed it into his coat pocket. Then he reached for the top button of his shirt and began to work it free of its mooring. "I hate those things," he said. "They choke me."

"I can imagine," she murmured, trying not to stare at the golden hair revealed in the V of his unbuttoned shirt. "So," she said, hugging her black clutch bag close to her stomach, "where did Heather and Jeff go?"

"To Wayfarers."

"Wayfarers? The restaurant?"

He nodded. "You know kids. They don't ask anymore. They just tell you what's going on."

"But...how am I going to get home?" Amanda asked.

"Hey," he said with a grin and an affronted tone. "Do I look like the kind of guy who'd leave a woman stranded?"

He didn't. He looked handsome and rugged and altogether solid and dependable. He looked like the kind of guy who could make a woman crazy with wanting. She shook her head.

"Okay, I'll come clean. I want us all to have dinner together—if that's all right with you," he tacked on. "I know I should have called this afternoon to ask you, but I honestly didn't think about it until the last minute."

He was lying, but Amanda didn't need to know that. Actually, he hadn't asked sooner because he'd been afraid she wouldn't agree to go. He continued his fabrication. "Of course, if it means time spent with Jeff,

Heather is going to go for it, so...when Jeff found her
a few minutes ago, she asked him and—''

"And if there's Heather *and* food involved, Jeff's
definitely going to go for it," Amanda interrupted dryly.

Way laughed. "Right. They wanted us to meet them
at the restaurant, and Heather told me she wanted to ride
with Jeff. Which means, Mandy, that you're stuck with
me."

The fact that he'd called her Mandy registered, but
somehow Amanda didn't find the nickname as objec-
tionable as she had at first. What kind of spell was Way
Dalton working on her? She took a steadying breath.
"Isn't that the other way around?"

"What do you mean?"

"*You're* stuck with me."

"Actually," he said in deep, pseudoserious tones, "I
think we've been manipulated, railroaded and out-
smarted. We're stuck with each other, so we might as
well make the best of it. What do you say? How does
some steak and lobster sound?"

As if the mention of food stirred her to new heights of
hunger, Amanda's stomach chose that instant to rum-
ble.

Way's mustache twitched as he schooled his features
into a facsimile of sobriety. "Is that a yes or no?"

Amanda bit back a smile of her own. "It's a yes."

"Good," he said, taking her elbow. "Let's go."

The restaurant, situated downtown, was in a reno-
vated building and boasted the original marble floors of
the offices that had been there more than forty years
before. The windows and door were shaded by curved
green-and-white striped awnings. The sign saying Wayfarers, written in what looked like handwriting, was
hung across the revolving front door. Amanda had never

eaten there, but she'd heard about the excellence of the food and the corresponding cost from friends.

Way's hand was warm at the small of her back as he ushered her through the door.

"Mr. Dalton, how good to see you," the maître d' said, a smile of welcome on his face.

"Hello, Phillip," Way replied. "How's business?"

"Never better."

"That's good to hear," Way said.

He urged Amanda ahead of him as they followed Phillip to a prime table, where they were seated and handed menus. Heather and Jeff, who were already seated, greeted them and they began to study the restaurant's offerings. Amanda put her menu down, looking around with interest and soaking up the ambience of the place, while the others decided.

The music of the San Sebastian strings wafted through air redolent with savory aromas. The quiet of conversation and the muted tinkling of silver against china was punctuated by an occasional quiet laugh. The decor, a careful blend of contemporary and traditional, made excellent use of large Boston ferns strategically placed atop columns of varying heights. Framed Erté reproductions and ornate mirrors hung on every available wall space, reflecting the glow of candlelight and faces animated with laughter and goodwill. The dining room was a masterpiece of understated elegance and taste.

"It's a beautiful place," Amanda said at last.

Way smiled. "You've never been here before?"

"On my salary—with a kid in college? Are you kidding?"

He rested his elbows on the pristine white tablecloth and propped his chin on his hand. "What about your dates? Where do they take you—McDonald's?"

Was he trying to see if she was involved with anyone? Amanda wondered, or was he just making polite conversation?

"I'm not dating anyone at the moment," she said.

Jeff, who had the advantage of being a man and the ability to pick up the vibes of another man on the stalk, didn't miss the masculine interest in Way's eyes. He hadn't believed Heather's story of her father's actions before they'd left for the graduation ceremony, but here, right before his eyes, was proof positive. Way Dalton was making a move on his mother, and she didn't even seem to be aware of it. Jeff looked at Heather, whose eyes seemed to say, "I told you so."

He wasn't certain how he felt about this new development, but Jeff said the first thing that came to mind. "She hasn't dated anyone on a regular basis in years."

Amanda's startled gaze flew to her son's. So did Way's. When would the boy ever learn to keep his mouth shut? Way wondered, the hard look in his eyes sending Jeff's eyes back to the menu. He could embarrass his mother without half trying.

Way looked at Amanda out of the corners of his eyes, He could almost see her gathering up her vulnerability and replacing it with the no-nonsense armor she'd worn when he first met her. He sighed.

Damn you, Jeff.

It promised to be a long evening.

IT HAD REALLY been a nice evening, Amanda thought as she peeled her hose down her legs two hours later. There had been that uncomfortable moment when Jeff blurted out the truth of her social life—or lack thereof—but by some sort of silent consent they had overcome it and turned the dinner into a true celebration for Heather.

The food was everything Amanda had been told to expect, from the green turtle soup to the strawberries Romanoff. Conversation had been lighthearted and pleasant. No one had spoken a word about Jeff and Heather's plight or what they planned to do about it; instead, they had dredged up memories of childhood pranks and other graduation nights.

Once, when she had pulled a gift for Heather from her purse, Amanda had surprised an almost grieving look on Way's handsome face. She had empathized. There was something inherently sad about graduations, knowing that the child you'd nurtured, consoled and guided was stepping out of the circle of home and love and into a hard, uncaring world.

She'd felt it when Jeff had graduated last year and again the day he'd left for college. It was a helpless feeling. A feeling of wanting to call all the years back and do them over, this time better. A feeling of knowing that although you'd given it your best shot, that might not be good enough. A feeling of wanting to take your child home and keep him away from the disillusionment and heartache that was inevitably coming. It was a feeling that had never really passed.

Unable to bear the silence of her own company, Amanda turned on her clock radio. The music was soft and romantic, and suddenly she was thinking about Way again. Tonight, when she'd seen the look on his face and he'd caught her looking at him, she'd wanted more than anything to say something to ease his mind about Heather.

She shook her head at her fanciful thoughts. Someone like Way Dalton didn't need any words of comfort from someone like her—or did he? They were both single parents, and being a single parent and suffering the

sorrows of bringing up a child alone was a hard job.
Until the past few weeks, she'd thought that maybe single parenthood was the hardest part of not having a
mate. Now, since she'd begun to reassess her opinion of
athletes in general and Way Dalton in particular,
Amanda was finding that these days the hardest part of
being single period was not having anyone to share those
sorrows with...or not having anyone to share your bed.

Amanda unhooked her bra and slid the straps down
her arms, staring at her reflection in the mirror. Her
breasts, though not full, were high and firm—evidence
of the only good thing about being small busted. Not
bad for thirty-seven, she thought. She was slim, maybe
too slim. Did Way like curvaceous women, women with
voluptuous breasts and tiny waists?

She closed her eyes and, reaching up, placed her hands
over her breasts. With eyes closed she could almost imagine Way's hands were her own. The nipples puckered
against her palms and her teeth caught at her lower lip
as a pungent need pierced her. How long had it been
since any man had touched her?

The soft love song on the radio ended and moved directly into "Sharp Dressed Man," the song the TV station had used when it did the show featuring Way and
Jose Delgato. Pictures from the television show flashed
silently through her mind. Pictures of Way with gorgeous, full-bodied women.

Stop it, Amanda!

With a groan of frustration, she opened her eyes and
yanked open her drawer, reaching for the first thing that
came to hand, the lavender-sprigged seersucker gown
she'd worn the morning Way and Heather had come to
discuss Heather's pregnancy...the first morning she'd
seen him. Angrily she pulled it over her head and re-

placed the white briefs she wore with the gown's matching bikini panties. Way Dalton meant nothing to her. Nothing! She managed to hold that thought close while she brushed her teeth, creamed her face and weighed herself, all part of her nightly ritual.

But when she crawled between the crisp percale sheets and pounded her pillow into a comfortable wad, Amanda couldn't deny her feelings anymore. As she'd done earlier that afternoon, she faced the fact that she wanted Way Dalton. She wanted him in her bed, wanted to feel his body become a part of hers. Him—not someone else, not anyone else—because no one but Way had managed to stir her in even the slightest way since... Deke.

Why Way? Why not Dale Patterson, who had been trying to get her to say yes to an affair for months? Was it because Dale was too available? Had these unwanted feelings for Way started with the old attraction-of-opposites theory? And had those first angry sparks they'd struck off each other ignited something more? She covered her eyes with her hands. Did Way feel it, too, or—heaven forbid—was she reading things in his actions, in his eyes that she only wished were there?

And if it is real, if he does feel it, what will you do, Amanda? He's a ball player. An athlete.

But he's nice.

So was Deke in the beginning.

But he isn't like Deke.

Or was he?

That was the problem. She didn't think Way was like Deke, but after being so wrong once she was afraid to trust her own instincts, afraid her judgment might be off again.

Forget the man!

Easier said than done.

Concentrate on the problem with Jeff and Heather.

Thinking of Jeff, she glanced at the clock. Midnight. He should be home in an hour or so. Way had brought her home and Jeff and Heather had stayed out, wanting to attend a graduation party one of her friends was throwing. Amanda had tried not to think about them going somewhere and making love.

Making love. Was everyone in the world making love but her? Disgusted at her one-track thoughts, Amanda rolled to her stomach and hit the pillow with her fist, damning her body, which ached with a hunger she couldn't fulfill . . . or deny.

MOONLIGHT STREAMED through the crack in the drapes, dissecting the brown-and-rust bedspread and shining on Heather's face. She lay on her back, Jeff's dark head cradled against her, his breath a warm tickle on her bare breast, a Mona Lisa-like smile of contentment curving her lips.

For the first time since she and Jeff had sneaked off to Oklahoma to get married almost a month ago, she felt truly married. This was the night they had been waiting for, the time they had been longing and planning for— the first time they had shared a bed for a full night. Tomorrow they would tell their parents.

They had been saving their money and had put down a deposit and first month's rent on an apartment in an old house. It was clean, not too fancy, and certainly nothing like the new, modern apartments that were springing up all over town, but neither of them cared. Heather could see the potential in the French doors leading to the single bedroom and the graceful arch that separated the dining room from the living area. She smiled again. It was their apartment. Their home. To-morrow would be their first real day as man and wife.

Filled to overflowing with love, she rubbed the tips of her fingers over Jeff's muscular shoulder in small concentric circles, a gesture that betrayed how hard it was to keep from touching him, even as he slept.

To her surprise she felt his head turn the slightest bit and his lips touch the tip of her breast.

"Are you awake?" she whispered.

Jeff raised his head and looked at her in the moon-light. He smiled. "No," he said facetiously. "You just keep me so hot I do that sort of thing in my sleep."

"Jeff!"

"Hey! I wasn't the one tickling," he said, nuzzling his face in her stomach and pressing random kisses over it.

"I wasn't tickling. I was...touching," she clarified.

He lifted his head and spread his hand over her abdomen. "When will it start moving?"

"I'm three and a half months now. I'd say in another month for sure."

"I can hardly wait. You know it's going to be a boy," he said.

"Yeah?" she asked. "Who told you?"

"A father's intuition."

She laughed. "And what are we going to name him?"

"Waylon Jeffrey," he said without pause.

"Waylon? You want to name the baby after my dad?"

"Why not? I sure don't want to name him after my dad. Besides, your dad has been really good to me."

"He'll love you forever!" Heather said, smiling widely.

Jeff looked into her face with its light sprinkling of freckles and felt a sudden surge of protectiveness and love so strong it brought the heat of tears to his eyes. He reached up and threaded his fingers through the silky skeins of her hair.

"No," he murmured. "I'll love you forever."

AMANDA DIDN'T KNOW what woke her, she only knew that she came awake instantly, fully. Turning her head, she glanced at the clock and saw that it was four o'clock in the morning. Had Jeff called?

Hardly daring to breathe, she sat up and cocked her head, listening, but there was no sound in the room except the rapid beating of her heart. The absence of sound did little to reassure her, though, and she swung her feet to the floor, using them to feel for the purple satin scuffs she'd left there. Rising, she scooped up the short robe lying on the foot of the bed and went to the door, flipping on the hall light and going to Jeff's room.

Careful not to make a sound, Amanda turned the knob. The door swung open on silent hinges. The light from the hall was more than ample to see the bed. The empty bed.

Jeff wasn't there! Gasping in surprise, she reached out and turned on the overhead light. The room was just as he'd left it to go to the graduation ceremony—dirty clothes in a pile near the bathroom door and his damp towel draped across the foot of the bed. A bed that hadn't been slept in.

In typical motherly fashion, visions of a car wreck catapulted into her mind. She forced herself to remain calm and struggled to slow her runaway heart. Maybe, she reasoned, Jeff was just late. Maybe he was in the kitchen having a snack, or asleep on the couch.

Turning, she raced down the hall and through the living room, turning on lights and calling his name as she went. He wasn't in the living room, and he didn't answer her calls. When she pushed through the saloon doors that separated the kitchen from the dining room, she really didn't have any hope of finding him there.

Amanda leaned against the cabinets and tried not to think about him being in an accident. Even though a lot of fun was usually poked at parents for daring to have the thought, she told herself that Jeff really *might* have had a wreck. That possibility was enough to send her to the phone. She called the police station, asking if there had been any wrecks involving a blue '57 Chevrolet.

"No ma'am," the night officer said, "not tonight. What's the matter? Missing a kid?"

"Yes," she confessed. "My son."

"I wouldn't worry about it," the masculine voice said with the soothing manner that told Amanda he probably gave the speech a dozen times a night. "He'll be there in a little while. He's probably been partying. Lots of graduation parties going on, you know. If he hasn't come home in twenty-four hours, you give us a call back, okay?"

Amanda started to say that Jeff wasn't the partying kind, that he didn't stay out all night, that he wasn't the type who did that sort of thing. Then, recalling that Jeff wasn't as perfect as she'd once thought him to be, she bit back the sharp retort. No sense taking out her worry on the policeman. He was only doing his job.

"Thank you, Officer. I appreciate your time," she said, cradling the receiver.

What now? she wondered, chewing her bottom lip. If he hadn't had a wreck, there wasn't any use calling the hospitals, was there? In the end, working on the assumption that he might have been in the car with someone else, she called every hospital in town. Jeff wasn't at any of them. Where could he and Heather be?

Heather. Why hadn't she thought of Heather before? Had Jeff taken her home and then gone out with the guys? No. He wouldn't do that. Should she call Way and see if Heather was at home? She glanced at the clock and shook her head. It was almost five. She'd make some coffee and wait until daylight before she broke down and called Way.

She reached for the coffee carafe, thinking about the other nights she'd lain awake worrying about Jeff— nights when he'd been sick, nights he'd cried, needing the father he'd never known, asking Amanda if the reason Deke didn't come back was because there was something wrong with *him*, a feeling she understood all too well. She'd spent several years bearing all the fault for the breakup of her marriage before she realized that Deke was the one with the problem, not her. Gradually, as he'd grown older, she'd made Jeff understand.

Damn you, Deke.

Amanda began scooping coffee into the paper filter with jerky movements, her anger at Deke surfacing in the face of her own need. She was tired of being strong. Tired of carrying the load by herself. It would be so wonderful to have someone to talk to. Someone to share the problems, the worry. Someone to hold her close and tell her everything would be all right.

Tears welled in her eyes. Swearing softly, she resolutely blinked them away. She turned on the coffeepot and sat down at the kitchen table, dry-eyed. Feeling sorry for herself wouldn't help. It never had.

WHERE IN THE HELL were Heather and Jeff, anyway? Way paced the length of the living room floor and back, glancing at the telephone for at least the hundredth time. Should he call Amanda and wake her up? he wondered, looking at the clock. He shook his head. It was too early to call. Only five-fifteen. It felt as if it should be noon.

After he'd taken Amanda home, he hadn't slept a wink. He'd lain there in the darkness and thought about how much he'd enjoyed being with her and how much he would like to be the one to awaken her dormant sexuality. Like her warmth and caring, it was there, hidden beneath sixteen years of garnered protection. Protection like her coolness, her sharp tongue and her no-nonsense attitude. But he was learning—gradually—that beneath it all was a woman who was afraid of making the same mistake twice, a woman afraid to trust her feelings.

Woman. All woman. He'd fantasized about how it would feel to run his hands through the soft ebony curls, to pull her close, closer, while he tasted the sweetness he knew her lips had to offer and tunneled into the softness of her body. Finally, the madness of his thoughts had driven him in desperation to the promised relief of a cold shower. But even that tried-and-true remedy had failed, lessening his agony, not erasing it.

After a while, as he'd looked at the clock in despair of ever getting to sleep, he realized that Heather hadn't come in. That had been three hours ago, and his concern was growing along with his anger. Where the hell were they?

Running a weary hand through his tousled hair, Way sank onto the couch and leaned his head against the striped upholstery. They hadn't been in an accident; he'd determined that by calling the police station, where a bored-sounding officer had told him that after twenty-four hours he could come down and fill out a missing persons' report. Way laughed, a bitter sound that echoed hollowly through the empty room. In twenty-four hours he'd be a prime candidate for the asylum.

He rubbed his mustache with his forefinger and stared at the empty fireplace. If he were Jeff and Heather, what would *he* do? The answer came to him in a moment of sudden clarity, an answer so simple he wondered why it had taken him the entire night to think of it.

He looked at the clock again. Five-twenty. He pushed himself to his feet and grabbed the keys to his Blazer from the glass-topped coffee table. It would take him at least fifteen minutes to drive to Amanda's. Surely by that time she wouldn't mind if he woke her up...especially under the circumstances.

AMANDA LOOKED OUT the window—for the two dozenth time since the night had begun to fade. It was light enough that she could see the birdbath, close enough to daylight to call Way. She was refilling her coffee cup when the front doorbell rang. She froze. Who was it? The police? The thought galvanized her into action. She set the cup down and almost ran to the front door, unlocking it and flinging it open without checking to see who it was.

It was Way.

He looked tired and hollow-eyed.

She started to ask what he was doing there, when it dawned on her that he was there for the same reason that she was just about to call him. Heather and Jeff. And from the look on his face...

"Are they all right?" she asked.

Way heard the stark panic in her voice and saw the fear lurking in the shadows of her wide violet eyes. "They haven't had an accident," he said, stepping through the threshold and closing the door behind him.

Her eyes filled with the tears she had refused to let fall all night. One slid down her cheek. "I know. I called the police station and the hospitals, too."

Way reached out and wiped the tear away with his thumb, letting the tips of his fingers brush the delicate curve of her jaw. He smiled. "They're okay."

"How do you know?" she wailed as the tears began to fall in earnest.

He let his hand fall from her face to her shoulder. Beneath his hand, her bones felt as fragile as her state of mind. Unable to bear seeing her cry, he grasped her shoulders with both his hands and pulled her into the shelter of his arms.

Amanda went willingly, reaching up and wiping at her cheek with the back of her hand.

"I know they're okay, because I know what I'd do if I were their age, in their situation, and I'd just been told by my elders that I was on my own, responsible for my actions and taking my first steps into the world of adulthood."

"Wh-what would you do?" she asked, speaking into the front of his yellow knit shirt.

Way tipped her head back and looked her directly in the eyes. "I think I'd elope."

CHAPTER EIGHT

"ELOPE!"

Way shrugged. "I'm not positive, but it seems likely. Heather and Jeff aren't the kind of kids who'd deliberately stay out all night and cause us to worry. I think it's possible that they planned to slip in about the time we'd get up and break the news to us."

Way's matter-of-fact tone failed to check the fall of her tears. The sight of the crystalline drops silvering her eyes and threatening to spill over the fragile dam of her lashes was more than he thought he could bear. Involuntarily he plunged his hands through her hair as he'd wanted to do for a long time, threading his fingers through it and cradling the back of her head in his palms. As he'd known it would be, her hair was silky fine, silky soft. He pulled her into his arms and pressed her face against his chest, rocking her back and forth with a slight sideways motion and crooning soft words of comfort to her while she dampened the front of his shirt with her tears.

The totally masculine part of him, the part that was governed by his hormones, wanted to tighten the hold on her hair, to tilt her face back and cover her mouth with his, to swallow those heart-wrenching sobs into his own mouth, to change them into throaty purrs of need. Thankfully, and through no conscious effort on his part, sanity and the more sensitive side of his nature prevailed—maybe because he had the feeling that she didn't indulge in the emotional release of tears often and that this deluge was way overdue.

After long moments Amanda's crying slowed to an occasional sniff and a sob. She sagged against him, her arms circling his lean waist, the soft expulsion of her breath warm through his shirt. She was exhausted, he thought as he brushed his lips against the softness of her hair and his fingertips rubbed her scalp with a gentle motion. She'd probably been awake the better part of the night, too. Without considering that she might protest, he bent and scooped her up into his arms.

The fact that she didn't stop him was testimony to her state of mind. Instead, in a gesture that seemed as right to her as it did to him, Amanda looped her arms around his neck and rested her head on his shoulder while he carried her to the couch and sat down with her still in his arms. She released her hold of his neck and allowed him to cuddle her close, her palm resting against his chest where his heart beat a strong, comforting rhythm.

"Better?" he asked, his voice a low vibration against her temple.

She nodded and, for the first time, he noticed the clean, fresh scent—peaches and cream?—wafting from her gleaming cap of black hair to his nostrils.

"Are you going to be okay...if I'm right?"

She tilted her head back to look at him. Way could easily have drowned in the liquid amethyst of her eyes.

Amanda noted with some surprise that his eyes—the same deep brown as her morning coffee—held quantum amounts of warmth and concern, something she hadn't seen in a man's eyes in a very long time. Because it had been so long and because of the circumstances that had brought them to this point, she couldn't help being touched by Way's concern, any more than she could change the fact that all her old hurts and antagonisms were undergoing a subtle change because of the man holding her so tenderly.

She sighed, a sigh of defeat, a sigh of surrender, a sigh of acceptance. But the measure of acceptance didn't negate all the worry. Her fingers moved restlessly against the waffle weave of his shirt. "I suppose I'll have to be okay, won't I? You said it yourself. They have to make their own decision. I only pray it's the right one."

Eyes meshed with hers, Way nodded and sent a prayer winging upward. Like Amanda, and as much for her sake as theirs, he prayed Heather and Jeff's decision was the right one. Amanda Farrell didn't need any more heartache. She needed security and the luxury of having someone to take care of her. More and more, despite his knowledge that his chances of making her reciprocate his feelings were less than zero, he felt a need to tackle the job himself. Wanting only to offer her a measure of comfort, he pressed his lips to her forehead.

Even in her distraught state, Amanda knew the reasoning behind the unexpected kiss, but instead of comforting her, it only sharpened her awareness of how alone and lonely she was. Alone. Lonely. The tears threatened to start afresh, and she burrowed against him, burying her face into his chest.

Feeling completely ineffectual in the face of her misery, Way tightened his hold on her and wished he knew a way to ease her pain. "Don't cry, Mandy," he murmured, nuzzling his lips against her hair. "Please, don't cry."

But she did. She cried, her slender body racked with sobs that tugged at his heartstrings. Gradually, the tears slowed, until only a random, hiccuping sob marred the stillness of the room. He held her tightly. She held him with equal intensity. There was no sound in the room but an occasional sniff from Amanda and a sporadic sigh from Way.

It was the even tenor of her breathing that finally alerted him to the fact that she'd fallen asleep. He tried not to move, tried not to wake her. Eventually, though, after more than half an hour, he slid down on his spine and eased his leg onto the sofa, shifting her to a more comfortable position and resting his head against the sofa back. She felt good in his arms, he thought, a small smile lifting the corners of his mustache. Real good. Soft . . . and warm . . . and totally feminine. . . .

IT WAS 7:35 when Jeff pulled into the subdivision where he'd grown up. Heather dozed at his side, her head resting on his shoulder. The late spring morning was clear, and the breeze coming through his open window was warm. There was still a soft, not-quite-awake feeling to the day. The bird song was sweet and hushed, and the sounds of trash cans clanging and cars starting throughout the neighborhood seemed hesitant to intrude on the quiet. Jeff braked to round the corner of his block, his mind filled with how to approach his mother.

"Oh, no."

The worry in his voice penetrated Heather's light sleep and alerted her to the fact that something was wrong. She sat up, pushed the hair from her face and looked around. "What is it?"

Jeff pointed to the Blazer sitting in front of his mother's house.

"Daddy!" Heather cried, looking at Jeff. "What's my dad doing here at this time of the morning?" Then, as a sudden thought hit her, she said, "Jeff, you don't think—"

Jeff gave her a quelling look. "No, I don't. Not my mother and your father—not that it would bother me a lot if it were true," he tacked on.

"B-but you said yourself that he was making a move on her last night."

"He was. But my mom is so naive she didn't even know that's what he was doing."

"Naive? Come on, Jeff," Heather scoffed. "She's forty years old."

"Thirty-seven."

"Whatever. She's old enough to know when a man is making a pass."

"Yeah, she is. But even if she gets past the fact that your dad plays baseball, she'd never believe that someone like him could ever be interested in someone like her."

"What do you mean? She's beautiful."

"And insecure. My dad really did a number on her."

Heather looked skeptical. "She doesn't seem insecure. She seems very together."

"Trust me," he said, turning into the driveway. "When it comes to her personal life, she's a mess." He shut off the engine and turned toward her. "I'll tell you what she needs."

"What?"

"A man to get her into his bed and keep her there about a week."

"Jeff!"

"Well, it's true," he told her with a grin. He put his arm around her shoulders and pulled her close. "Just look how sweet and docile you are after only one night."

Heather pinched his side. "You no-good, sorry, chauvinist..."

"...pig," he finished for her, leaning forward and taking her mouth in a series of light kisses. When he drew away, the love in his eyes was mirrored in Heather's.

"I love you," they said simultaneously.

They smiled at each other and Jeff sighed. "No time for this right now. Come on, Mrs. Farrell. Let's get it over with."

"What do you think she's going to say?" Heather asked as they walked hand in hand through the garage to the back door.

"Who knows?" Jeff said with a shrug. "What about your dad?"

"Daddy just wants me to be happy. He likes you."

"I'll try to remember that while he's chewing me out." Jeff drew a fortifying breath and unlocked the door, only to find the kitchen empty. He raised his eyebrows. "She's usually up by now," he said in a low voice. "I thought she'd be awake and meet us at the door."

"She's got to be awake, Jeff," Heather whispered back.

"Why?"

"If she isn't...where's my dad?"

"Oh. Right." Jeff's grin was almost a leer. "Come on. Maybe we can catch them in the act, and then they won't dare preach to us."

"Jeeeff!" Heather said, elbowing him in the ribs.

He flinched but didn't lose his naughty smile. He mimed a kiss at her and headed for the swinging saloon-type doors that led to the dining room, Heather tiptoeing along behind him. The house was quiet, and there was no sign of anyone around. He started down the hall, but stopped when he felt a hard tug on his shirt. Pivoting on the ball of his foot, he gave her a questioning look, his gaze moving past her.

Across the living room, on the sofa, were both their parents. Asleep. Way was slumped in the corner, his right leg stretched out along the length of the couch, his left foot on the floor. Amanda, still in her shorty gown—which had ridden up so that the panties showed—slept on her side, wedged in the V of his legs, her head resting on his thigh, her face embarrassingly near the masculine bulge in his Levi's. Her hands were clasped beneath her chin, as if she couldn't find another place to put them, and Way's free hand lay across her waist. To anyone just walking in, it might look like a very compromising position, but Jeff took it exactly for what it was.

With Heather following, he approached them and, reaching out, shook his mother's shoulder. "Mom."

The sound of Jeff's voice came from far away, as if it were filtered through layers of cotton batting. Amanda stirred and reached to push away the weight of the covers at her waist. But it wasn't the brushed polyester of a blanket that her hand came into contact with, but warm hair-dusted flesh. Her eyes flew open, expecting to see familiar flower-covered walls. Instead, she saw faded blue. Faded blue...denim? She moved her head back a fraction of an inch and saw the same wavy undulations created in the zipper of Jeff's jeans when he sat down. Jeff's jeans? She frowned and moved her head back even farther. A yellow cotton-knit shirt came into view above the waistband of the Levi's. Far above that was a strong chin and a sexy mouth framed by a drooping blond...mustache....

Way frowned in protest when he heard Jeff speaking to his mother, but did his best to ignore the sound that threatened his light sleep. He felt movement against his thigh and warm...was it hands? Yes, he thought with sleepy satisfaction. Hands. Warm, soft...feminine hands touching his bare forearm. The movement stopped and then started again, something sliding down his other thigh. He lifted his lashes slowly, his sleepy gaze colliding with eyes filled with the same shock he might have seen in his grandmother's eyes if she'd visited the Chippendale show.

But these weren't his grandmother's eyes. These eyes were violet. Amanda's eyes.

At precisely the instant he recognized that the eyes belonged to her, she made the connection that the eyes she was looking into belonged to the man wearing the shirt tucked into the faded Levi's. She also realized they were the same eyes that belonged to the body that filled the Levi's out so well, and that her head lay on his lap.

Before she could gather her wits enough to make a comment on the situation, she heard Heather say, "Daddy?"

At the sound of the girl's voice, Amanda's mind made several startling realizations more or less at once. Heather was here. Jeff must be, too. And here she was, asleep on the sofa with Way Dalton. More specifically, with her face...

Before the thought was even coherent, Amanda scrambled guiltily away from Way toward the other end of the couch. Startled by her sudden movement, Jeff took a few steps back.

Way, fully aware of the censure in his daughter's voice, struggled to his feet, unable to stay the guilt sweeping through him. Close on the heels of the guilt came the resurgence of the anger he'd felt the night before. The difference was that now, rather than being angry with Heather and Jeff, he was angry at being caught in a situation that could look even the slightest bit compromising. He raked both hands through his tousled hair and concentrated on his anger. *He* hadn't done anything wrong; why should he feel guilty? *They* were the ones who hadn't come home all night.

"Where in the hell have you been?" he snapped.

"What are you doing here?" Heather asked.

They spoke simultaneously, their body language that of two fighters circling each other in the ring. Jeff simply looked at Amanda with a considering light in his eyes while Amanda tried her best not to show how mortified she was.

"Don't try to third-degree me, young lady," Way said, his voice harsh, his eyes narrowed to angry slits. "I want to know where you and Jeff have been all night."

Jeff stepped forward and drew Heather to his side. "We were at the Holiday Inn, sir," he offered.

"What!"

Jeff's gaze moved from his mother's shocked face to Way's. "Yes, sir. We were married almost a month ago. We decided to make last night our honeymoon night."

"A month ago?"

"Yes, sir. We drove to Oklahoma the night Heather was supposed to stay with her aunt in Saint Louis."

Way felt the announcement working its way through his intellect, erasing his anger. He hadn't been too far off base. He turned to see how Amanda was taking the news. She hadn't spoken since Jeff had, and her features wore a total stillness as she tried to absorb that the thing she had dreaded and fought against happening was no longer a threat, but a fait accompli.

Finally aware that she was being scrutinized by the other three people in the room, Amanda's gaze found them each in turn. Way looked concerned; Heather looked fearful; Jeff pulled Heather closer, waiting to see if his mother would fly into them as he half expected, or if she would take her defeat with grace.

What could she say? Anger and recriminations would serve no purpose now. It was done. There was nothing she could do but accept their decision and try to help them however she could. A smile—forced, but a smile nevertheless—curved her mouth as she looked at her son.

"Well," she said in a subdued tone, "I guess that's why you haven't been pushing marriage this past month."

"Yeah," Jeff said with a shrug. "I guess so."

Amanda stood and went to him. Jeff released his hold on Heather to pull his mother into a bone-crushing embrace that lifted her from the floor. When he released her, there were tears in both their eyes.

"Be happy," she whispered, reaching up and smoothing a lock of hair from his forehead.

"I am."

Then Amanda turned to Heather and, after giving her a hug, said, "All I ask is that you love him."

Tears sprang up in Heather's eyes at the plea she saw in her new mother-in-law's. "I do, Mrs. Farrell."

To her credit, Amanda managed a ragged laugh. "You're Mrs. Farrell, too, now. Why don't you call me Amanda?"

Heather nodded. Then she sought Way's gaze and said hesitantly, "Daddy?"

Way swallowed back the emotion clogging his own throat. He smiled. "Congratulations," he said, and Heather flew into his arms. He pressed a kiss to her temple and murmured something to her. Heather nodded. Way smiled and looked up, his gaze snagging Amanda's.

She still had a tumbled, sleep-warm look that lent a rosy tint to her cheeks and a young vulnerability to her eyes. Her beauty struck him with the same force he put behind each swing of the bat, and his senses reeled under the strength of the desire he felt for her.

Amanda didn't see the need in his eyes. She was too wrapped up with her own thoughts, her own needs. Only the day before she'd grudgingly acknowledged the fact that she was sexually attracted to Way Dalton no matter who or what he was. Yet the more she saw of him, the clearer it became that there was more to him than she'd ever imagined.

She watched him holding his daughter close and recalled the feel of his arms when he'd comforted her only hours before. They were strong but gentle. She'd felt secure and comforted at the same time. She also knew that despite his reputation on and off the ball field, there was a gentleness inside him that augmented his strength. Amanda watched him hold Heather and dared to wonder how those arms would feel under different circumstances, how they would feel holding her close... with nothing separating them but the ragged beating of their hearts.

As TIRED as they all were, they spent the rest of the morning over coffee, talking about the future. Neither Amanda nor Way could believe that the kids had already rented an apartment, and when they learned that it was in an old two-story house, both parents looked at each other in a way that clearly said they wondered if their children knew what they were doing. Jeff and Heather were so excited they didn't notice.

Way left before noon to go to the stadium, offering the use of the Blazer to the newlyweds so they could begin moving some of Jeff and Heather's things to the apartment. He promised to meet them as soon as he could in order to help Jeff with the heavy stuff.

Amanda walked with Way to the door, gripped by an unexpected shyness. What did you say to a man whose arms you'd found comfort in so recently? Who you'd *slept* with in the purest sense of the word? A man who, by anyone's standards, was a relative stranger?

Way must have felt the strain, too, because he shoved his hands into the pockets of his jeans and offered her a half smile. "See you later."

Amanda nodded and watched him turn to go down the sidewalk. After taking a couple of steps, he stopped, turned where he stood and retraced his steps.

"Thanks," he said simply.

"For what?"

"For accepting all this with such good grace when I know you're disappointed."

Amanda smiled wanly and shook her head. "I'm not disappointed. I was disappointed with Jeff when I heard Heather was pregnant. Now I'm just worried about them and how they'll manage."

"They love each other, and as they say, love covers a multitude of sins. If it's real, and it seems to be, it'll be enough to get them over the rough spots."

"I hope you're right," she said.

He smiled. Making a loose fist, he reached out and put his knuckles beneath her chin, raising her gaze to his. "I'm right. Trust me. You just keep your chin up and be there when Jeff needs you."

Without thinking, Amanda reached up and curled her fingers around his wrist, extracting an unexpected strength from his words and the touch. No matter what, she thought, they were bound inexplicably together now through Jeff and Heather. As long, at least, as love was enough.

AFTER WAY LEFT, Amanda and Jeff loaded the Blazer to the hilt with what he wanted to take, and dropped Heather off at her house to pack her things. Then mother and son drove to the apartment, which was situated in an older, residential section of town.

"Oh, Jeff, it's wonderful!" Amanda said as he pulled the Blazer to the back of the house, which, despite its age, was well maintained.

"Don't make any rash statements until you see the inside."

They each took a box and started down the sidewalk and up a short flight of stairs. Jeff unlocked the door and they stepped into the compact kitchen.

Amanda looked around critically. The apartment was old but clean—which in her mind was something. She'd moved into some pretty grungy places while she was married to Deke. There was new Formica on the countertop and a new stainless-steel sink, but the refrigerator was avocado green and didn't really go with the gold stove or the old-fashioned red-and-pink wallpaper. With different wallpaper to tie the colors together, and new curtains, the room could really be cute, she thought.

"I like it," she said at last.

Jeff took the box Amanda had carried in and set it on the countertop. The worry on his face eased somewhat at the enthusiasm in her voice. "Yeah? I thought you might like it, since you've always liked fixing places up, but I'm not sure what Heather's dad's gonna think. It sure isn't like living at some of those fancy new apartment complexes."

What would Way think? Amanda wondered, looking around at the faded wallpaper and worn carpet. Not everyone could afford a home like his. She evaded the question in Jeff's voice. "I think he'll be happy with the apartment if Heather is."

"Heather loves it. She can't wait to start fixing it up. I know it needs some paint and new wallpaper," Jeff said, his insecurity back, "but Mr. Collins said that we could do whatever we wanted to the place and take it off the rent."

"That's nice of him," Amanda said. She wandered into the dining room, taking in the built-in china cabinets on either side of the arched doorway that led to the living room. She turned and gave Jeff an encouraging smile. "We can strip this old paint off the china cabinets and varnish them. They'll be beautiful."

"That's what we thought."

"Heather shouldn't do it, though," Amanda cautioned. "She shouldn't breathe those fumes. If she doesn't mind, I can come over and do it whenever it's convenient, since I'm out of school now."

"Gee, Mom, would you? That'd be great!"

Amanda looked at him and saw the familiar twinkle in his eyes. He was happy. That would have to be enough for now. Pushing her doubts to the farthest reaches of her mind, she said, "I can't believe you're married, that you have a wife and are going to make me a grandmother."

Jeff grinned. "You'll be the prettiest grandmother in Kansas City," he predicted.

"Yeah?" she asked doubtfully.

"Mr. Dalton obviously thinks so."

Amanda could no more stop the flush of excitement that raced through her than she could have denied herself her next breath. "What do you mean?"

"You tell me," Jeff said. "You two were on the sofa together."

Amanda saw the teasing look in his eyes. "Oh, you!" she said, throwing a playful punch at his midriff. "He came over about daylight because Heather wasn't at home. He told me he figured you'd eloped."

"He thought that?"

"Yes."

"He's pretty sharp, huh?"

"So it seems," Amanda said dryly. "Anyway, I sort of went to pieces and he..."

"Comforted you," Jeff finished for her, but his tone of voice gave the two words new meaning.

"You don't have to make it sound X rated," Amanda said. "We fell asleep waiting for you. That's all."

"Is it?"

"What do you mean?"

"I mean, are you interested in him?"

Amanda felt the heat returning to her cheeks. She struggled to sound nonchalant. "Oh, Jeff. Way Dalton is a very handsome, worldly man who doesn't normally give women like me the time of day. If it weren't for you and Heather, he wouldn't even know I'm alive."

"That isn't what Heather says."

Amanda's eyes widened. Her heart beat a rapid tattoo against her ribs. "Wh-what does Heather say?"

"She said that he was awfully concerned about how he looked last night, and when she asked who he was trying to impress, since he wouldn't be seeing anyone but me and you, he changed the subject."

"She was probably imagining things." *The way I do when I think he's looking at me a special way.*

"The way I am?" Jeff reached out and touched a curl that lay against her neck.

"What do you mean?"

"I mean that you're different. That you're...restless. Nervous, almost."

Restless? Nervous? If Jeff could see it, who else did? Heather? Or—heaven forbid—Way himself? Amanda took refuge in cool common sense. "We're both adults here, Jeff, so stop beating around the bush. What are you saying?"

The change in her wasn't lost on him. He'd run into that controlled wall of hers plenty of times in his nineteen years, and by now was almost immune. He smiled, a smug sort of smile. "I'm saying that I think you sorta like him."

"Well, of course I like him."

"You know what I mean. I mean I think you're... attracted to him."

Good grief! She must be as transparent as glass. Maybe she could laugh it off. "Oh, you do, do you?" Amanda asked with a saccharine smile.

"Yeah."

"Well, if I am, that's none of your business."

"I know. Like you said—we're both adults. I just want you to know that I understand."

Amanda was beginning to feel as if they were dancing all around the basic thrust of the conversation. "Understand?"

"Yeah. You've been single a long time, and there haven't been any men...I mean that I know of. You're awfully pretty and you aren't old or anything, so...it's only natural that you..." Jeff paused, gesturing with his right hand, searching for the right word. "You know...and it's okay with me," he tacked on.

Amanda stood stock-still, her hands clasped tightly together, unable to believe what she was hearing. "Let me get this straight. You're giving me permission to...sleep with some man if I want to?"

Jeff looked relieved that she'd spoken the words he'd been unable to verbalize. "Well, I know you have... urges."

"Yes, I do," she acknowledged with a nod. "Urges I've controlled rather admirably over the past sixteen years, I might add." Amanda had the satisfaction of seeing Jeff blush. "Let me tell you something, Jeff. The only urge I have right now is to slap that smug smile off your face. And I don't need your permission if I want to sleep with a man."

Jeff's grin was unrepentant. "Well, now that we've got that straight, I guess we can drop the subject."

"I wish you would."

"Done."

But it wasn't done. Amanda worked throughout the afternoon, thinking about what Jeff had said. She was wondering if it was true that Way had wanted to look nice for her, wondering if Way could see through her as easily as Jeff could.

WAY WAS STILL on Amanda's mind when Jeff left to take Heather's bed apart and bring her back along with the last of the small stuff so he'd be ready to get the bedroom furniture when Way came. She was unpacking a box of books and Heather was going through a box of high-school mementos when the girl said suddenly, "I really appreciate you doing this."

Amanda looked up from the box of paperback romances she was putting on a shelf. "I'm glad to help."

"Jeff said you'd also help with some painting and stuff around here."

"I'd be glad to, if you don't mind."

"Mind? Why should I mind?"

Amanda shrugged. "This is your home, Heather. I don't want you to think I'm trying to intrude, or that I want to do things my way."

Heather smiled, and Amanda saw what had initially attracted Jeff. Hers was a beautiful smile, filled with sunshine and good humor.

"I don't think you'd ever do that, and I appreciate everything you've done for us."

They shared a smile that was the first tentative step toward their new relationship. Then, like a typical teenager, Heather glanced at her watch and asked, "Wonder what's keeping Jeff? I'm starving."

"What time is it?"

"Five-thirty," Heather replied.

"Look, there's a Kentucky Fried Chicken down the street. Why don't I go get us a bucket, and maybe by the time I get back, Jeff and your dad will be here. We can eat before they go get the last load. What do you think?" Amanda held her breath. She knew her offer was a ruse, a means to get her out of the apartment, to escape contact with Way.

"I think it's a good idea."

Amanda rose. "Then it's as good as done." She grabbed her purse and started for the back door. "I'll be back in a jiffy."

She escaped the apartment with a sense of inevitability dogging her heels. What did she think she was doing? She had to face Way sometime.

CHAPTER NINE

"WHERE'S AMANDA?" The words, directed to the top of Heather's bent head, were out of Way's mouth the instant he came through the kitchen door.

Heather looked up from the box of things she was sorting through. "Oh, hi, Daddy. Where's Jeff?"

"I asked first," he reminded her with a patient smile. He'd been able to concentrate on the game only because he knew that when he got to Heather and Jeff's apartment Amanda would be there. His disappointment when he'd driven up and seen that her car wasn't in the driveway was more intense than even he would have believed.

If Heather saw the disappointment in his eyes, she ignored it. "She went to get some chicken for dinner. I was starving."

"As usual."

"I'm eating for two, remember?" Heather teased.

"How can I forget?" he said, but the lightness of his tone took out any sting the statement might have held. "And now that you've told me where Amanda is, I'll tell you that your better half stopped by the landlord's to ask him something."

Heather groaned. "Do you mean we're going to have all those old corny things said about us now?"

"What do you mean?" Way asked, pushing back the curtain at the window to see if Amanda's car was back yet.

"You know—'the old lady,' 'your old man,' 'your better half,'" she singsonged.

Way grinned. "It goes with the territory."

"He really is, you know," Heather said suddenly.

"What?" Way asked, his mind divided between the conversation with his daughter and wondering when Amanda would be back.

"My better half," she said, rising from the floor and thrusting her hands nervously into her pockets. "Unlike me, Jeff sees both sides of things. I pout, and he's usually even tempered, but he doesn't let me push him around," she hastened to add.

The undisguised seriousness he saw on Heather's face and heard in her voice demanded his full attention. He listened to her list Jeff's virtues with mixed emotions—wondering how anyone could be so perfect, yet remembering how he'd felt the same way about Carol.

"He's smart and sensitive and funny," Heather continued. "He makes me laugh, Daddy. At the world and at myself, whenever I get too stuffy."

Stuffy. A strange word to use about a seventeen-year-old. A strange word, but, in many ways, true. Way thought of what a solemn child Heather had become after Carol's death, how she'd tried so hard to do what he wanted, to be what he wanted. He remembered the good grades she'd stayed up late studying for, when she might have gone out with the other kids her age, the piano recitals at which she'd excelled, even though she'd had no real love of music. And, as she'd grown older, there were the nights she'd waited up for him, just to talk. Had Heather tried so hard to please because she'd wanted his attention? Attention he'd neglected to give because he'd been so wrapped up in his career and his own feelings of loss? That keen sense of failure he'd been experiencing lately returned with a vengeance.

"He's terribly talented, too. He's written some really good songs. He taped a couple of them and sent them to Whitesnake."

"Whitesnake?" Way dragged himself from the precipice of his thoughts and forced his attention back to what she was saying.

"It's a rock group," Heather explained. Then she added confidently, "They're going to love his songs."

Way wanted to tell her that Jeff's chances of making it as a singer or songwriter were slim to nothing, but kept his own counsel when he remembered that they'd told him the same thing about his chances of ever playing professional baseball. The truth of the matter was that all of life was a gamble, from crossing the street to choosing a career...or a mate.

"He's good to me, Daddy," Heather said, the sound of her voice breaking into his thoughts once more. "And he wants a home and family, the same way I do."

The feeling of inadequacy that had plagued him moments before resurfaced. Way's throat tightened with emotion, and there was no mistaking the hurt in his eyes. "Didn't I give you a good home, baby?"

"Oh, Daddy!" Heather cried, going to him and sliding her arms around his waist. "Of course you did. You've given me everything a girl could want."

Pulling her arms from around him and grasping her wrists, Way held her far enough away to look into her eyes. "Everything except a father to rely on?"

"No!" Heather denied. "That isn't true. You're wonderful! You've been there when I really needed you.

I understand that you had to work...to make us a living. You're good and handsome and—'' her voice broke "—and I've always been so proud of you.''

"Then, what, baby? What didn't I give you that Jeff has?''

Heather's smile was bright and beautiful, and her eyes glowed with happiness and that special look of a woman in love—a look that Way realized, with a sense of sadness, he hadn't seen in years.

"Oh, Daddy, he makes me feel like I'm the most important person in the world. He makes me feel prettier and smarter than anyone. And he needs me and wants me.'' She ducked her head, unable to meet his eyes.

"I know we shouldn't have...made love, but he makes my heart beat faster and my skin feels all tingly and my legs go all weak and trembly when he touches me. No one else has ever made me feel that way. Making love with him seemed like an extension of what I feel for him, a way of expressing how much I do love him.''

Once guilty of falling into the same trap himself, Way couldn't find it in his heart to say anything to tarnish what his daughter was feeling. Besides, he'd said everything there was to say the night he'd found out she was carrying Jeff's child. Actually, he was humbled by the trite simplicity of her answer. Trite or not, it was an honest answer. Who could argue with love? And who said it took a six-figure income, two cars and a house with a swimming pool to be happy? Way pulled her close and sighed, feeling old and jaded and the slightest bit envious of her happiness, a feeling he squelched as soon as he recognized it for what it was.

Heather tipped her head back and looked up at him. He smiled down at her, the same smile that had broken dozens of hearts across the country. "You're a lucky young woman, Heather Dalton."

"Farrell," she corrected with a cheeky smile.

"Farrell," he said. "You and Jeff have something special. Something few people ever find. My advice is that whatever comes your way, you fight to keep your love to the bitter end."

Her eyes filled with tears. "I will, Daddy."

The sound of voices outside the apartment effectively put an end to the seriousness of their conversation. "Come on," he said, taking her hand. "Give me the grand tour." Heather led Way through the apartment. The place definitely had potential. "Not bad," he said, nodding. "It has possibilities."

She stopped dead in her tracks. "Really? You like it?"

Way's eyes were soft with memory. "It reminds me of the first apartment your mom and I had. I guess it's that archway."

His approval gave free rein to Heather's enthusiasm. "Isn't it neat? Amanda said she'd strip the old paint off the china cabinets."

"She did?"

"Yeah." Heather grew quiet once more. "You know, Daddy, I like her. I know she was upset at first, but she only wants the best for Jeff."

Way was glad that his daughter was mature enough to see Amanda's actions for what they were. "That's natural. She's been through a similar situation."

"I know." Without warning, the memory of Amanda asleep with her father on the sofa flashed through Heather's mind. "Do you like her?"

The question caught him off guard. "Well, sure I do, baby. What's not to like?"

"You are interested in her!" she declared, as if his answer justified her suspicions.

"Interested in her? What are you getting at?"

Heather heard the irritation in his voice. She shrugged. "Nothing. But she is pretty."

"Yes, she is," Way agreed with more patience than he was feeling.

"She's single. So are you."

"I may be forty. I may be on the brink of grandfatherhood, but I'm not blind, baby, or senile. I'm aware that we're both single. I'm also aware that you've never been overly concerned about my love life before. Why now?"

Confusion and uncertainty clouded Heather's face. "Because she's different. She's not a glamorous party girl. She's real."

"And that's cause for worry?"

"Not worry, exactly," she hedged.

Way laughed. "I think what we have here is a case of role reversal. Unnecessary role reversal."

Heather couldn't help smiling. "Butt out, huh?"

"If you don't mind."

"Okay. End of conversation. That sounded like Jeff's voice outside. Let's go see what's holding him up."

They retraced their footsteps back through the apartment, and Way was halfway across the kitchen when the door was thrust open and Amanda stepped through the threshold carrying a bucket of chicken and balancing a couple of bags on top. Above the sacks, their eyes met and clashed—coffee brown to soft violet.

Way's heart slammed into fifth gear. She looked gorgeous. Her hair curled untidily around her face, which was almost devoid of makeup, leaving her with a young, fresh appearance. The utter femininity that was such a part of her was enhanced by the purple-flowered pedal pushers that clung to her slender thighs and hips and accentuated the shapely length of her calves. Staring at a woman who was the very epitome of her sex, Way had never been more glad to have been born a man, to have been born the direct opposite of the person looking at him with nervous expectancy shining in her eyes.

"Thank goodness you're back," Heather said. "I'm starving!"

The sound of her voice brought Way back from the certainty that he'd narrowly escaped a brush with some sort of emotional and mental revelation. Pushing aside the feeling that something special, something exciting, was just within grasp, he strode across the room and reached for the packages. "Here, let me give you a hand."

Amanda ducked her head in much the same embarrassed manner Heather had done only moments before and looked up at him from beneath her lashes. "Thanks," she murmured, relinquishing her light burden.

Way carried the food to the small table centered in the dining room, setting it down and turning back toward her. "Where's Jeff?"

"He's coming."

As if on cue, Jeff burst through the door. "Where's the food?"

He spied Heather, who was already taking out corn and rolls and coleslaw, the last of which earned the comment of "Yuk." Going to her and grabbing her from behind, Jeff swung her away from the table. "Outta my way, woman. I'm hungry."

Heather punched Jeff in the stomach with her elbow and, narrowing her eyes, snarled up at him with mock ferociousness. Jeff yelped in kind and released her, looking at both startled parents with a happy gleam in his eyes. Assuming a serious tone, he said, "And that, ladies and gentlemen, is a classic example of a mother protecting her young."

If Way looked surprised at Heather's actions, he was stunned by Jeff's reaction. And, while Amanda could understand his astonishment, she couldn't help the laughter that spilled from her lips at the way Jeff's sometimes wacky personality surfaced at the most unexpected moments.

"You're crazy," Heather said calmly, but there was a smile toying with the corners of her lips.

Jeff reached into the bucket of chicken and pulled out a piece of white meat, holding it to her mouth as a peace offering. "Crazy about you, babe."

With the same ease that things had changed from serious to hilarious, the mood between them now changed back. Jeff and Heather might have been the only two occupants of the room. Eyes locked with his, Heather took the chicken, tossed it negligently back into the cardboard bucket and slid her arms around Jeff's neck, tilting her head back for his kiss and arching into him with a breathtakingly sensual familiarity.

Amanda couldn't help the gasp that escaped her any more than Way could stop his hoarse, "Heather!"

At the sound of his voice, Jeff pushed his new bride away with an abruptness that bordered on the comical.

"Daddy!" Heather cried, whirling around to face him with her hands on her hips. "We're married... remember?"

A chagrined look crossed Way's handsome features. He scraped his hand through his thick blond hair and propped the other on his hip. "I'm sorry," he said.

Amanda could relate to what he was feeling. She was experiencing the same reactions herself: shock at the intimacy they flaunted with such innocence, regret that the same happiness had slipped through her fingers, and an awareness that went beyond Heather and Jeff, that transcended uncomfortableness and encroached the sacred boundaries of her own latent sexuality.

Hoping to smooth things over, she said, "Jeff, why don't you get the paper plates out of that grocery bag so we can eat? We have a lot of work to do before bedtime."

The awkwardness of the moment passed in the confusion generated by four people filling plates and glasses and trying to find places to sit. Neither Amanda nor Way forgot their children's intimacy; it was there between them every time their eyes met...which she didn't allow to happen often. Still, the impromptu meal was pleasant and filled mostly with talk of future plans.

"I wish we had another room for the baby," Heather said, reaching for a French fry.

"What about that little laundry room?" Jeff said.

"Where would we put the washer and dryer?"

"Couldn't we go to the Laundromat?"

"Too expensive," Heather mumbled around a mouthful of chicken.

"Is there room for the stackable kind of washer and dryer in the kitchen?" Way asked. "If there is, I could always get the set for a wedding gift."

"That's a good idea," Amanda said. "The other room is small, but it would be okay for right now."

Heather's face glowed with excitement. "It would need a lot of work. We'd have to do some painting and papering."

"I can hire it done," Way said.

"No way!" Jeff said hastily. "Mom can do it—can't you, Mom?"

Amanda saw the gleam of masculine pride in his eyes. It was one thing to accept a wedding present, and quite another to let his new father-in-law pay for something that he considered to be his debt. She wanted to praise him for his stubbornness, and berate him for being so hardheaded. She wanted to tell him to let Way do whatever he wanted, because he could afford it. But she couldn't. She hadn't been brought up that way, and that wasn't the way she'd raised Jeff. The Farrells paid their way, and they didn't take advantage.

"Sure," she said. "I'd be glad to."

Jeff leaned toward Heather, who met him halfway for a kiss. Again, there might have been no one in the room but the two of them. Jeff reached out and placed his palm on her still-flat stomach. "Don't worry, babe. I'll bust my butt to get everything you need for the baby."

There was such promise in his voice—promise that she knew he made because of the hard time the two of them had had—that Amanda felt her throat tighten with tears. She looked askance at Way and saw him looking at their children with a considering light in his eyes. She hoped that he saw the pride that was such a part of Jeff's personality. She prayed he respected it.

The remainder of the meal passed quickly. Heather and Jeff's happiness was both heartwarming and sad. It was a special feeling to witness their contentment and their very real joy over the prospect of becoming parents despite the circumstances. Yet Amanda couldn't help praying that it would last, couldn't help thinking that she had once felt the same way, once had the same dreams, the same goals. And somehow, some way, she had lost them, because she hadn't been clever enough to see them slipping from her grasp.

Way's misery stemmed from the fact that every time Jeff and Heather touched, kissed or smiled at each other, it only made him want to do the same thing with Amanda. Ever since she'd fallen asleep in his arms and he'd had a glimpse of what it would be like to hold her— really hold her—he had been able to concentrate on little else. He couldn't remember feeling such a need to see a woman, to be with one, in years. Not since Carol. It was a sobering, frightening way to feel about a woman who'd made it very clear what she thought of the men in his line of work.

Both Amanda and Way were glad when they finished eating and resumed their respective tasks. Leaving Heather to clean up the kitchen, and Jeff and Way to unload more boxes, Amanda went to work in the bedroom, unpacking what had already been brought in. Recalling Jeff's instructions—"We'll change stuff around later, just get it unpacked"—she meticulously put things in the chest of drawers that he and Way had carried in. She also hung clothes in the closet and juggled space on the shelves for everything from blankets to tennis rackets.

Amanda was searching through a box that Heather thought held the mattress pad and sheets when a deep voice said, "I've been given orders to come give you a hand."

Red faced at being caught with her rear end in the air, Amanda whirled around and faced Way, who stood with his arms crossed, leaning against the doorjamb. He looked more masculine than any man had the right to look. A faded sweatshirt with the sleeves cut out covered his broad chest and exposed his bare arms, arms that were tan and lightly dusted with blond hair from elbow to wrist. Arms that she knew firsthand could hold a woman so very tenderly.

His feet were crossed at the ankle, one toe of his battered Reeboks resting against the carpet. His long, well-muscled legs looked as if he had been melted and poured into the tight jeans he wore—or dipped into a denim vat and coated with the blue fabric that clung to his thighs and the proof of his manhood with heart-stopping accuracy. With the scene on the sofa ingrained on her memory, it was an effort to keep her gaze above his zipper.

"I can make the bed by myself, thanks," Amanda said, surprised at the husky, breathless quality she heard in her own voice.

Oh, Mandy, if you only knew how much I'd like to make you . . . on that bed, to throw you onto that mattress and strip those sexy pants off you.

"Uh-uh," he said, shaking his head and lunging away from the door frame. "You aren't getting rid of me that easily."

Amanda's heart began to race at the intimacy of his words, but she didn't speak. She couldn't. *I don't want to get rid of you at all. I'd like for you to come over here and pull me into your arms the way Jeff did Heather. I'd like to see if we fit together as well and as easily as they do.*

"They're doing the kitchen stuff," Way said, jerking his thumb back over his shoulder toward the other room. He smiled. "I don't do kitchens."

So much for him wanting to be with you, Amanda.

She forced her heart to resume its normal, placid speed and urged a lightness to her voice that she hoped didn't sound as phony as it really was. "Then by all means, help me with the sheets."

"I think I remember seeing them in here," he said, going to a large box. He pulled back the flaps and began to rummage around inside. Amanda, still calling herself forty kinds of fool for having the audacity to even think he might want to spend time with her, stood across the bed from him, watching as he unearthed the missing sheets and laid them on the dresser.

They worked silently together, putting the mattress cover on first and then the bottom, fitted sheet. Deke had never helped her do any household chores, because, she supposed, he thought it might tarnish his masculine image. But there wasn't a man alive more masculine than Way Dalton, and here he was, flipping sheets out with the practice and skill of any woman, doing it without a fuss and without any apparent damage to his ego.

"You do this pretty well," she said, speaking her thoughts aloud.

"I come from a family of five," he told her with a smile. "Mom made us all do our share."

"And doing housework isn't . . ." She paused in her efforts to smooth the wrinkles from the top sheet and to find the right words.

"Demeaning to my macho image?" he finished for her, divining the turn of her thoughts.

"Yes," she said, turning the top sheet back so that the lacy border showed.

Way copied her actions on his side of the bed. "Not really. Carol always worked, and I felt that if I was home and she wasn't, it was only right to try to ease her load." He grinned. "Which brings me to the real reason I came in here."

"You mean you didn't come in here to help me?"

The unexpected teasing quality in Amanda's voice came as a pleasant surprise, another aspect of her personality that was so intriguing. The list was growing. Way crossed his arms over his broad chest. "Actually, I came to offer you an apology."

"Apology?" she asked. "For what?"

"For putting you in an awkward situation this morning."

Amanda didn't want his apology. She didn't want the memory of waking up in such an intimate situation with him spoiled by taking it apart and discussing it. "You didn't put me in an awkward situation. It was a perfectly innocent situation."

"I know that and you know that, but I'm not sure Jeff and Heather believe it was innocent."

Jeff's questions about her interest in Way and his "advice" flashed through Amanda's mind. Her heart sank. Had he said something to Way? "Why? What happened?"

"What happened is that Heather cornered me and asked me point-blank if I was interested in you."

Are you? Amanda's first thought was quickly replaced by a soul-deep thankfulness that Jeff had kept his mouth shut. Following rapidly on the heels of that was a picture-perfect recollection of the shocked look on Heather's face. She hadn't been happy about finding a woman in Way's arms. "Oh, Way!"

I wanted to tell her yes, Mandy. "Yeah, she did. Can you believe it?"

A heated blush stained her cheeks. "As a matter of fact, under the circumstances, I can," she said, compelled to tell him the truth since he seemed so concerned about her.

Way correctly interpreted the reason behind the gleam of humor in her eyes. He tugged a pillowcase onto a fat feather pillow. "Don't tell me Jeff put you through the inquisition, too."

Determined to make light of the whole issue, she offered him a brittle smile. "He wasn't questioning me as much as he was giving his blessing."

"What!"

Amanda nodded, drawing a pillowcase onto the other pillow. "He told me that he knew I had urges, and if there was something going on between us, he understood."

"Well, that's damn big of him, considering his own circumstances," Way said sarcastically, plopping his pillow down near the headboard.

The aggravated tone of his voice struck Amanda as funny, as did the fact that both their kids felt the need to caution them about getting involved. She felt her mouth curving upward at the corners. "It is, isn't it?"

Way must have seen the funny side, too, because he began to laugh—a low, bass sound that triggered her own laughter and sent a frisson of desire trickling down her spine.

"Hey!" Jeff called from the other room. "What's so funny in there?"

Way and Amanda sobered abruptly, and feeling as she had that morning, as if she'd been caught doing something she shouldn't, she began to search her mind for something mundane to cover the brief intimacy they'd shared. That something turned out to be a big wrinkle near the middle of the bed. She reached to smooth it out at the very moment that Way got the same idea. His hands brushed hers a millisecond before their foreheads collided.

"Ouch!" she said in tandem with Way's mild curse.

"You okay?" he asked, his hands closing around hers and holding her where she was.

Leaning over the bed with her palms pinned to the floral sheets by his, their mouths mere inches apart, Amanda nodded, steeling herself against the warmth in his brown eyes.

"Show me," he murmured. Still holding her hand in his, he straightened and rounded the end of the bed.

Amanda drew herself up as he came nearer and willed her body not to tremble as he pushed the hair back from her forehead, revealing a red place just above her left eyebrow.

He reached out and feathered his thumb across the spot. The gentleness of his touch sent her eyelashes drifting downward and started a helpless longing inside her. What would it be like to have him kiss her?

"No bump," he announced softly. He drew in a deep breath, filling his nostrils and his senses with the scent of her shampoo. He was no more able to stop his hand from moving to the soft curls above her ear than he could have denied himself his next breath.

His touch was feather light, as soft as a whisper and nerve shattering. Amanda raised her lashes and looked up at him. "I'm okay," she assured him, her voice as soft as his touch.

The smile on his lips matched the smile in his eyes. "Yes, you are, Mandy. You're more than okay."

A quivering anticipation began in her middle as his head lowered. He was going to kiss her. And heaven help her, she wanted him to. Wanted it more than anything she could remember wanting in a long time. She forgot that he was an athlete, forgot that he was Heather's father, forgot everything except the fact that his mouth was only a heartbeat away from hers. Her eyes fluttered shut, blocking out the sight of him, blocking out the light, blocking out the tiny voice inside her that taunted her for a fool.

"Mom!" Jeff yelled, bursting into the room unexpectedly, coming to a halt just inside the door.

Amanda's guilty, startled gaze met her son's over the bulky shape of Way's shoulder. As usual, her first instinct was to put as much distance between herself and Way as was humanly possible. She made a halfhearted attempt to pull free, but this time, Way wouldn't let her. The hand cradling her cheek slipped around to the back of her head, and his left hand gripped her upper arm, holding her still in his grasp. The stillness in the room was so thick it could be cut, dried and sold.

"Hold still, Mandy," Way growled in a soft voice. Then, he turned and looked at Jeff, the barest hint of challenge in his eyes. "Your mother got some lint in her eye while we were putting the sheets on the bed."

"Oh," Jeff said with a nod. "I see."

Without another word, he turned and left the room, but not before Amanda had seen the I-told-you-so gleam in his eyes.

The fragile emotion binding her and Way was broken. Disappointment welled up inside her as she allowed her gaze to meet his and found, with a bit of surprise, that he looked as disappointed as she felt.

His eyes searched hers with a thoroughness that left her shaken to the roots of her soul. In a move of unstudied provocation, her tongue darted out and slicked across her lips.

With a groan Way dragged his thumb gently across the tantalizing moistness, pulling her bottom lip down the slightest bit and brushing the sensitive, inner portion of her mouth with the rough pad.

She felt the touch deep inside her, and it was all she could do to keep from touching Way's thumb with the tip of her tongue. It was only the sound of Jeff's voice in the other room, as he spoke to Heather, that stopped her. She looked up at Way with tortured eyes that begged him to make her understand. What did he want from her? Where would a kiss lead them?

"Those eyes of yours are going to get you in trouble one day, Mandy-mine," he told her. "And stop trying to put a mile between us every time one of the kids comes into the room. We haven't done anything wrong, have we?"

Amanda shook her head, shocked at the strength of the emotions Way's touch generated. She wanted to ignore—to deny—the longings he stirred inside her, but she couldn't, not while her blood was racing recklessly through her veins.

She dragged her gaze from his and busied herself with turning back the bed. It promised to be a long evening.

Way reached out and took her shoulders, turning her around to face him. "We didn't do anything wrong, Mandy, and whatever we do is really none of their business."

CHAPTER TEN

THE NEXT MONTH was torture for Amanda, who wrestled with the knowledge that her growing feelings for Way Dalton, while undeniable, were ridiculous. She was a fool for feeling the way she did about him, but fool or not, she didn't seem to be able to help herself. When she was near him, she felt breathless, nervous, excited and alive. Since they'd first met she'd experienced more disparate emotions than she'd felt in years, and every bit of wisdom she'd gleaned about the opposite sex had flown from her mind like a home-run ball out of the playing field.

As a matter of fact, she thought, as she drove over to pick Heather up, she felt as young and inexperienced as her new daughter-in-law.

So where does that leave you, Amanda?

It left her wondering how Way's lips would have felt against hers if Jeff hadn't come in and interrupted them that late-May night. And there was no doubt that he had been about to kiss her. Amanda was as sure of that as she was that the sun would set in the west every evening. It left her with the unbelievable possibility that Way wanted her, too. The thought that he might reciprocate her feelings—the desire, at least—left her sleepless. Sleepless, with an aching, empty feeling that burned at the heart of her femininity and spread until its heat left her wanting, restless and irritable.

Where it leaves you, Amanda, is scared. Scared that you're imagining what you see in his eyes, that you're putting the wrong name to his actions. You're scared that if something did develop between you, it would be nothing more to him than the fact that he'd added your scalp to his belt.

It also left her with the lonely certainty that she'd done herself an injustice by letting her bitterness over Deke's defection color her view of the opposite sex—men who might have been decent if she'd only given them the chance to prove themselves. Men like the seven-year-old Jeff's scoutmaster. A man recently divorced himself, a handsome, rugged type who played soccer in his spare time. He'd tried to date her, but Amanda had cut him off short and, after a few attempts, he'd given up. Then there had been Jeff's junior high school basketball coach, a man Jeff had adored at the time, yet another man she'd refused to even consider dating. She sighed.

It had been wrong to judge all males by Deke, and she wouldn't make the same mistake with Way. Even though their relationship—if you could call it that—had developed because of their kids, he'd already proved that he wasn't the self-centered, glory-seeking man Deke had been. Way was a good father, a good first baseman and incredibly... sexy.

Amanda groaned at the frustration eating away at her, thankful that the apartment was just around the corner so she wouldn't have to put up with her own company much longer. With all the woodwork stripped, varnished and painted, and all the cracks filled up at last, she and Heather were finally going shopping for wallpaper. Amanda hoped—prayed—the trip would erase thoughts of Heather's handsome father from her mind... at least for a few hours.

UNFORTUNATELY, THE WALLPAPER expedition didn't take as long as Amanda had anticipated. Heather had already scouted out the offerings of several places that handled in-stock paper and made tentative decisions. All Heather really needed Amanda to do was to give her okay and list what else she needed.

"Do you mind if we stop in the mall a few minutes so I can look at some sale-priced maternity clothes? It won't be long before I need them," Heather asked as they stashed paper and tools in the trunk.

"Of course not," Amanda said, impressed that Heather was concerned enough about money that she was looking at sale items.

The store was filled with women in varying stages of pregnancy—from those who, like Heather, weren't showing yet, to those who looked ready to deliver at any moment. Heather found three shorts-and-tops outfits, a pair of maternity jeans and a dress, all of which Amanda insisted they put on her charge card. Then, with Heather declaring that she was starving, they headed back to the car.

They were nearing the mall exit when, lured by the vibrant colors on the mannequins in the window of a rather exclusive boutique, Heather stopped with an envious sigh. "Wow. What I wouldn't give to be able to wear one of those."

Amanda turned, regarding one of the strapless dresses, the top of which appeared to consist of a wide piece of fabric attached at the waist only at the front. The place where the material was wrapped and tied once in back would leave a generous portion of flesh exposed above and below. The cloth was then brought back to the front and tied between the breasts. The skirt was straight, but the material looked as if it had been wrapped and tucked in at the waist, falling in loose folds to almost the hemline. The dress was classy and sexy, and not at all the type of thing found in Amanda's closet.

"It's pretty," she admitted.

"Why don't you try one on?" Heather suggested. "It would look great on you."

"Oh, no," Amanda said with a shake of her head. "That isn't my style at all."

"Why not? You certainly have the figure for it."

The compliment came as a surprise. "It's too...bare. Look at that open place in the back."

"That deep turquoise would be great with your hair," Heather shot back.

Would it? She was supposed to wear those bright colors, but the style was so...provocative. "I don't know."

Heather took her arm. "Come on. Go try it on. No one says you have to buy it."

"Okay," Amanda said with a sigh. "I'll try it."

Heather was one hundred percent right, Amanda thought a few moments later as she adjusted the knot between her breasts. Even though the strapless dress wasn't her style, it did look good with her hair...and the cut was flattering. The pockets that opened parallel to the waist were located so that their slight flare emphasized her small waist, and the draped hemline accentuated her slender calves.

The saleslady stood with her hands on her hips and studied Amanda with as much pride as if she'd created the dress with her bare hands. "Very nice. You certainly have the figure for it," she said, echoing Heather's sentiments.

"It's great!" Heather said, and then added with a laugh, "But the tennis shoes have got to go."

Amanda looked down at the offending shoes and met Heather's eyes in the three-way mirror. They laughed, and for a moment Amanda was held by a feeling of déjà vu so strong it was almost frightening. How many times had she gone shopping for new clothes with friends when she was Heather's age? And how long had it been since she'd treated shopping as an adventure instead of a necessary evil connected with her job and her desire to convey a professional image?

"Buy it," her new daughter-in-law said.

Amanda regarded her image in the mirror and tugged at the fabric above her breasts. "Oh, Heather, I don't know...."

"But hurry. I'm really starving now."

The dress did make her feel prettier...and desirable, things that Amanda admitted, in a moment's honesty, she liked feeling. "Okay," she said with a dubious smile, "I'll take it."

Later that night, while Jeff and Heather were out, Amanda—exhausted from hanging the pastel-hued teddy bear wallpaper but determined to finish—was still wondering if she'd done the right thing buying the dress. Where would she wear it, for goodness' sake?

The radio, tuned to whatever station Jeff had listened to last, filled the soon-to-be nursery with one of the songs that she recognized from a movie she'd seen recently on television.

Amanda judged just how far she could reach and decided that she really did need to move the step stool the landlord had provided for her use when they couldn't find a ladder. Stretching, she took a long, flat brush and smoothed the bumps and wrinkles from the strip of paper she was hanging. When it was as smooth as possible, she took a small roller from the back pocket of jeans so old and faded that she used them only to work in the yard and to paint in—jeans that, in fact, Jeff declared were right in style again because they were so worn. Roller in hand, she sealed both seams as far up and down as she could reach without climbing down and moving the stool. Her leg muscles were already sore and aching.

Flexing and rubbing her tired shoulders, she calculated that she needed three more strips of paper to finish. The border, she decided with a weary sigh, could wait until tomorrow. She reached into her front pocket, drew out the small retractable razor and opened the blade, stretching up on her tiptoes to trim the excess paper.

She was never sure later whether she'd heard a sound behind her or if she caught the suggestion of motion from her peripheral vision, but something brought her head around with a suddenness that played havoc with her balance. Waving her arms in an attempt to regain control, she tipped the stool. A shriek of surprise and terror escaped her, and with no thought but to rid herself of the sharp razor before she fell on it, Amanda hurled it across the room and closed her eyes, trying to prepare herself for her imminent fall.

She didn't see the startled look on the face of the man standing in the doorway and didn't hear the sound of his footsteps as he raced across the room toward her. All Amanda knew was that instead of crashing to the floor as she'd expected, she was gathered into a close, secure embrace that elicited a deep, masculine "Umph!"

Way! When had he come in? What was he doing here? Trembling as much from his nearness as the fact that she'd narrowly escaped a hard fall, Amanda tilted her head back and lifted her lashes. Worried coffee-brown eyes probed hers.

"Are you okay?" he asked, the softly uttered words stirring the silky strands of black hair at her temple.

She nodded. The tension left his body all at once, and the sudden relaxing of his muscles only made the intimacy of their position more evident. His right arm held them chest to warm chest. One of Amanda's arms was hooked around his neck, the other clung to his waist in a death grip. For the first time she realized that his left hand partially covered her denim-clad bottom and that the lower part of her body was cradled firmly by that hand into the V of his legs, which were braced apart to take her weight.

Awareness, like wildfire in dry summer grasses, sprang up between them, igniting their senses with a raging heat, a heat that consumed old misconceptions, former passions and lingering fears, leaving only the pure, bright flame of desire burning between them. Desire that began in her heart and left the deepest core of her hot and melting. Her eyes meshed with his, her body languid and relaxed against him, Amanda felt—in direct contrast— Way's body growing hard against her abdomen.

She saw his head begin to lower, felt his right hand join his left on her bottom in a slow caressing motion that drew her up even closer. Without conscious thought, Amanda shifted her legs slightly apart and, with a groan of frustration, Way pulled her up flush against him, closer, tighter, fitting their bodies together like two pieces of the same puzzle.

His mouth took hers then, not in the sweet, tentative kiss of exploration they would have shared that night in the bedroom, but in a scorching touch of lips that seared her emotions and her heart with the taste and feel of him. Amanda, so long without a man—dear heaven, too long without a man—and hungry, so very hungry, responded to the first touch of his mouth by arching into him and parting her lips. She granted his tongue entrance without any preliminary, seeking forays, taking it into her mouth as she longed to take him inside her body, knowing intuitively that he would fill both places equally well.

Way's tongue stroked the roof of her mouth, slid over her teeth and entwined with hers in the perfect, yet unsatisfactory, mimicry of what they both wanted. The slight abrading of his mustache against her mouth only enhanced the fiery sensations his lips ignited. Her breasts felt full and heavy, aching for his touch. Lost in the mastery of his kisses, she imagined him drawing her nipples into his mouth and stroking them with his tongue in that skillful, maddening way.

A car door slammed outside, and the sound of laughter came in through the closed window, cooling Amanda's heated senses as effectively as a dousing of cold water. Jeff and Heather! Shocked at the wantonness of her response, she twisted her mouth free of his.

Way's mouth released hers, but he didn't let her go. There was no hint of victory on his face, no censure in his eyes. Instead, they held a heavy-lidded, passion-induced haze, and his lips, as she knew hers were, were shiny wet from their kisses.

"Mandy," he breathed, shaking his head in a fashion that wordlessly said he was having a hard time grasping what had just happened between them.

Amanda lowered her arms from around his neck and pushed against his chest in an effort to put some distance between them. The strength of his arousal still pressed against her as she heard Jeff's and Heather's voices getting nearer.

"I . . . don't know what to say. . . ."

Way released her then, and Amanda could see by the slight smile on his lips and the teasing gleam in his eyes that he was rapidly regaining control. That was par, she thought with a sinking heart. He was more used to dealing with this sort of thing than she was.

"Don't say anything," he warned in a husky voice that bespoke his own need. He reached out and touched his index finger to the tip of her nose. "You're quite a woman, Amanda Farrell, and as much as I'd like to kiss you again, it's time to see how good a liar you are."

Amanda blinked. "What?"

He jerked his head toward the sound of the back door opening. "You go out there and keep them entertained a couple of minutes while I try to get things under control here." Then, with a wicked smile that gave no quarter to her sheltered sensibilities, he took her hand and guided it to the hard thrust of his manhood against the barrier of denim.

Amanda's eyes widened and hot color rushed into her face. Jerking free, she whirled and rushed from the room, the sound of his soft, mocking laughter chasing after her.

CHAPTER ELEVEN

AMANDA TIED THE BOW of the strapless sundress, never stopping to question why she was taking such care with her appearance or why she was wearing a dress that by her own admission was too daring. It was ridiculous to be so nervous. It was only a dinner date, and not really a date at that. She had simply agreed to have dinner with Way, Heather and Jeff at Wayfarers again. Still, she knew her bout of nerves stemmed from the fact that ever since Way had kissed her more than five weeks ago, she had gone out of her way to stay out of *his* way. She hadn't been able to stop her feelings for him from growing, but she could certainly keep him from knowing about them.

The first few moments after Jeff and Heather had come home that evening would forever remain a blur to Amanda. She had been so wrapped up in her own feelings of shame and embarrassment that her excuse to keep them from going into the nursery was almost forgotten.

She remembered asking Jeff to get her something to drink and questioning them about the movie, which they both raved over. Other than that, she drew a blank, except for noting with an acute feeling of relief that when Way stepped through the door there was no outward sign that they'd been necking in the room that was to be their grandchild's.

Necking! Groaning with frustration, Amanda sank onto the velvet-covered chair that matched her built-in vanity. She rested her elbows on the swirled travertine surface and raked the nails of both hands through her hair, pressing her head between her palms in a vain effort to stop the tormenting thoughts.

It was disgusting to think of how she'd responded to Way's kiss like a teenager who'd just discovered the pleasures of sex. Her lips twisted wryly. Or, more aptly, she'd behaved like the sex-starved divorcée she was. What must he think of her?

She was going to be a grandmother, for goodness' sake. Way was going to be a grandfather. It wasn't normal to have such strong and uncontrollable feelings at her age—no, *their* age—was it? Was it even decent? But decent or not, he aroused feelings in her Amanda had thought she'd never feel again.

Face it, he arouses feelings in you you've never felt before.

It was true. While sex with Deke had been good at the time, the vantage point of age and maturity told her that much of what she'd experienced back then had a lot to do with an awareness of her body, natural curiosity and the lure of the forbidden.

Forbidden. Way was the kind of man she'd forbidden herself to have anything to do with, but somehow he'd overcome every obstacle she'd created, and she was helpless to stop the feelings his very presence brought to vibrant life.

Still, she was an adult who had garnered adequate reserves of worldliness through the years, one who'd managed to keep her life in immaculate order...until now. There was no reason this unaccountable attraction for Way should cause her to disappoint Jeff and Heather and their plans for the evening. She knew life had given her more than her share of self-possession, and there was no reason she couldn't pull off dinner with her normal aplomb. She would be polite, friendly, and conduct herself as Jeff's mother should. It was only dinner. Just a couple of hours spent with Way, with Jeff and Heather as buffers. She could and she would do it.

WAY PULLED into Jeff and Heather's driveway at exactly seven o'clock. The early-evening sunshine caught the metallic gleam of his gold watch and flung it momentarily back into his eyes. He shut off the engine and opened the door, hoping the kids were ready, because after five of the longest weeks he'd ever lived through, he was more than ready to see Amanda. He'd started to call her a dozen times, but always managed to stop himself before going through with it. The kiss they'd shared had shaken him as much as it had her, even though he thought he'd been able to cover up that fact . . . and the likewise disturbing fact that he was scared.

He wasn't conceited, and he'd never had any complaints from the women in his life, but *no* woman had ever responded to him with the hungry abandon Amanda had. While he'd always suspected that there was hidden fire in her, the knowledge that he was able to elicit such a response was a sobering and heady feeling. Heady because he wondered just what other surprises he might discover in her, and sobering because he knew what that response must have cost her in terms of self-respect later.

He'd needed this time to come to grips with the fact that she had come to mean more to him than he'd ever thought she would. She was more than Jeff's mom. More than Heather's new mother-in-law. She was, as

he'd discovered, a woman to challenge him, to capti-
vate him, to constantly surprise him. She was the woman
he was beginning to think he might want to grow old
with.

Heather was right, he thought, knocking on the back
door. Amanda was different. Amanda was real. She was
a threat to his state of self-imposed bachelorhood, a
menace to the heart he thought he'd never lose again.
After Carol, he'd felt certain he'd never find anyone else
who would make him feel the way she had, and up until
Amanda, he hadn't. Losing control was a frightening
feeling, and he wasn't sure he liked it any more than she
had. Quite simply, he hadn't made any contact with her
because he felt that they both needed time to think, time
to get perspective on what was happening to them.

Jeff opened the door, a smile of welcome on his face.

Way looked at his new son-in-law, who was still
dressed in a pair of cutoffs and a pocket T-shirt. Way
sighed. He'd just got into town and hadn't called to
check with Jeff about the plans they'd made more than
a week before. "Did you forget we were going to dinner?"

Jeff moved aside for Way to enter and closed the door
behind them. "No. We didn't forget, but I think we're
going to pass," Jeff told him. "Heather's really
bushed."

Concern gouged the creases in Way's cheeks deeper.
"She's okay?"

"Yeah. But this August heat is really draining her.
She's pretty tired. I don't think she's asleep, though.
Why don't you go in and say hello?"

Way made his way to the bedroom, but despite Jeff's
prediction, Way found Heather fast asleep. Tiptoeing
into the room, he bent and dropped a light kiss to her

cheek, grimacing at the pain that shot through his back as he straightened. His slide into home the previous day had cinched the game, but it had cost the usual pound of flesh. He left the room wondering how much longer he could keep up his grueling life-style.

"She's sleeping," he told Jeff. "How has she been feeling?"

"Pretty good. She isn't sick, but she sleeps a lot. She feels kind of drained... you know?"

"So how's everything going?" Way asked, sitting down at the small dinette table that boasted a silk floral bouquet in a small basket.

"Fine. Did you see the baby's room?"

Way shook his head and loosened his tie. "I'll see it before I go. How's the job?"

Jeff shrugged, but there was no disguising the bleak look in his eyes. "It pays the rent and puts groceries on the table. By the way, thanks for the washer and dryer."

"You're welcome." Way paused, and then plunged ahead before he could lose his determination. "School will be starting in about three weeks, and I've been wondering what you planned to do about it."

Jeff didn't even look up from the potatoes he was scrubbing with unnecessary force. "I think I'm going to stay out this year."

"Why?" Way asked, already knowing the answer.

"There's no hurry."

"Your mother will be devastated if you don't go back this fall."

"Yeah? Well, there's always next year, or I might take some night courses at the community college."

"Is it money?" Way probed gently.

Jeff turned, and there was a look in his eyes Way remembered feeling only too well. Despair. Hopelessness. Entrapment.

"Do you have any idea what it costs to have a baby?"

Way shook his head, his heart saddened that the happiness he'd seen in Jeff's eyes that first night had been wiped away by the harsh hand of reality. "No, I'm afraid I don't. It's been a long time since Heather was born."

"Eight hundred and fifty friggin' dollars," Jeff told him in an awe-filled voice. "And that's just the doctor. I haven't had the guts to check with the hospital. Not only that, but the doctor wants his money up front." He laughed bitterly and flung his head back to look at the ceiling. "I think I'm right in the middle of what my friend, Casey, calls a real-life situation."

"Regrets, Jeff?" Way asked in a gentle voice.

The question brought Jeff's honest gaze back to his father-in-law's. "No sir. Not about marrying Heather. About my own lack of consideration for the future, yes. I never wanted to make her worry or do without." There was a suspicious glitter in his eyes, and his voice held the barest tremor as he added, "All I wanted to do was love her. To make her happy."

"I think she is happy, don't you?" Way queried, wanting, *needing* to take away the helplessness he heard in Jeff's voice.

"I don't know," he said with a shake of his head. Then he shrugged. "I guess so. Yeah."

"I want you to go back to school," Way told him.

"No way. I can't."

"Your mother and I can help. We want to."

Jeff held his palms up and his eyes held the same determination Way had seen in Amanda's. "Oh, hey, man.

No way. I'm not taking charity. I got us into this—it's my responsibility to get us out."

"Don't let your pride stand in the way, here, Jeff," Way cajoled. "It's a commendable attribute, and I'd think less of you if it weren't such a part of your make-up, but sometimes pride can keep us from seeing things clearly."

The very pride they were talking about faded slightly from Jeff's features.

"I'm not talking about charity, either," Way said. "I'm talking about a loan. Call it an investment in my grandchild's future, if you want. It's important that you get your education, for everyone's sake. I want to pay your tuition, so you can finish school on schedule. I think your mother will loan you the money for the doctor. If you have to, you can pay the hospital bill out. Once you get your degree and get a good job, you can pay us back in monthly installments. What do you say?"

Jeff crossed his arms across his broad chest. "I say my mom will have a fit. If you think I'm proud, wait till you run this by her. She cornered the market on pride."

Way smiled, looking more confident than he really felt. "I think I can deal with your mom. What do you say?"

Jeff began to pace the small room. "I don't know...it just doesn't seem right."

"Why?"

He stopped and faced Way. "It seems like it *ought* to be tough, you know? Like I ought to have to scrimp and sacrifice. Like it ought not be as easy as you want to make it."

"You mean you feel like you should have to pay for Heather getting pregnant?"

"I know it sounds crazy, but yeah, I guess so."

"Just because you made a mistake doesn't mean that your life should be hell," Way said. "And even though your mother and I are financially able and willing to help, believe me, you're still going to have to sacrifice and scrimp. There are a hundred and one things that come up that you never think about. You're going to have to go to school every morning after being up half the night with a colicky baby. You're going to have to stay at home with a wife and kid while your friends are out carousing around. It isn't going to be easy, any way you look at it."

Jeff nodded. "I know."

"So what do you say?"

Jeff plowed his fingers through his hair. Then he grinned, a relieved yet embarrassed lopsided quirking of his lips. "Yeah, yeah. Okay."

Way smiled back. "Good. I understand you're a whiz at math."

"I do all right," Jeff said, the wary look in his eyes asking without words what Way was getting at.

"I have an opening for a bookkeeper at Wayfarers, if you're interested."

Way saw the stubborn light gleaming in Jeff's eyes again. "I don't think..."

"It's a real job, Jeff, not charity. I need someone. The lady who works for me is moving to L.A."

"Well..."

"It beats minimum wage, and there's a medical plan." Way could see Jeff's resolve wavering. One corner of his mustache inched upward in a half smile. "You'll still be free at night, so you can play whatever gigs you have, and if it will make you feel any better, I promise to fire you if you don't pull your weight."

Suddenly, Jeff smiled. "You just hired yourself a bookkeeper."

Way felt as if a load had been lifted from his shoulders. "Good." He shot back the cuffs of his white dress shirt. "It's getting late. You'd better call your mom and tell her dinner's off."

"Hey! There's no reason to cancel because we aren't going. Why don't you and mom go on without us?" Jeff suggested.

Way considered the option for a second. He couldn't believe he hadn't thought of that option himself—but then, maybe he'd been afraid to consider it. He looked at Jeff, anticipation at seeing Amanda again glowing in his eyes. "Sounds like a good idea."

Jeff smiled, the kind of smile one man gives another when they're in tune with each other's thoughts and motives. "I thought you might like the suggestion."

"Show me the nursery," Way said, "and then I'm outta here."

AMANDA PACED the living room, twisting her hands. She went to the window and peeked between the miniblinds to see if the car had arrived. Then she went to the mirror hanging over the sofa and stared at her reflection. Without any conceit, she knew she'd never looked better. She tugged the strapless top up and wondered for the hundredth time if she should go change, but before she could make a decision, the doorbell rang. Tucking a curl behind her ear and taking a deep, fortifying breath, she flung open the door, a smile of welcome on her face, a faux smile of dazzling brilliance that died a swift and merciless death.

Standing there alone, his hands in the pockets of his gray suit pants, stood Way—taller, blonder and more handsome than she'd remembered.

"Hi," he said with a slight smile.

Her manners flew by the wayside as Amanda realized that the kids were nowhere to be seen. "Where are Jeff and Heather?"

"Heather isn't feeling well," he told her with a small shrug. "So I guess it's just you and me."

"You and me?" Amanda echoed.

"You and me," he repeated. "Is that okay?"

"I...uh...yes, I suppose so," Amanda said, not knowing what else to say. She certainly couldn't tell him that she didn't want to go with him because she was embarrassed to have acted so uninhibitedly. Or worse, that she was afraid to be alone with him because the attraction felt for him put her at a distinctly vulnerable disadvantage.

"Good," he said with a smile that warmed her already heated blood. "Are you ready? Do you need to get a purse or anything?"

She nodded and turned back to the room to get her matching handbag, cursing the naive excitement coursing through her. What she felt was ridiculous. Way was a baseball star—rich, famous and as out of reach as that first star glittering in the evening sky behind him. She was just Amanda Farrell—divorcée, mother, teacher. It was a hopeless situation, but even recognizing that hopelessness, her heart was pounding as fast as any excited fifteen-year-old's.

DINNER WAS SHRIMP SCAMPI and a Bibb lettuce salad. The wine was an exhilaratingly dry, green-gold Riesling. The fruity fragrance tickled her senses as Amanda raised the bell-shaped glass to her lips once more. Never much of a drinker, the wine, which the waiter seemed intent on pouring when her glass became the slightest bit low, was going straight to her head. Which, she thought with a smile, might have been part of the reason the dinner she'd dreaded was developing into a very pleasant experience.

Way, knowing that she hadn't forgotten their kiss any more than he had, also knew her well enough to realize that she was still uncomfortable about it. That knowledge and being acutely conscious of the subtle shift in his own feelings for her made him go out of his way to be pleasant, polite and entertaining—not, he reminded himself, that it was hard to enjoy the time he spent with her. It tried his social prowess to keep the conversation on mundane things when he really wanted to tell her just what he was feeling.

Instead, he praised the work she'd done on the apartment and told her of his talk with Jeff. Surprisingly, rather than the anger Jeff had led him to expect, Amanda seemed relieved that Way was offering financial help. And, as Way himself had predicted, she offered to lend the money to pay the doctor bill.

"I appreciate all you're doing to ease Jeff's load," she said as they topped off their dinner with bananas Foster.

"And I appreciate all you've done to make their place a home."

"Love and people make a place a home," she corrected, "not wallpaper and pictures."

Way recalled the emptiness of his own house since Heather had left. The thought of going back to it after he took Amanda home held about as much appeal as not making it to the play-offs. "You're right. There's not much happening at my place since Heather moved out."

Amanda's smile was sympathetic. "I know. It took me a long time to adjust when Jeff left for college."

She was an attentive listener, he realized, something more rare than a good bed partner as far as he was concerned. She turned her face slightly toward him and the candlelight glazed her shoulder with pearlescent light. And besides being a good listener, she was also easy on the eyes.

The dress she wore was something of a shock, considering that her wardrobe seemed to consist of tailored suits, slacks with knife-sharp creases and blouses with bows at the neck. The dress she'd worn to Heather's graduation had been becoming, but it couldn't touch this one for drop-dead effectiveness.

Her shoulders were a pale creamy white above the strapless bodice, and he was willing to bet a month's paycheck that she wasn't wearing a bra underneath. The vivid turquoise did wonderful things to her skin and hair, which, he noted with a flicker of pleasure, still hadn't been cut.

"I like the dress," he told her, smiling over the rim of his coffee cup. "It's very becoming, very...sexy."

Amanda's eyes met his. "Sexy?" she said breathlessly. Then she laughed, a soft rush of air that shivered down Way's spine in a frisson of desire. She turned her head as if she were looking for someone. "You must be talking about someone else. I've never been called sexy in my life."

Way's voice was filled with conviction as he said, "Then lady, you've been keeping company with men who are either blind or very unobservant." He leaned back in his chair and regarded her through tender half-closed eyes. "I think you're probably the most feminine-looking woman I've ever come across. And you're sexy because you've sold yourself so short for so many years that you don't have any idea of your attractiveness."

Amanda's eyes clung to his. She'd never wanted to believe anything so much in her life. "I don't know what to say," she confessed, the totally sober portion of her mind wondering why she was engaging in such suggestive small talk.

He smiled. "Say, 'Thank you, Way,'" he teased.

Amanda's tone and smile matched his. "Thank you, Way."

"You're more than welcome. Did I tell you I like your hair?"

She shook her head, an action that brushed the curls against the curve of her neck and set her head to spinning dangerously. "Not in a while."

"That's because I haven't seen you," he said at last. "Where have you been keeping yourself, Mandy?"

The vivid memory of their kiss spun out between them, a memory so clear it was visible in both their eyes.

Out of your way.

"You can't ignore it, you know."

"Ignore what?" she asked with studied nonchalance.

"The fact that I kissed you and you responded."

She lifted her chin a fraction of an inch. "We can try," she quipped lightly, emboldened by the wine.

"I don't want to try."

The soft declaration set Amanda's heartbeats into high gear and made her realize with sudden clarity the danger involved in the game she was playing. Way was a seasoned veteran of love games, while she'd sat on the sidelines so long she was nothing more than a rookie. "What?"

"I don't want to forget it," he said. "I want to do it again."

"Way..."

He reached across the table and took her hand in his. "Sh. Don't say it. I know every reason you have for not...getting involved with me. I've already thought of them."

"Then you know it won't work."

He shook his head. "I don't know that, and neither do you."

"Heather and Jeff—"

"Have nothing to do with this," he told her firmly. "What we do is our business."

Amanda swallowed hard at the suggestiveness of his tone. She struggled to maintain their bantering mood, but the seriousness in her eyes belied the lightness of her voice. "And what are we doing?"

Way laid his napkin next to his plate, aware of her inner turmoil. He glanced at the gold Rolex strapping his left wrist, and grinned engagingly. "Right now, we're going dancing. The night, as they say, is young."

While she was relieved that dancing was the most immediate thing on his mind, Amanda couldn't help confessing, "I'm not much of a dancer."

"Me either," he told her, "but I'm not ready to go home."

If the truth was known, Amanda wasn't, either. For some crazy reason, she wanted to prolong the exquisite agony of being with him, wanted to push her feelings and his to the absolute limit. "How about a movie?" she suggested instead.

"Sounds good to me," he said. "What was it Jeff and Heather saw a couple of weeks ago? Heather said she thought I'd enjoy it because of all the old songs they played."

Amanda named the movie, and after deciding it seemed worthwhile, she made a visit to the powder room while Way took care of the bill and rid himself of his tie and jacket.

The movie theater was dark and, by a streak of luck, they got there just as the coming attractions were being previewed. Amanda tried to ignore the fact that ninety percent of the other people in the small room were under twenty-five.

Taking her hand, Way led the way down the aisle, and, when they sat down, he didn't offer to release it. The simple gesture made Amanda realize with something of a shock that she hadn't been to the movies with a man in twenty years. She could only surmise that the few men she'd dated must have had more sophisticated tastes, but she wouldn't have traded all those dates for this one evening spent in Way's company.

The previews soon ended, and the studio logo filled the background. Music started and the opening credits faded in, black-and-white images of young people dancing...dancing that looked to Amanda as if they were making love standing up. Even though they dipped and swayed in some sort of computerized superslow motion, their hips still gyrated to the beat of the music in a suggestive way. The whole effect was one of total abandon, total sensuality. She shifted uncomfortably in her chair and, without turning her head, tried to gauge Way's reaction from the corner of her eye. All she could see was his strong profile, which didn't give away anything.

Way was trying to concentrate on the screen and forget the woman sitting beside him, but it was impossible. The two meshed in his mind. He watched a boy lift a girl's leg, saw their hips moving in slow synchronization and pictured himself doing the same to Amanda as he plunged into her warmth and softness. Without voluntary thought, his thumb began a slow caressing of the back of her hand, and he was glad the darkness of the theater hid the natural response of his body.

It was a relief when the opening credits came to an end and the picture started. Once they were into the story, both Way and Amanda knew why the picture had come so highly recommended. It was a love story—a classic good girl/bad boy tale that clearly portrayed the innocence of another era. A time when pregnancy outside of marriage was the exception—not the norm, when abortions were done illegally in the secrecy of the night, when a teenager's problem was what dress to wear to the prom instead of whether she should do drugs or not. It was a story both Way and Amanda could relate to, because they had both known teenaged sexuality and because they'd just experienced its consequences again through Jeff and Heather. When they left the theater hand in hand ninety minutes later, Amanda couldn't shake the feeling of having stepped back into time.

"Good movie," Way said, altering his ground-eating stride to match hers.

She glanced up at him. "It really was."

"The dancing was good."

Amanda glanced at him sideways. "No one I knew danced like that."

Way laughed. "Me either. You can't deny the sound track was good."

"It was," she said with a smile. "It brought back a lot of memories."

Way unlocked her door. "What it did was make me feel my forty years."

Amanda laughed softly in response. "Why don't you put the top down?" she suggested when he helped her into the convertible.

"What about your hair?"

She shrugged. "I'm going home. It won't hurt if it's windblown."

Obligingly he lowered the canvas top, slid in beside her and pulled out of the parking space. He reached for the radio knob, searching for a station and stopping when the theme song from the movie came on. He glanced at Amanda, his eyes questioning.

"Leave it," she said, more than willing to have the film's nostalgic spell continue. The wine had long since ceased to make her head swim, but the soft breath of the summer night, the music playing on the radio and the nearness of the man beside her combined to leave her feeling as light-headed as if she'd finished the whole bottle. She relaxed against the upholstery and closed her eyes, letting the heady feeling course through her. An effervescent happiness bubbled through her veins, a giddiness she hadn't experienced since she was eighteen and in love for the first time.

In love. It didn't seem possible that she could be falling in love, not after all these years. Turning her head, she opened her eyes and looked at Way. Falling in love—when she was about to become a grandmother! A soft girlish giggle escaped her lips.

The sound brought Way's head around. Their eyes met and clung and, in that moment, Amanda knew that it didn't matter what came of her love for him. She was an adult, a responsible adult whose behavior had always been above question. Why couldn't she just take whatever he offered? One night? Two? This was the eighties. Who needed promises of forever and avowals of undying love? Why should she worry about tomorrow and whether or not Way felt the same as she did? Other women began a relationship on shorter notice and with less commitment....

Which was precisely the problem. She was in love. Way was...what? He wanted her, but wanting was a long way from loving.

"Come here," he said, breaking into her thoughts before she could come to any conclusion about his feelings.

Acting on an impulse that was far removed from her usual analytical forethought, and without stopping to question where her actions would lead, Amanda scooted nearer and leaned against him. Just once, and for the first time in twenty years, she was going to let her heart—not her mind—guide her. She was going to risk an affair with a totally unsuitable man. Way's arm closed around her shoulders, sheltering her in a warm embrace. Her eyes drifted shut. She felt his lips touch the top of her head and heard the sound of the engine as he let out the clutch and pulled away from the light.

CHAPTER TWELVE

THE DRIVE to her house was the longest twenty minutes Amanda had ever lived through. Way pulled into her driveway and turned off the engine. She expected him to open the car door, but instead, he sat looking at her. The night was dark and moonless, and the distant streetlight threw shadows on her features and gilded her eyes with silver.

"I want to kiss you," he told her simply.

She nodded. "Please..." she begged, "please...do."

The hint of pleading in her voice was his undoing. Without another word Way drew her close and lowered his mouth to hers.

It was the kiss they'd bypassed before. It was the stuff that first kisses and dreams of white knights were made of. The touch of his lips was soft—his mouth was soft, but somehow firm—as they met the yielding readiness of hers. He kissed the corners of her mouth, the bow of her upper lip, and then turned his head to the other side to take her lips from a new angle, teasing the seam of her mouth with the barest touch of his tongue. Amanda's lips parted beneath the subtle persuasion, and her own tongue tentatively met his.

It was all the encouragement Way needed. He pulled her across his lap, turning her to face him and wrapping his strong arms around her. Her arms circled his neck, and she threaded her fingers through his blond hair as he took her mouth in a dozen kisses that warned of his increasing hunger.

They kissed minutes...or maybe hours. Amanda wasn't sure. They shared kisses that were soft nibbles, kisses that teased and taunted and promised hidden, forbidden delights, kisses that were hard and hungry and bruised her soft, willing mouth.

At one point she realized that Way's hand was beneath her dress, moving caressingly over her hip. She didn't care. Nothing mattered but her need to sate herself with the taste and feel of his lips...an impossibility that was still worth the attempt.

Way dragged his mouth from hers and trailed moist kisses along her cheekbone to her ear. The hand beneath her skirt moved suddenly; a coolness invaded the place warmed by his hand. Then, unexpectedly, she felt it sliding between their bodies, stopping at her breast. Her heart, already racing, shifted into a reckless gear, and her breast seemed to blossom beneath his touch. She bit back a moan of desire.

She felt his chest rise in a deep indrawing of breath that was expelled on a whispered confession. "I want you, Mandy."

Amanda stilled in his embrace. She didn't move...not even to breathe. She'd known it would lead to this, wanted it to, but hearing him say the words made it all so real. All so *now*. This was nothing she could weigh and ponder, as the hardness of his body beneath her hip testified.

"I want you so badly."

"Yes," she murmured back, inhaling the masculine scent of his cologne and pressing her lips to his cheek.

For a moment Way only held her, his face pressed against the warm hollow where her neck and shoulder met, as if he were trying to absorb the reality of her answer. Amazingly, Amanda felt him trembling almost as much as she was. He helped her out of the car and, with Way's hand tightly in hers, Amanda led him through the garage to the back door then through the dark house. She paused in the hallway just outside her bedroom door.

Way sensed her hesitation. "Afraid, Mandy?"

"Yes." Her voice was a wisp of sound in the darkness.

His hands fell warm and heavy on her shoulders, and he pulled her near. "Don't be."

He touched his lips to her temple and then, as if he'd waited as long as he could, he swung her up into his arms and carried her across the room to the double bed. Lowering her to its center, he stretched out beside her and covered her breasts with his hands, a touch that wrung a throaty groan from her.

"Do you like that?" he asked.

Amanda wasn't used to conversation during lovemaking, but for some reason it seemed right, acceptable—even desirable—with Way. She nodded in the darkness. "Too much."

"No," he said. "Never too much."

She placed her palm against his cheek, brushing her fingertips over the crest of his cheekbone. Her voice held a deprecating humor as she said, "After the way I kissed you at Jeff and Heather's, you must think I'm sex starved, or that I go around..." Her voice trailed away. When she could speak again, it was unsteady, filled with a growing need that battled her uncertainty. "You may as well know that it's been a long time for me."

Amanda knew he smiled because she felt the movement beneath her hand. He turned his head and kissed her palm.

"And here I was thinking your response had something to do with me."

His teasing tone didn't escape her, and neither did the fact that his fingers were busy working the bow between her breasts free, but the moment held too much import for her to treat it lightly. "It does," she confessed, sliding her hand to the back of his head and drawing his mouth nearer hers. "It has everything to do with you."

Way's lips touched hers, sipping at their sweetness and taunting her with darting forays of his tongue. Amanda felt the sudden loosening of the dress bodice as the knot gave way, and she was unable to stop herself from gasping as he pushed the fabric from her body.

"You're perfect, Amanda," he told her, brushing his thumbs experimentally across the aching tips of her breasts and finding that they responded to his first real touch as quickly as she'd responded to his first kiss. He rubbed the button-hard nipples with a tight, circular motion and lowered his head to brand one taut tip with a passionless kiss. Her upper body arched at his touch, as if drawn by the string of a master puppeteer. Then he felt the tension leave her in a long shuddering sigh that signaled her total surrender.

Amanda held his head tightly to her, and when he raised his head to transfer his mind-destroying attentions to the other breast, she moaned his name in protest. His free hand moved downward, over her rib cage and past the flatness of her abdomen. His hand covered her, feeling her heat even through the soft fabric of her dress.

She made a sound almost like a sob, and Way realized with sudden clarity just what her acceptance of this night truly meant. He wanted to tell her not to worry, that he thought he loved her, but he wasn't certain that his confession might not create more problems than it would solve.

Instead, he tried to show her with the gentleness of his touch, his mouth, and the low words of encouragement he whispered while his hands continued to work their magic.

After a while—Amanda had lost track of time long before—Way turned her to her side, nuzzling the hair at her nape aside with a rain of gentle kisses. Then she felt his mouth against her shoulder and heard the descent of her zipper. Way ran his finger lightly down her bare spine from her shoulders to the place where her back curved into her hips, and then blazed a fiery trail down the same path with his mouth. Then, turning her onto her back once more, he grasped the dress bunched at her waist and, instructing Amanda to raise her hips, peeled it down her slender form, leaving her with no covering but a pair of the sheerest panty hose.

In the room's darkness she saw his shadowy bulk as he stood. Her heart began a slow, sluggish rhythm as she realized that they'd reached the point of no return. Closing her eyes, she cataloged the muted sounds of his undressing—the rustle of his shirt as he pulled it off, the soft grind of a zipper, the whisper of slacks drawn down hair-dusted legs. She felt the bed give beneath his weight as he sat back down—to take off his socks, she supposed. Finally, she forced her leaden eyelids upward to see what was taking so long, and instead saw him reach toward the nightstand. There was a click and the room was suddenly bathed in soft incandescence.

Amanda blinked in the unexpected brightness, crossing her arms to shield herself. Her first impression was that he was totally naked, but she didn't have the courage to lower her eyes enough to make sure. Instead, she lost herself in the warm brown of his gaze. There was tenderness there . . . and passion, more passion than she could ever remember seeing.

Reaching out, Way grasped her wrists and uncrossed her arms, baring her to his hungry eyes, eyes that made a leisurely journey from her wind-tousled hair, over her mouth—kissed free of lipstick—to the pert thrust of her breasts and beyond, to the proof of her femininity taunting him through the hazy mesh of her panty hose.

Slowly, as if he were afraid of frightening her, he slipped his fingers beneath the elastic band and drew the wispy nylon down her slender, well-shaped legs.

"You're beautiful," he told her huskily, skimming his hands up her firm thighs. "Beautiful."

Lacing his fingers through hers, Way held her hands pinned to the bed and, with agonizing slowness, lowered his mouth to hers and his body into the cradle of her thighs. Amanda couldn't help the moan of pleasure from her lips when she felt the weight of his chest against her bare breasts. She moaned more loudly as she felt his hardness resting intimately against the most feminine part of her. Way swallowed the sound when his open mouth met hers.

Amanda's hips arched against him in a never-forgotten movement that proclaimed her need. With his lips still devouring hers, Way released her hands and trailed his fingers lightly down her side. They tickled her waist and smoothed over the slight flare of her hip, moving unhesitatingly toward the hidden heart of her desire.

A sound fought its way past the emotion thick in his throat. She was more than ready for him.

As he was her.

Moving back the slightest bit, Way poised his body and began a slow, questing entrance. Mindful of Amanda's confession that it had been a long time, he didn't want to hurt her.

Amanda lay perfectly still beneath his probing thrust, her body and her heart opening to him. She realized suddenly that something was . . . different.

"Way?" she questioned, raising up on her elbows, her forehead puckered into a frown. "What . . . ?

Smiling slightly, he took her hand and guided it to the hard fullness of his arousal. And then she understood.

"You aren't on the pill, are you?"

Amanda shook her head.

"One day when you're better protected, I'll make love to you with nothing between us, but until then . . ." His voice trailed away as he kissed her tenderly on the mouth.

Amanda feathered her fingers through Way's hair and felt a gladness fill her heart at his consideration. If she hadn't known before, she knew now. She loved him.

Buried snugly, deeply inside her, Way was completely still. He could have wept for the "rightness" of it. She was tight, almost virginally tight, and for the first time in years, he felt as if he'd come home. Fighting the huskiness in his voice, he asked, "Are you all right?"

She nodded.

Kissing her lightly, he began to move—slowly at first, wanting to make the moment last, wanting to hold on to it forever. But all too soon he found that his body's demands could override his mind's desire. Thought stopped; time stood still. The sounds of harsh breathing and low moans filled the quiet of the room.

Amanda's hands, restless, questing, roamed at will over him, while he moved in synchronization with her quiescent body, fighting the need to empty himself as long as he could, wanting to ride the wave with her, not alone.

He felt the exact moment her climax began. Her body tightened around him, and she clutched at his bare bottom convulsively. Quickening the rhythm guiding him, he plunged them both into the shimmering sea of sensation and let the force of their desire pull them under....

AMANDA AWOKE to the sounds of an angry blue jay chattering outside her bedroom window. Lethargic and contented, she opened her eyes slowly. The early-morning sunshine beaming through partially closed blinds bounced off the mirror of her dresser and into her eyes. Blinking, she turned to her side to escape the blinding light and found herself staring into brown eyes filled with an emotion as brightly blinding as the reflected sun had been.

Way.

Fully awake, she realized that she was completely naked beneath the sheet tucked primly over her breasts. Memories of the night before came to her in tantalizing bits and pieces. How could she have forgotten the reason for her contented feeling for even one instant? She and Way had loved each other far into the morning, trying without success to quench the insatiable hunger gnawing at them. She had been anxious at first, and then, under his tender tutelage and soft encouraging words, she had grown more confident, even adventurous, exploring his hard, fit body with the same attention to detail he had shown when charting each curve and valley of hers.

It had been a glorious night, a night when she'd rediscovered the power and joy of being a woman. If Way had taken her with a gentle forcefulness, he had also given her back the self-esteem Deke had taken with him when he left. For the first time in years, she felt like a totally feminine, desirable woman.

So why now, in the clear light of day, were those old feelings of doubt creeping back in? Why did she feel as if she'd just made the greatest mistake of her life?

Attuned to Amanda as only a person in love can be, Way was aware of the emotions warring inside her. Wanting only to allay her fears, he reached out a gentle hand to cradle the side of her face. "Good morning."

"Good morning," she said unsteadily.

"Regrets, Mandy?" he queried, lifting her chin until their eyes met.

"Maybe. A few," she confessed, unable to be anything but truthful to him after the night they'd spent together.

"Why?"

She lifted one bare shoulder, an act that also brought one rosy nipple into view. Without thinking of possible repercussions, acting solely out of the need to see if her skin was really as soft as he remembered, Way's hand moved from her cheek downward. His hand cupped the yielding underside of her small breast, his thumb and index finger automatically rolling the sensitive tip to button hardness.

Amanda gasped, completely surprised at the quickness of her response.

Way's gaze clashed with hers, and then, somehow knowing that the only way to overcome her fears was to nip them in the bud, he lowered his head in slow deliberation and took the tender peak into his mouth.

Amanda tangled her hands through the thickness of his blond hair, bent on pushing him away, but somehow, the instant she touched him, her determination to stop him was swept away by the need to experience the raging passion he evoked. Instead of pushing him, she arched her back and held him to her.

Just once more. Just one more time.

She made the promise to herself, and at that moment, she fully intended to keep it.

LATER, AS SHE LAY sprawled breathlessly across him, the sound of his heart thundering beneath her ear, Amanda wondered at the power he held over her, unaware that Way reciprocated her feelings. His hands slicked over her perspiration-damp body from the curve of her bottom to her shoulder. The gentleness of his touch made her feel . . . content. Wanted. Loved.

Loved? She stirred restlessly in his embrace. No. She shouldn't fool herself. Love had nothing to do with the night they'd just shared . . . from his point of view, anyway. It had meant nothing more to him than a night spent in a woman's arms, had been no different from a dozen others. That sobering thought brought her feet back to the ground. Pulling away from him with an abruptness that shattered the intimacy of the moment, she moved to her side of the bed and started to get up.

Way grabbed her wrist and their eyes locked—turbulent violet with determined brown. "I'm not going to let you do this, Amanda," he told her, pushing himself to a sitting position and holding her hand tightly in his.

"Do what?"

Irritation flashed through his eyes. "Pull away from me as if our lovemaking hadn't happened. It did happen. And we both enjoyed it."

"Did I act as if it didn't happen a few moments ago?" she asked.

Way wanted to shake her, but he knew he had to be careful, that he had to handle the situation gently and with tact. She'd taken her capitulation hard. He urged his voice toward a lightness he didn't feel. "You would have, if I hadn't . . . talked you out of it."

Amanda saw the smile tugging at his lips, saw the hint of teasing in his eyes and felt the beginning of an answering lightness start to take possession of her own heart. She'd never met anyone like him. How could he be so . . . carefree? And worse—why did he have the ability to make her forget the seriousness of their relationship? Why did he make her feel as if everything would work out, when her heart, still laden with old hurts and bitter memories, nagged that it never could?

Her eyes were still troubled, but there was a tiny smile on her lips as she said, "Well, you certainly have a way with . . . words, Mr. Dalton."

Way sobered abruptly. He laced his fingers with hers and drew her toward him. "No, Mandy, I don't. If I did, I'd know what to say to make you feel better about what's happened between us." He lifted her hand and pressed a kiss to her knuckles. "I'd know the right words to tell you not to worry."

"I'm not worried . . . exactly," she told him, rubbing his thumb with hers.

He carried her hand to his chest. "I'd tell you that I don't kiss and tell . . ."

Sweet relief flooded her.

" . . . and that whatever this is that we feel will sort it-self out."

"What is it we feel?" Amanda asked candidly. She didn't want to back him into a corner; she just wanted to gain some sort of perspective on where they stood.

Evidently sophistry was foreign to her makeup. Smiling at her straightforwardness, Way pulled her back into his arms. "I don't know what you feel. Maybe you do kiss and tell."

She tilted her head back and looked up at him with surprise in her eyes.

"You look shocked, but believe me, there are a lot of women out there who like to brag about sleeping with anyone in the public eye. And athletes are prime targets."

The thought had never occurred to Amanda, but she could see the validity of his statement. She'd known a few women like that herself. "Well, I don't kiss and tell, either," she assured him.

"I know that. Why do you think I decided to make a move on you—" his mustache inched upward as he smiled crookedly "—besides the fact that I knew you'd be dynamite in bed?"

"Dynamite? Me?"

"You. Which gets us back to your original question of what we feel." He nuzzled his lips against her hair, and his voice was hardly more than a soft vapor against her ear. "What I'm feeling is...right. Good. What about you?"

"I...don't know," Amanda told him truthfully. Her fingertips rubbed lightly over the blond hair curling against his chest. She drew in a deep breath that was laden with a montage of masculine scents. "It was certainly...good. But right? I'm afraid to trust what feels right."

"Don't be."

"I can't take this lightly, Way. I'm not made that way."

"I'm not asking you to take it lightly, because I'm sure not. What I'm asking is that you don't worry about tomorrow. That you take one day at a time so we can see where it is we're going."

The phone beside the bed shrilled, causing Amanda to jump in surprise. The world was intruding, as she'd known it would. Way's eyes, too, held a wry regret. Was he as sorry as she was to have their time interrupted? Careful to keep the sheet tucked across her bare breasts, she reached for the offending instrument, interrupting the second ring. "Hello?"

"Mom?"

Amanda's guilty, startled gaze flew to Way's. "Jeff?" she squeaked, holding the receiver away and looking at it with an expression closely akin to horror.

Way smiled and drew her resisting form back down beside him.

"Yeah. What are you doing?"

"Uh...doing?" she repeated. What she was doing was trying to push her lover—who was trailing a string of kisses across her shoulder—away. "I'm...uh...I...just woke up."

"Just woke up? Are you sick?"

"Sick? N-no, of course not." She moved the phone from her ear and held it out toward Way, a look of pleading in her eyes.

"Then why are you still in bed?" Jeff asked.

Way clutched his head and rolled his eyes.

Amanda dragged the receiver back into place. Way dragged the sheet down her body. What on earth was he trying to do? she wondered frantically.

"Mom...what is it?" Jeff asked again.

"I...uh, woke up with a headache, so I thought I'd sleep in," she lied.

"Oh," Jeff replied, satisfied with the answer. "Well, how was your evening?"

"My evening?" she said, beginning to feel like an echo. Oh, Lord, what could she say?

"Yeah. You did go out with Way, didn't you?"

Amanda, whose eyes again sought the villain of the drama, nodded. Way dropped a kiss to her thigh. "Oh. Yes. It was very nice." His lips inched upward. Her legs moved restlessly. "We went to Wayfarers and I had shrimp scampi. It was—" her voice broke as Way's mouth moved to her navel "—nice." She grabbed a handful of his hair and pulled. "Afterward, we went to a movie. It was really very—"

"Nice," Jeff interrupted in a dry tone.

Amanda glared at Way, who smiled back unrepentantly. "Yes."

"Look, Mom, go on back to sleep. You don't sound like yourself. You didn't take one of those woozy pills, did you?" he asked.

Those "woozy pills" were the muscle relaxers Amanda had taken for her shoulder pain the year before. They'd tended to make her a little crazy. "No."

"Well, don't," he warned. "Look, if you need me for anything, give me a call. I don't go in to work until late this afternoon."

Relief spread through her like warm sunshine. "Thanks, Jeff. I will. G'bye." She cradled the phone and turned to Way, a fighting light in her eyes.

"That was Jeff."

"I heard."

"What do you mean, doing that while I was on the phone?"

"That, what?" he asked with butter-wouldn't-melt-in-his-mouth innocence.

"Way!"

He laughed. Amanda didn't think it was funny.

"He wanted to know what I was doing," she told him, her eyes holding that same uneasiness he'd seen there earlier.

"I know," he said, beginning to feel sorry that he wasn't treating the situation with the seriousness she felt it deserved.

"What do you imagine they'll think when they find out?" she asked.

"It's our lives, Mandy. They don't have to know right now," he told her.

"They already suspect something."

"So we'll let them worry about it a while longer."

"You make it sound so easy," she said with a sigh.

"It is," Way told her, pulling her back into a loose embrace. "It is."

And he made her believe it.

They showered together, something Amanda had never done with Deke. It was an experience that made her realize just how much she'd missed by not having a lover like Way all these years. Then, pleasantly exhausted and at his insistence, she accompanied him to practice. Watching him was enjoyment in its purest form. She was able to indulge in endless fantasies as he stretched and leaped and cracked the bat against the ball. And in every one of them, he belonged solely to her.

After practice, he insisted on introducing her to his teammates, and the next thirty minutes became a blur of faces and names she knew she'd never be able to match up later. Only one face stood out—Jose Delgato, Way's closest friend and one of the Royals' pitchers.

"He looks happy," Jose observed, watching Way, who was standing across the room, laughing at something the third baseman was saying. "And he hasn't been happy in a long time."

Amanda met his gaze squarely, wanting to ask Jose if he thought she was the reason for Way's happiness. Instead, she said, "You've known him a long time, then?"

"Since Heather was six," the wiry Puerto Rican said. "Just before Carol was killed. We played for the same team for a while. Then we both went in different directions and finally wound up here about four years ago."

"What was she like?" Amanda asked, thirsting for knowledge about Way's past. She wondered what kind of woman had made a man like Way so happy that in more than ten years he hadn't found a replacement.

Jose didn't have to ask who Amanda meant. "Carol was pretty. A lot of fun. And totally devoted to Way and Heather. He's missed her."

Amanda sighed. While she had stayed single out of fear of repeating the mistakes of her marriage, Way had remained so because he was afraid his happiness couldn't be duplicated.

"He's due some happiness," Jose said, rubbing his dark mustache with his forefinger. "Thanks for giving it to him."

"Oh, but..." Amanda began, a becoming blush staining her cheeks. "We're not...serious."

"Yeah?" Jose said with a knowing smile. "Then why did he bring you down to meet us? He's never brought a woman—other than Carol—to meet the team in all the years I've known him."

Amanda let the implication of Jose's statement and a tentative feeling of hope wash over her. Was he right? Did Way feel more for her than she realized?

"Mandy?" Jose said, drawing her attention back to him by calling her Way's pet name.

"Yes?"

"Be good to him." Jose looked uncomfortable, as if he wished he hadn't opened himself and Way up to such close scrutiny. He gave her a jaunty salute, and tossing a "Good to meet you" over his shoulder, ambled across the room to join his friends.

CHAPTER THIRTEEN

"I DON'T WANT to go," Way said later that night, after he and Amanda had spent the entire day together.

They stood at her front door, his forehead resting against hers, both of her hands clasped tightly in his. He wanted to tell her he loved her, because somehow, during the course of the past twenty-four hours, that already-suspected fact had come to rest on his soul as softly and sweetly as the brush of a butterfly wing.

"I know," Amanda replied.

"I should be home in a week or so."

She nodded. *What then?* It was easy to say you wanted to stay while the perspiration still dampened the sheets, but Amanda knew that things often looked different with a little time and space. What would Way want when he came back? Anything?

"Do me a favor?" he asked, drawing back so that his smiling eyes could meet hers, which glowed with soft contentment from behind her glasses.

"What?"

"No—two favors," he corrected.

"Anything you want," she murmured, still high on the love they'd shared during the night and earlier that morning.

Way released her hands and, splaying his hands over the roundness of her bottom, drew her lower body up against him. "Anything?" he growled through clenched teeth.

"The favors, Dalton," she said, teasing.

Way smiled. A few months ago, he'd never have suspected that she could banter as well. "First, don't worry about this. It's going to be all right. I promise."

She nodded with more force and conviction than she really felt. "And?"

"And second...think about me while I'm gone."

Amanda let the soft request seep through her troubled mind. He wanted more than a one-night stand. The thought both pleased and frightened her. Still, she felt obligated to repay his honesty in kind. "I can assure you that your request will be no problem," she told him with a slight smile. "No problem at all."

And it hadn't been. He called every night, no matter how late. She looked forward to his calls with all the excitement of a child waiting for Christmas, because in and of itself, each communication told her he missed her and wanted to be with her. Their conversations were lengthy, and Way brushed aside her worry about cost with the airy dismissal, "Easy come, easy go."

She told him that Jeff liked his new job, that Heather's latest doctor's visit had been routine. She herself was doing fine, just waiting to see if the university would renew her teaching contract.

Way told her that her kisses went to his head like the best Scotch, that he loved the way her breasts felt and tasted, and that he felt as if he'd come home when he was buried deeply inside her. Her pleas that he talk about something else did little good. His blatantly sexual observations embarrassed her, thrilled her and left her with a restless yearning burning deep inside her.

She did dream about him. Nightly. Sometimes several times a night. The dreams were always the same, Way kissing her... Way taking her to the edge of ecstasy... Way telling her he loved her. And when she woke up, Amanda's reactions were always the same, too. She chided herself for being a fool to think that he would ever really care, and damned herself for letting him scale the carefully constructed walls she'd placed around her heart. Sex was sex, she reminded herself grimly each morning, and it had absolutely nothing to do with love.

"WHERE HAVE YOU BEEN keeping yourself?" Heather asked when Amanda finally showed up on Thursday evening.

Amanda couldn't tell her new daughter-in-law that a combination of guilt and a feeling of wanting to shield her tentative happiness from outside eyes had kept her secluded at home all week. "I hate to bother you newlyweds," she said instead, hoping the flimsy excuse held up since she'd spent so much time there immediately after their marriage, helping fix up the apartment.

Heather patted her burgeoning stomach. "I don't feel like a newlywed."

Amanda smiled and took the glass of iced tea—sweetened iced tea—Heather offered her with a bland acceptance and a sense of inevitability. What was a little sugar compared to the other things she'd accepted into her life?

Heather got her own tea and joined Amanda at the small table in the dining room, her movements still graceful despite her advancing pregnancy. At six months, Heather's height held her in good stead. She was carrying the baby well and had just begun to wear maternity clothes.

"You look wonderful," Amanda said impulsively, taking note of the clarity of the younger woman's complexion and the gleam of happiness in her eyes. She had blossomed the past couple of months, and Amanda didn't know whether to cite her pregnancy or marriage as the reason.

"Thanks," Heather replied. "You look pretty good yourself . . . different."

Amanda took a sip of her tea, hoping its icy coldness would combat the heat she felt rising to her cheeks. She forced her eyes to Heather's. "It must be my hair. I haven't worn it this long in years."

"Maybe," Heather said with a considering nod. "Whatever it is, you look . . . I don't know . . . happier."

Amanda's laughter sounded strained to her own ears. "It's probably because I haven't had to go to school every day. Where's Jeff?" she asked, hoping to turn the conversation to a less touchy subject.

"He had to go to the airport to pick up Daddy. The Blazer wouldn't start, so they're going to have to see what's the matter. They should be here soon."

"Way's home?"

"Yes."

"He didn't tell me he was coming in," Amanda said, a distracted look in her violet eyes.

Heather didn't miss the relevancy of the comment. Whenever her father and Jeff's mother were in a room together, the atmosphere was always charged. At first it had been anger and animosity sparking between them, but lately—like Jeff—Heather wondered if the sparks might not be originating from a different source.

"I never did ask how your dinner was the other night," she said, fishing for information.

"Dinner?" Amanda asked, giving Heather her full attention.

"Yeah. Didn't you and Daddy go to dinner?"

Amanda nodded; her smile felt stiff, unnatural.

"I'm glad to see that you two are getting along," Heather said, wanting to give Amanda some sense of approval. "You *are* getting along, aren't you?"

A picture of Way's face as he made love to her flashed through her mind. She supposed one could say they were getting along. "There isn't any reason we shouldn't get along now that you and Jeff have married," Amanda hedged. "Marriage was supposed to make things better for you and Jeff, and harboring any resentment toward your father just because we originally shared opposite views would only defeat the purpose."

"He thinks a lot of Jeff," Heather said.

"I know. And I really appreciate his giving Jeff the opportunity to go back to school this fall."

Heather, who had been around adults a major portion of her life, saw the changes that were gradually taking place in Jeff's mother. It was amazing what one tiny unborn child could do to people, and the changes ran deep in Amanda Farrell. Once she'd accepted the marriage, her mother-in-law seemed to become a completely different person—instantly accessible, available when Heather needed her, whether it was to ask something about a recipe, a pain she was having, or just to go shopping with. Heather saw how Amanda could, in time, easily take the place of the mother whose memory was becoming more nebulous with each year. She was glad the animosity between her father and Amanda was over, and was accustoming herself to the fact that there might be more between them than either was letting on.

"My dad's a nice guy," Heather said. "Offering Jeff the money doesn't surprise me, but offering him the job at Wayfarers does."

Amanda's head snapped up. "What do you mean, Way offered Jeff the job?"

"My dad owns both Wayfarers restaurants," Heather said, wondering how that fact could have escaped Jeff's mother all these months.

Amanda recalled the easy camaraderie between Way and the maître d' on the occasion of both visits to the exclusive restaurant. She remembered how the waiters had taken special care with the service and the food, and she could still see the gleam of pleasure in Way's eyes as he had looked around the room. She should have known. But from the beginning of her association with him, she had been unfairly steeped in her own self-righteous bitterness, assuming that he had no thought beyond the next game, no goal but to upset Hank Aaron's home-run record. She owed him an apology. As she'd already come to realize on more than one occasion, there was more to Way Dalton than one might suspect.

Heather watched the emotions flitting across Amanda's face. She was about to speak when she heard Jeff's car in the driveway.

"They're back!"

Way! The fact that he owned Wayfarers paled in significance to the fact that she would be seeing him for the first time since they'd—Her thoughts came to a sudden halt.

Say it, Amanda. Since you made love.

The door burst open and Jeff stepped inside. Amanda missed the kiss he gave Heather, missed their secret smiles as his hands moved over her swelling abdomen.

Amanda had eyes only for the tall blond man behind him.

Way closed the door and smiled. Not at the tenderness between his daughter and her husband. He smiled straight into Amanda's eyes.

"Hi," he said, his own dark eyes drinking in the sight of her.

"Hi."

"What are you doing—"

"I didn't know you—"

They spoke simultaneously, stopped and smiled at each other again.

"I didn't know you were coming in today," she said.

"The game got rained out."

"Oh."

"Hey!" Jeff said. "You guys are both staying for dinner, aren't you?"

Way's eyes never left Amanda's face. The message she read there said that he had ideas more to his liking. Courtesy demanded another answer. "Sure. Sounds great," he agreed.

"How about it, Mom?"

"Why not?" she said. Then, because she was dying to touch him and afraid Jeff and Heather could see how much, she asked, "Do you need any help, Heather?"

"I thought I'd fix spaghetti. Is that okay?"

"It's fine. Would you like me to do the salad?"

Heather cast Jeff a bland look. "That's Jeff's job."

"Well, as long as Mom's here—"

"Jeff Farrell, you worm!" Heather said, flinging a wet dishrag at him. Instinctively Way stepped sideways and stretched out his left hand, catching the cloth with a deft movement and tossing it into the sink.

Jeff cupped his hands around his mouth and intoned nasally, "And it's a magnificent effort on the part of first baseman Way Dalton, who zings the ball back to the pitcher!"

Heather groaned and turned back to the sink with make-believe embarrassment. Way and Amanda laughed, a sound that miraculously drained the tension from the room.

"I had to put up with this for nineteen years before you got him," Amanda said.

"Want him back?" Heather retorted, shooting Jeff a teasing look over her shoulder.

"Hey!" Jeff said, properly affronted. "I don't want to go back." He looped his arms around Heather's middle. "If I let Mom entertain your dad and help you make the salad, can I stay? Huh? Huh? Huh?" he begged, punctuating each question with a kiss to her neck.

Heather's meager control of her mirth dissolved, and she collapsed into a fit of giggles, turning and throwing her arms around his neck.

Amanda swallowed the lump of emotion in her throat. They were so happy. She turned to look at Way and saw that his eyes held the same sense of loss she felt. Sensing her scrutiny, he turned and silently held out his hand; wordlessly, she took it and followed him into the living room.

Way sat down on the sofa and, without thinking of the consequences, Amanda allowed him to pull her down beside him. Then, keeping one eye on the door, he put his arms around her and bent to kiss her.

"Way..." she protested.

"Shut up, Amanda," he said thickly, placing his index finger over her mouth. "Do you know how long it's been since I've kissed you?"

She shook her head.

"Five days, fourteen hours and forty minutes," he said seriously. Then he grinned. "But who's counting?"

Moving his hand to the side of her face, he lowered his head and pressed his mouth to hers in a soft kiss.

Amanda wanted more. She let the tip of her tongue score the separation of his lips, seeking and finding the soft inner flesh of his mouth.

With a moan of need, Way swept her into a tighter embrace, one hand sliding beneath the soft cotton of her sleeveless sweater to cup and stroke her lace-encased breast. Amanda pressed against him instinctively. At almost the same moment she remembered where they were. She tore her mouth from his in an effort to salvage her sanity.

Framing her face with his hands, he gave her an incredibly slow, incredibly sexy smile. "You make me so damned hot I can hardly stand it," he murmured in a husky voice.

Amanda smiled back.

Neither heard the soft whisper of tennis shoes against the carpeted floor as Jeff stepped through the French doors into the living room, stopping dead in his tracks at the scene before him.

Heather's dad and his mother on the sofa. Way's hands cradling her face. Both of them smiling the soft, intimate smile of lovers. As Jeff watched, Way closed the scant few inches between his lips and Amanda's.

Rooted to the spot, Jeff watched them kiss. Then, without a word, without a sound, he backed out of the room and went into the kitchen.

Heather noticed the sudden change in Jeff's actions, which she chalked up to a headache. Neither Way nor Amanda noticed. They were both too interested in getting the meal over with so they could go to Amanda's and take up where they'd left off a few days before.

Once the dishes were done, Amanda pleaded weariness and said she was going home.

"I think I'll head out, too," Way said, rising and stretching.

"I'll take you," Jeff offered.

"There's no need for you to do that. I'm sure Amanda won't mind driving me home."

Amanda tried not to let her surprise show. "I don't mind at all," she said with a shake of her head.

Jeff looked from his mother to Way and back at his mother. He plunged his hands into the pockets of his Levi's. "Fine," he said with a short nod. "I guess we'll see you tomorrow."

"Before I leave, for sure," Way said, putting an arm around Heather and dropping a kiss to the top of her shining blond head.

Amanda kissed Jeff on the cheek, and amid a chorus of goodbyes preceded Way out the door to the car. Way got in the passenger side and Amanda slid behind the wheel. They waved to the kids, who stood in the open doorway, and Amanda backed out of the driveway. Neither spoke until they got to the corner.

"Do you think they suspected anything?" she asked.

Way stretched his left arm across the back of the seat and smiled. "Naw. Not a thing."

"I NEED TO TALK to you," Jeff said, closing the door and ushering Heather to the living room.

"What's the matter?" Heather asked, picking up on the fact that something was wrong.

"Our parents."

"What about them? They seem to be getting along okay."

"I'll say."

Heather dropped to the sofa and patted the place beside her. "Jeff, don't talk in circles."

Jeff sat down beside her and, leaning forward, rested his elbows on his knees. He turned his head to look at her. "You like my mom okay, don't you?"

Heather's brow pleated and her head bobbed in a nod. "Yeah, I do, now that I'm getting to know her better. She's changed a lot since we got married. I think she likes me more."

"Mom's hard, sometimes—hard on herself, too—but she's okay."

Reaching out, Heather put her hand on his shoulder. "Jeff, what's all this about?"

He turned to look at her. "Do you remember how we were a little suspicious when we found them together the morning after your graduation?"

"Yeah? So? There wasn't anything going on."

"Then."

"What do you mean, 'then'?" Heather said, but, as his meaning dawned, her eyes widened in disbelief. "Jeff, you aren't saying that—"

"Yeah, babe, I am."

"You mean they—"

Jeff rose and began to pace the room, his agitation apparent. He stopped and locked his gaze with hers. "I saw him kissing her before dinner, Heather. Draw your own conclusions.''

Heather looked stunned. ''But I asked Daddy and he said...'' Her voice trailed away as she remembered what her father had said.

''Yeah?'' Jeff prompted.

''He said she was pretty, and to mind my own business.''

Jeff smiled. ''I even talked to my mom about it, too. I told her that I knew her age didn't stop her from having sexual feelings.''

''What!'' Heather squealed.

Jeff planted his hands on his hips and regarded her with amazement. ''Sexual feelings. You know what sexual feelings are, don't you, Heather? You look like you do.''

''Your mom and my dad having sex?'' She shook her head. ''I don't believe it.''

''Yeah, well, it's the eighties, babe.'' He shook his head, too, still not believing what his eyes had seen. ''I could see it coming—I knew he was interested—but I thought it was sorta funny. I never really thought it would happen...if that makes any sense. I thought my mom was stronger. He must be pretty persuasive.''

''You aren't blaming him?''

''All I know is that she's been celibate for a long time.''

''How do you know?''

''Because I know!''

''Well, my dad hasn't—''

''Whoa! Whoa!'' Jeff said to silence her. Heather looked up at him expectantly. Jeff knelt at her feet and took her hands in his. ''I don't want to argue with you about this. I love you. And they're right. It's none of our business."

"But he's my father!"

"And she's my mother. But they have a right to their own life and their own choices."

Heather sighed, her eyes troubled. "I guess so. What do you think is going to happen?"

Jeff shook his head. "I don't know. I sure hope they've thought this through, because if they haven't, things could get really sticky. And if it doesn't work out, we'll be caught in between them—taking sides."

"Oh, Jeff!"

Jeff saw the worry in her eyes and was sorry that he'd brought it about, even though he felt she had a right to know what was going on. He deliberately made his tone light.

"But on the other hand, if it does work out and they decide to...get married, my father-in-law will also be my stepfather."

Heather thought about that for a moment and began to laugh. It was laugh or cry.

"YOU ARE AN INCREDIBLY giving woman," Way said when he could once again think coherently.

"And you're an incredibly sexy man," Amanda told him, propping her elbow on his chest and her head in her hand.

Laughter rumbled deep inside him. "Sexy? Considering I'm going to be forty next month and a grandfather in November, that's nice to hear."

"What does that have to do with anything?" she asked him, smoothing his mustache with the fingers of her free hand.

"I'm not getting any younger," Way said bluntly.

"None of us is," she reminded him.

"Yeah, but what you're doing with your life can be done at any age."

Amanda suddenly understood. "You're worried that you won't be able to play baseball much longer."

"Yeah," he told her, a faraway look in his eyes. "A couple of years after this...maybe. Maybe I'll forget about breaking Aaron's record and set a new one of my own."

"What's that?"

"First and only grandfather to play professional baseball. What do you think? The moniker has a certain authority, doesn't it?" he said with a cocky smile. But Amanda saw beyond the smile.

"You've had a good year. One of the best in a long time."

He smiled. "And how do you know that?"

"Because I've become a Waylon Dalton fan. I watch all his games, listen to all his interviews—"

"Really?" he asked, a pleased smile curving his mouth.

"Really."

"Since when?"

"Since...right after I met you," she confessed, throwing caution to the wind. "Because of my first husband, and the situation I was dealing with at school, I told myself that I hated you and all you stood for. I think at first I watched so I could look for things to hold against you."

"Tell me about him," Way encouraged, strangely pleased that she was opening up at last.

Amanda lifted her eyebrows, and her mouth twisted in wry humor. "You've heard most of it—thanks to Jeff."

"That you had to get married because you were pregnant."

"Yes. And he left me when Jeff was three to pursue a golf career."

"Did he make it?"

"No."

"So you hated athletes."

"Yes. I hated athletes."

"What happened at school?"

Amanda gave him an abridged version of her run-in with the university faculty over Steve Harris, explaining how she'd finally managed to salvage the situation. "I was worried that they might let me go, but I finally got a notice yesterday that they want me back."

"Do you want to go back?"

"I honestly don't know. I don't like threats and innuendo and someone trying to make me compromise my principles. Besides, I've been offered a position with the community college, where I won't have to worry about passing undeserving athletes, because they don't have sports."

"You do whatever you want, but don't ever think you're going to go anywhere that you don't find this sort of pressure. I've known a lot of rich people who give a healthy donation or set up a scholarship to a school, and then when their kid doesn't make the grade, they remind the board of everything they've done. It's the same principle in a different guise."

"I hadn't thought of that," Amanda said, "and you're right. I appreciate a different perspective. Thanks."

"You're welcome," he told her, pulling her down for a brief kiss that threatened to break the bounds of tenderness. He drew a deep breath and said, "Now that we have all that serious stuff behind us, can we get on to more important things?''

"Certainly," she agreed with a smile. "Like what?''

"Like the fact that since you've admitted to being interested in me from the first time we met, I'll do likewise."

"Oh, you will? How magnanimous."

"Now, Mandy," he said, shaking his head, "don't use such big words. You're talking to a bat-swingin', bubble-gum chewin' ball player, not one of your fancy professors."

"You're no dummy, Way Dalton," Amanda told him, shrewdly recalling Heather's statement about his two restaurants. "And speaking of which, why didn't you tell me you owned Wayfarers?''

"You didn't ask."

"Way—"

He circled her wrist with his hand and jerked her arm out from under her. The action brought them breast to chest and face-to-face. "How about if you take me to task about it later?" he suggested, running his hands down to her hips and pulling her over on top of him. "Right now I'm busy telling you about the first time I saw you."

Amanda nodded, trying to suppress a smile. "Right. Go ahead. You were interested that first time, too, you said."

"Interested? Lady, I had the hots for you when I saw you in that shorty gown with the little purple flowers on... What?" he asked when she began to shake her head.

"No, no, Way, you don't say, 'I had the hots for you,'" she told him with a seriousness belied by the mischievous gleam in her eye. "You say—"

"Oh, yeah. That I was hor—"

Her hand shut off the rest of his graphic comment. "You say that your heart began to pound and you were filled with an unanticipated feeling of wonder and—"

"Lsst," he mumbled from beneath her hand.

Amanda uncovered his mouth. "What was that?" she asked innocently.

"Lust. An unanticipated feeling of wonder and lust."

Amanda buried her face against his neck, her happiness manifesting itself in peals of laughter.

"You make me happy," she said, serious at last, but with a smile still on her lips and in her eyes.

Way brushed the hair from her face and said simply, "I'm glad."

Her face held the wonder of a child beholding his first Christmas tree. "I didn't know it could be like this—fun and carefree and . . . happy." She trailed a fingertip over one bushy dark blond eyebrow. "I've never met a man like you before."

"No?"

She shook her head. "Never."

Way drew her down until their noses rubbed Eskimo-style. "I've never met a woman like you before, either, Mandy. Not ever."

CHAPTER FOURTEEN

THE FOLLOWING WEDNESDAY, Amanda asked Jeff and Heather over for Chinese food, which she was fixing herself. The newlyweds were setting the table in the dining room, and Amanda was stirring egg into the soup stock when Jeff spoke without warning.

"So what's going on between you and Way?"

The casually posed question shattered Amanda's composure like a rock tossed into a placid lake. The spoon she was using to stir with slipped from her fingers into the bubbling broth. Soup forgotten, she set the bowl of beaten egg onto the counter and turned to face her son. Her first thought was that it had been easy to ward off his questions when there *hadn't* been anything going on between her and Way, but now that there was...

"What do you mean?" she asked.

"I mean, are you..." Jeff's throat closed on the verbal display of his suspicions. Instead, he said, "I saw him kissing you the day I picked him up at the airport."

The room gave a sharp lurch to the right, and Amanda eased down on one of the bar stools until she could regain her equilibrium. "Oh."

"What's going on, Mom?"

Unable to meet his eyes, yet touched by his interest, Amanda answered honestly. "I don't know."

Jeff pulled out another bar stool and, sitting down beside her, turned her face so that their eyes met.

She saw concern in his usually serious brown eyes. Concern and cautiousness. There wasn't a drop of censure.

"Do you love him?"

Amanda's teeth clamped down on her bottom lip. She nodded.

The breath Jeff had been holding came out in a long sigh.

"I don't know how it happened, Jeff," she told him, clutching his hands tightly in hers. "I never meant for it to. He's not my type at all, you know that, but he just—" Her voice broke and her eyes filled with tears.

Jeff felt like crying, too. He couldn't stand seeing his mother so miserable. She'd always been the strong one, the one who could see things so clearly, who'd never let personal feelings cloud her judgment. The one who never ever cried . . . until the past few months.

"Don't cry, Mom," he begged gruffly. "Please."

Amanda disengaged one hand and swiped at the tears spilling over the fragile dam of her lashes. She nodded and sniffed, and Jeff could see her visibly regaining control of her emotions.

"Does he love you?" he asked.

Amanda reached for a paper napkin and dabbed at her eyes. "I don't know. H-he acts as if he does, but . . . Oh, Jeff, I know it's silly to feel the way I do about a man like him. He's way out of my league." She made a helpless gesture with her hands. "I . . . I couldn't seem to help it."

"I understand."

"You do?"

"You need someone, Mom." At the surprise in her tear-bright eyes, he continued. "You need someone—not because you can't cope, because you can, you have. You need someone to love. I've always known you have a lot of love to give, and I always wondered why you never...dated more."

"I was bitter. And afraid."

"And you're not afraid with Heather's dad?"

Amanda attempted a smile, which crumpled into a teary mask before it was hardly more than a thought. "I'm scared. I'm scared to death. My heart tells me that Way is nothing like your father, but my mind is afraid to trust those feelings, because I never thought Deke would turn out the way he did, either." Her smile was little more than a wry twist of her lips. "I'm afraid, Jeff, but I have to hang on to see where all this is taking me, because I don't have any other choice."

"YOU AREN'T GOING to fight, are you?" Heather asked, her unease reflected in her eyes.

Jeff turned from the window, where he could see Way coming up the walk, and gave her a brief hug. "Right. Pistols at dawn," he said facetiously. "I'm not mad at him, babe. I just want to know what his intentions are, so you stay in the bedroom until I have a chance to talk to him. Now, scat!"

Heather disappeared from the kitchen, and in a matter of seconds, Way was knocking at the back door.

Jeff let his father-in-law in and tried to picture him through the eyes of a woman, acknowledging that Way's regular features and trim physique were no doubt attractive to the opposite sex. And he was a nice guy. He tried to imagine the man before him making love to his mother and couldn't.

"How's it going?" Way asked, shaking Jeff's hand.

"Fine, sir. Fine," Jeff said, indicating the dinette table through the doorway. "Have a seat."

"Where's Heather?" Way said, sitting down and crossing his legs ankle to knee.

Jeff busied himself with pouring Way a cup of coffee. They'd brought Way to the apartment by using the ruse that Heather was getting nervous about her delivery—which was less than three months away—and wanted to talk to him.

"She's ... taking a shower, I think," Jeff said, entering the adjoining dining area and setting both cups on the table. Never one to beat around the bush, Jeff seated himself across from Way and dove in. "Actually, I was the one who wanted to talk to you."

Way saw the determination in the younger man's eyes. Some inherent masculine instinct told him what the problem was. He breathed a troubled sigh. "How did you find out?"

Jeff didn't bother asking how Way had figured out the reason for his summons. "I saw you kissing her when you were home last week."

"I see," Way said with a nod. He took a sip of the scalding brew. "And?" he asked at last.

Jeff forced himself to meet the penetrating intensity of Way's gaze. "My mother is a sensitive person with a tender heart, no matter what kind of front she puts on."

"I know that."

"She hasn't dated much."

"That's what she told me," Way said, patiently fielding each of Jeff's statements but knowing what the ultimate question would be.

"What I'm trying to say is that she doesn't ... she's ... inexperienced about ... things."

"Yes, she is, and that's very refreshing."

Jeff took a nervous gulp of his coffee, which, he found out suddenly, was hot . . . so hot it brought tears to his eyes. He forced the coffee down and wheezed, "I'd like to know what your intentions are . . . sir."

"Honorable."

"Honorable?"

"I love her, Jeff," Way said. "At some time in the future, I hope I can persuade her to marry me."

"What?" Jeff couldn't believe his ears. Famous rich baseball star Waylon Dalton married to his mother?

"I want to marry her, if she'll agree. And with your blessing, of course."

"Well, uh . . . sure. Yeah. That's great," Jeff said, rising and heading for the bedroom. He got to the door and cut loose with a loud "Heather!"

Heather stuck her head out the door. "What?"

"Come here. We have something to tell you."

Heather entered the room with a wary expression on her pretty face, but the calm look on her father's features went a long way toward reassuring her that he and Jeff hadn't had any harsh words.

She looked from one masculine face to the other. "Well?"

"Remember our conversation last week?" Jeff asked. She nodded.

"Well, how would you like to have your mother-in-law for your stepmother?"

AMANDA TOOK one day at a time, even though another hurdle had been overcome when Jeff and Heather had taken the news about her relationship with Way with such surprising equanimity. She lived for the hours he was in town and missed him like the very devil when he was gone.

In her burning need to provide for herself and Jeff, she'd forgotten that there were such things as teasing, practical jokes and laughter, and Way did more than remind her of what she'd been missing; he was teaching her how to experience those things again.

They picnicked and went swimming. They doubledated with Jose and his latest girlfriend, a California model who was known simply as Chantée. Way procured prime seats and Amanda went to the home games and cheered along with Heather and Jeff and the rest of the Royals' fans. They cooked together and cleaned up together.

He sprayed her with the mist of the water hose through the open kitchen window; she stood on the commode and dumped a pan of cold water on his head while he showered—which resulted in him dragging her in with him, clothes and all. Amanda retaliated by pushing him—fully clothed—into the pool the next time they swam at his house. Not to be outdone by a mere slip of a woman, Way stripped them both to nothing and carried her to the shallow end of the pool, where he made slow, sweet love to her. He claimed that she brought out the best in him, and the best of Way Dalton was totally irresistible.

Amanda was happier than she'd been in years, and Way seemed to be happy, too, yet neither of them was willing to broach the subject of what the future might hold. They were both content to wait, to let the feelings between them grow.

MORE CONTENT with her life than she had been in years, Amanda crossed the campus toward the English building with a sense of anticipation. Last year's problems might never have been. She was in love. That, and the memory of Way making love to her far into the night, brought a smile to her face and put a spring in her step in spite of the draining heat of the late-August days.

She entered her office and looked around, feeling a welcome sense of familiarity. Stowing her purse in the bottom desk drawer, she opened her briefcase and began to drag out papers, pens and paper clips. She put the picture of Heather and Jeff on the desk and set a small plant she'd brought from home on the opposite corner. Every personal item she put down made her feel more certain that her decision to return had been the right one.

A tapping on the glass of the door brought her head up, and before she could speak, the door opened and a blond head of hair came into view.

"Steve! Come in," Amanda said, curiously touched by the fact that he'd stopped by to see her, and a bit surprised and embarrassed that her life had taken such a turnaround that she hadn't so much as thought of him during the summer. It was a side effect, she was sure, of love and the way it pushed everything else to the background.

"Are you busy?" he asked, stepping through the door and closing it behind him.

She glanced at her wristwatch. "I'm not doing anything that can't wait, and I have about fifteen minutes before the hordes descend," she said with a smile. "Come in and tell me how your summer went."

Steve took a seat directly in front of her desk. "What have you done to yourself?" he asked. "You look great."

Amanda tugged self-consciously at a strand of hair that curled against her cheek. It was beginning to look as if she had no intention of cutting it. "Thanks. You look good yourself. Where'd you get that tan—California?"

"The Bahamas," he answered. "I spent the summer with my mother."

"That's nice."

Steve's lips twisted into a bitter smile. "Maybe I should have said that I went to the Bahamas to try to spend the summer with my mother. I hardly saw her."

"Oh?"

"Yeah."

Amanda could have wept for the misery she saw clouding his blue eyes.

"She's got a new boyfriend. About seven years older than me. He's the tennis pro at the place where we stayed. She couldn't spend any time with me because she was too busy with her...tennis lessons. What it amounts to, Ms Farrell, is that she was too busy making it with the guy to pay any attention to me."

"Oh, Steve, I'm sorry."

"Yeah. Me, too." He straightened in the chair and said, "But them's the breaks, huh? I've tried everything I know, but she just doesn't care. But that's not my fault." He gave her a tentative smile. "There is some good news, though."

"What's that?"

"I met a girl. Just a couple of weeks before school started. She doesn't run with the fast crowd, but she's pretty and smart. And she likes me. Me. Not my parents' money or the prestige."

Genuinely happy for him, Amanda smiled. "That's great, Steve."

He laughed. "She's even going to help me with my math. I'm going to get my degree, Ms Farrell. And I'm going to work for it, because I've learned something from all this."

"What's that?"

"That I'm going to be different when I have kids. I'm going to love them no matter what. And do you know why?"

Amanda shook her head.

"Because someone I respect very much told me that you don't earn love. It comes with no strings attached."

Amanda remembered her own words, surprised that they'd left such a strong mark on him. Which was just another reason that Steve Harris had been worth all the time she'd spent with him. In spite of his upbringing, he'd become a decent human being.

"Good for you," she said.

Steve smiled in earnest at the sincerity he heard in her voice. "I didn't come here to cry on your shoulder," he told her. "I came to ask if you'd tutor me again this year. Stacey said she'd help, but she's carrying a heavy load and working, too, and I'm afraid of putting too much on her."

Surprise caused Amanda's mouth to drop open a fraction of an inch. She'd never dreamed that Steve would want tutoring again—or that he would want her to do it. As she'd explained in the spring, there were always students who excelled in a class and who made extra money by tutoring. Normally, she turned over problem students to them. It was a mutually beneficial arrangement, but somehow, Steve was different. Amanda couldn't shake the feeling that he needed more than help with his English. He needed to be around someone who would show him some attention, someone who would make him feel like part of a family. A mother.

Sensing her hesitation, he said, "I can pay for it."

"Payment isn't necessary, Steve."

"Then will you do it?"

"Sure," she said. "Why not?"

IT RAINED during the first week of September, and the heat, which had gripped the city for three long weeks, loosened its hold. It was still hot, but there was a difference now. The daily high wasn't so high, and the evenings held the breath of fall.

As Way had predicted, the Royals were in the midst of a pennant race. Feelings of jubilation ran rampant through the city, and T-shirts and caps bearing the Royals' colors and logo were de rigueur among the most loyal fans. Like the rest of the team, Way had psyched himself into believing that they would take not only the league championship, but would snare the coveted World Series in October. And, like the rest of the team, when he was allowed precious time to himself, he wanted to unwind, relax. And that, he told Amanda when he was at home in early September, he could do best when he was with her.

"Are you kidding?" she teased as he carried her—clad only in the briefest underwear—to the corner of the pool that doubled as a hot tub. "There is no way this can be restful."

"Describe 'this' for me, Professor Farrell," he said, stepping into the water.

"This," she said, waving her hand in an encompassing gesture. "You. Me. Making—"

"Mmm," Way said, easing them both into the hot, frothy water. "You mean making out." He settled her on his lap, her bottom resting against the proof of his arousal.

"Crude, Dalton. Very crude."

Way unhooked the front clasp of her bra and released her breasts to his heated gaze. Her nipples puckered in the air, and Way bent his head and pressed a kiss to each one.

Amanda held him close and said breathlessly, "I went to the doctor and everything's taken care of."

Way lifted his head and met the undeniable need in her eyes. "Meaning?"

"Meaning that I want to feel you...you...inside me."

Way lowered his mouth to hers. When they were a mere heartbeat apart, he whispered, "Crude, Farrell. Very crude."

He kissed her then, and slid them both lower into the water. "Boy, was I wrong," he murmured.

"Wrong about what?" Amanda asked.

"Before I met you I thought you would be some masculine type with thick glasses, a mustache and a hormone problem."

"Ugh," Amanda said with a smile. "So much for first impressions."

"You have to admit you were pretty... hard-nosed in the beginning."

"I know. But I was so afraid... for them."

He rubbed her nose with his in an Eskimo kiss. "I know. But they're doing great—thank God."

"Yes," she agreed, and then added, "I do wear glasses."

"Yeah. They're cute. They make you look like a little owl." At her disgusted look, he added hastily, "I like owls."

"Sure."

"Well, you certainly aren't masculine, and if you have a hormone imbalance, it works just fine with my hormones," he told her huskily.

"You're insatiable."

"You're right," he said, lifting her so that he could pull the wisp of lace down her slender legs. "I also remember thinking that you probably wore starched underwear."

"Starched?"

Way shrugged and, lifting her even higher, tumbled her naked form over the dividing wall into the shallow end of the pool, hoisting himself over after her. The water, warm, but not nearly as hot as the hot tub, felt good to her heated flesh. Leaning his back against the tiled side, he caught her by the hips and eased himself inside her. His breath hissed out through his clenched teeth slowly. He hadn't thought it could get any better; he'd been wrong. His eyes drifted shut and his head fell back against the rim of the pool.

"You feel so good, Mandy," Way moaned. "So damn good."

Amanda contemplated the intense pleasure on his face through her own passion-slitted eyes. The look and his confession sent her own libido into high gear. His hands covered her breasts, and he joined her in a seductive dance that grew increasingly faster, wilder. Her hands clutched the edge of the pool as the feelings inside her grew. The look of ecstasy etched on his face bordered agony. It was a feeling she understood perfectly.

Amanda felt the tension in Way reach its zenith. He gripped her waist and surged upward. Her fingers tightened convulsively on the tiled edge of the pool, and their cries of pleasure became one sound of satisfied joy.

Gradually, the emotions raging within her lessened to gentle shuddering aftershocks. Her arms were around Way's neck, holding his face against her as she fought back the prickling sting of tears. His hands traveled the well-known path from her knees up her thighs to her spine and back again. He turned his head and kissed her neck.

His voice was hardly more than a whisper as he said, "Marry me, Mandy."

Amanda froze. For long seconds she was still in his embrace, allowing the full implication of his words to hit her.

Marriage. After sixteen years of being single, did she want the responsibilities that went with a serious relationship? Was she ready to risk her heart to another man who was in many ways like Deke?

"Mandy?" he said, disengaging her arms and forcing her to meet his eyes.

Way saw the turbulence in her gaze, recognized the doubt, the fear. "I love you, Amanda. And I haven't said that to any woman since Carol died."

"I wasn't sure I'd ever hear you say that."

His smile was rueful. "I wasn't certain I'd ever find a woman I'd want to say it to."

"I never thought you'd want to marry me."

"Did you think I only wanted an affair? With my daughter's mother-in-law?" His laughter sounded hollow. "Give me some credit, Amanda. That would have brought about a terrible situation when it ended."

"I ... I hadn't thought about that. I hadn't thought about any of it. I was just ... taking it one day at a time. It's the way I had to live for so long that I—"

"That's over," he interrupted. "I want to take care of you. I don't want you to ever have to worry about *anything* again."

"I don't know how to be a baseball star's wife," she said with a self-conscious laugh. "I'm not geared for that . . . life-style. . . ."

Her voice trailed away, leaving Way with the feeling that he was about to lose something very important. He sighed, a deep indrawing of breath that somehow saddened her. "So the answer is no," he said in an attempt to clarify his position.

She shook her head. "The answer is a request. Can you give me some time? Let me think about it? I don't want to be a liability. I've been single for so long, I might make a terrible wife."

Way took her face in his hands. "You could never be a liability or a terrible wife, but yes, you can have some time. Just don't take too long. I'd like for us to be married before Thanksgiving so that we can celebrate the holidays as a real family."

"Thanksgiving?" Amanda echoed. "But that's only a couple of months away."

"I know."

"All right," she said. "Before Thanksgiving." She tilted her head and covered his parted lips with hers in a kiss of promise and passion—her thanks for giving her the time and space she needed. Then, with him still buried inside her, she smiled against his lips and moved her hips suggestively.

"Starched underwear, huh?" she said through gritted teeth.

"An honest mistake, Man . . . Ah, God, you're going to kill me," Way groaned as he felt his body surging to new strength under the insistent urging of hers. His face wore a look of mock-martyrdom that was completely at odds with the mischief in his eyes. "Be gentle with me," he pleaded. "I'm almost a grandfather."

"Gentle isn't in my vocabulary, Dalton. Starched underwear, indeed! You're going to pay..." Her lips touched his. "And pay..." She tightened her body around him. "And pay..."

CHAPTER FIFTEEN

AS SPORTS PEOPLE in the know had predicted much earlier in the year, the Royals took their division and the play-offs, and were expected to take the Series, as well, even though the Atlanta Braves had a hard-knocking team. The first game had been played the day before in Atlanta, and the Braves had taken it, 5–4, which meant the Royals were under a self-imposed pressure to win the second game. They would come home for games three and four and five and everyone believed that with the home field advantage, they might be able to win the next three games.

Amanda hadn't seen Way in three days, which, she thought as she tuned in to the second game of the Series, was as good a reason to watch the television as any. His proposal of more than a month ago was still fresh in her mind, and she found herself fantasizing at the strangest times about what life would be like as Mrs. Waylon Dalton. When he was gone, thoughts of her past crept back in to taunt her with her mistakes, but when they were together, her heart told her that she'd be a fool to turn him down. When she accused him of not being fair by making her decision harder with all the small proofs of love he showered on her, he reminded her that all was fair in love and war.

Still unable to come to a clear-cut decision, she focused her attention on the game—more specifically,

Way's turn at the plate. She watched as he chose a bat and swung it experimentally a couple of times. Then he took his place and swung the bat over the plate. The Braves' pitcher looked over his shoulder, wound up and threw a slider. Way didn't swing. A strike.

The catcher threw the ball back to the pitcher, who caught it with easy nonchalance and then took off his cap and made an ordeal out of wiping his face with his shirtsleeve. When he was ready to throw again, Way stepped away from the plate and straightened his shirt.

This time Amanda recognized his actions for what they were: mind games. When Way stepped back to the plate, the pitcher threw again, but before the announcer could call what type of pitch it was, Way swung, connecting with a loud thwonk that sent the ball sailing up and out.

As soon as they'd seen that he'd hit the ball, the runners on the other bases were flying toward home. Way hesitated just a second, and then, when it was apparent that the ball was going into the crowd, he leaped into the air like a kid, his fists clenched in a sign of victory, the smile on his face bringing one to Amanda's. He loved it, she realized for the first time. He really loved the game and the competition, not only with other teams, but with himself.

She watched as he made the obligatory run around the bases, and smiled at the enthusiasm and joy on the faces of his teammates when he crossed home plate and entered the dugout to a round of hugging and backslapping.

The phone rang and Amanda reached for it, mumbling dire consequences to the caller. She didn't want any interruptions.

"Hello."

"Mom? It's me," Jeff said.

Amanda heard the panic lacing his voice. "Is everything okay?"

"I think we need to go to the hospital."

"Hospital!" Amanda cried, visions of all sorts of terrible things running helter-skelter through her mind. "What's the matter?"

"I think Heather's water broke."

Amanda forgot the game. "What happened? Did she fall?"

"No. Nothing happened. She went into the kitchen to get something to drink, and the next thing she knows there's a puddle of water on the floor. What should I do?"

"Just stay calm," Amanda said, feeling her own nerves jangling. "Get some towels for her to sit on and take her to the hospital."

"Towels. Right." Amanda could almost see him running his hand through his hair, and there was no denying the worry in his voice. "Mom, is she going to be all right? I mean it's almost a month early."

"She's going to be fine, Jeff. Now, go on."

"Okay."

"Jeff!"

"Yeah?"

"Drive carefully, and I'll meet you there."

"Okay, Mom. Thanks."

Amanda switched the television off, all thoughts of the game forgotten. She was almost out the door when she realized that she should try to get hold of Way. She called the number of the hotel where the team was staying and left a message that they'd taken Heather to the hospital and for him to call her there. That done, she grabbed her handbag and glanced at the clock. Two-thirty. The game should be over and Way should be back at the hotel in a couple of hours—three, tops. She wished he was with her. And despite the pep talk she'd given Jeff, she prayed Heather and the baby would be all right.

HEATHER, WHOSE EPIDURAL had already been started, was watching television when Amanda arrived, while a fetal monitor kept track of the baby's heartbeat.

"Hi," the younger woman said when Amanda entered the room.

"Hi yourself." Amanda went to the bed and kissed Heather's cheek. "How do you feel?"

"Not a thing from the waist down," Heather told her with a smile.

Amanda returned the smile and looked around the beautifully appointed LDR unit, the place where Heather would stay during her labor, the baby's delivery and for the two hours after birth, during her recovery, after which she would be moved to a private room. The decor was beautiful—aquas and watermelon hues and a lot of nubby fabric and wood. Besides Heather's bed, there was a hide-a-bed sofa for Jeff if the labor was prolonged, a telephone, television, a dining table and cabinets that housed the accoutrements the doctors would need during delivery.

"Things have sure changed since I had Jeff," Amanda commented. "Where is Jeff, anyway?"

"He can't stand the pressure," Heather said with a smile. "I think he went to get a Coke."

AS THE DOCTOR PREDICTED, Heather's labor promised to be a long one. Jeff was a wreck, and his worry seemed to agitate his wife. At five-thirty Amanda sent him to get something to eat, as much to get him out of their hair as to assuage his hunger pangs. She and Heather were watching a game show when the phone rang. Amanda pulled off her button earring and lifted the receiver to her ear. "Hello."

"Mandy?"

Pleasure gleamed in Amanda's eyes as her gaze flew to Heather's. "Way! You got the message."

"Yeah. I just got here. How is she?"

"She's fine," Amanda told him with a wide smile. "Would you like to talk to her?"

"In a minute. First, I love you and miss you like hell."

Amanda cast a glance at Heather, who appeared to be involved with the show. "Me, too," she told him.

She heard him sigh. "This is really it?"

"It really is."

"The team is flying back tomorrow morning at nine. Should I come earlier?" Amanda could hear the hesitancy in his voice. She knew he wanted to be with his daughter, but she knew he was tired, too.

"I don't see any reason why you should. I can reach you in your room, can't I?" she asked.

"Yeah. I'll send out for dinner." Like Jeff, Way couldn't hide his concern. "Keep me posted, will you?"

"Surely. Let me give the phone to Heather. By the way," she asked, "who won?"

"They did," he told her in a disgusted tone.

"I'm sorry."

"Yeah. Me, too."

"I'll get Heather," Amanda said, standing and holding the phone out toward the younger woman. But before Heather could take the receiver, Amanda heard his voice call her name. She brought the phone back to her ear. "Yes?"

"Thanks for being there."

AT TEN MINUTES PAST MIDNIGHT, Jeff, hands plunged palm-out in the back pockets of his jeans, stood staring out the window of the maternity floor waiting room. He and Amanda had come there when it had become apparent that the baby's birth was getting closer. Jeff was afraid that he'd pass out if he saw the whole ordeal, and, the closer delivery seemed, Amanda found that she wasn't ready to be that "modern," either.

She was pretending to read an article about giving any kitchen a new look for one hundred dollars, when a green-outfitted nurse appeared in the doorway. "Mr. Farrell?"

Jeff whirled. "That's me."

The woman smiled. "You have a beautiful little girl. Five pounds, three ounces, born at 12:05."

Amanda saw Jeff's body actually sag as the tension that had held him prisoner for the past nine-plus hours fled. "Is everything all right?" he asked.

"Mother and baby both look good," the nurse replied. "Your wife will be in recovery for a couple of hours, and then we'll move her to her room. If you'll go knock on the window of the nursery in about thirty minutes, they'll let you have a peek at the baby." She smiled again. "Congratulations."

Jeff's eyes found Amanda's. "A girl," he said softly. He smiled, a white slash of a smile that threatened to split his handsome features. "A girl!"

Amanda felt her own tenseness leave. Laughing, she went to Jeff and gave him a tight squeeze. Then she went to call Way.

AMANDA LOOKED at her watch and cast a furtive, side-long glance at Jeff who, with his elbows propped on his knees and his clasped hands dangling between his thighs, was beginning to look worried, too. It was closer to three hours than the predicted two, and the doctor still hadn't moved Heather to her room. Not even the happy thoughts of their laughter and joking when she and Jeff had gone to look at the baby or the memory of Way's rebel yell when she'd called him could dissipate the cloud of unease that was beginning to rain on Amanda's happiness.

Jeff turned and caught her looking at him. "Do you think something's wrong?"

"I doubt it," Amanda said, sounding far more cheerful than she felt. "Maybe they've moved her and forgot to come and tell us. Would you like for me to go to the nurses' station and check?" She purposefully ignored the obvious—that the birthing room was just down the hall and they would have seen Heather being wheeled by.

"Please," he said, lifting his hand and rubbing his eyes in a gesture that was poignantly reminiscent of his childhood. Amanda's heart constricted painfully, as if a giant hand were intent on squeezing the life from it. She wanted more than anything to lift the burden of worry from his shoulders and place it on hers. She was used to it. Jeff wasn't.

"I'll be back in a minute."

The nurses' station was comparatively quiet, and a plain-looking woman filling out a chart looked up at Amanda's approach. "May I help you?"

Amanda smiled. "I hope so. I'm Heather Farrell's mother-in-law, and we were wondering if you'd moved her to her room yet."

"Not yet," the woman said without even checking on a chart. "She's still in recovery."

"Is something wrong?" Amanda asked, the tension—hand in hand with an irrational fear—creeping insidiously back.

"Her uterus is still a bit boggy...that's soft," the nurse clarified, "and she's bleeding a little more than we'd like. We want to keep a close watch on her until we get her condition corrected."

Amanda struggled to put the seemingly serious words into a balanced perspective. Was Heather's condition serious, or was it as routine as the nurse's voice suggested? Dear God, what would she tell Jeff—and Way?

"Thank you," she said, turning back toward the waiting room. "You will keep us informed, won't you?"

The nurse smiled, a gesture that transformed her plain features to almost pretty. "Sure."

Jeff stood in the doorway, his hands braced on either side. "Well?" he asked anxiously when he saw the stricken look on his mother's face. "What is it?"

Amanda linked her arm through his and ushered him back inside. And then, displaying as little negative emotion as she could manage, she repeated the nurse's words. Repeated the words that with one unmerciful thrust killed forever the last vestiges of innocence Jeffrey Farrell would ever know.

THE MINUTES CRAWLED by. Jeff and Amanda took turns pacing the room and staring out the window. They both prayed. At three forty-five the nurse passed on the information that the doctor had ordered an IV and some lab work to check Heather's blood count. Jeff continued to prowl the small room.

Four-twenty...four-thirty.

Twenty-till-five. Jeff had collapsed into a chair and sat staring at a spot across the room. Amanda had just decided to call Way when she glanced up toward the nurses' station and saw Dr. Palmer standing there, looking over a chart.

"Jeff!" she cried softly, the urgency in her voice and the direction of her gaze drawing his attention to the man who, even as they watched, entered Heather's room.

The last bit of color in Jeff's haggard face vanished, and he sprang to his feet, tearing down the hall toward the room, his tennis shoes making a squeaking sound as they came into contact with the polished marble floor. Amanda followed him, dogging his footsteps as fear dogged hers.

"Sir!" the night nurse said sharply as Jeff raced past the station. "You can't go in there."

The sound of her voice must have penetrated Jeff's single-minded quest, because he stopped just outside Heather's door and looked back at Amanda with a blank gaze that quickly mutated to desolation. She reached him and put her arm around his waist.

"I'll have the doctor come and tell you her status when he finishes," the nurse said to Amanda.

She nodded. Jeff allowed Amanda to lead him back to the waiting room, where he sank into a chair and buried his face in his hands.

Her heart, already filled to overflowing with her own pain, threatened to break. "Jeff, don't," she begged in a voice thick with her own emotion.

He lifted his head and looked at her, the tears in his eyes already making tracks down his cheeks. "It's my fault."

"It *isn't* your fault. It's no one's fault."

"It is! If I hadn't—"

Amanda went to him, kneeling at his feet and taking his hands in hers. "You made a mistake. Not just you— *both* of you. But this has nothing to do with that," she told him earnestly. "Things just happen."

He drew a shaky breath and held on to her hands so tightly she flinched. "If anything happens to her, I don't know what I'll do."

Amanda brought one of his hands up and cradled it to her cheek. "It won't. You have to believe that."

"Yeah," he said, nodding. "I guess so."

Giving his hand a pat, Amanda stood. "Will you be all right while I go give Way a call? I think we need to let him know what's going on." *And I need him to be here. I need him so badly.*

Jeff nodded, a new wave of despair washing over him. "He's going to hate my guts, isn't he? He's the closest thing I've ever had to a father, and I've screwed that up."

"No, you haven't," Amanda assured him. "Way isn't like that. You just sit tight until I get back."

She picked up her purse and left Jeff sitting there, praying with every step she took that she was right—Way wouldn't blame Jeff, and Heather would recover. As she passed the elevator, it pinged to a stop, but intent on finding the pay phone, she was oblivious to the sound.

"Amanda!"

The masculine voice calling her name was achingly familiar and blessedly sweet. She whirled around. Way, tall and handsome and solid looking in jeans and a heavy sweater, stood near the elevator. She realized with something of a start that she was tired of being strong, tired of carrying the burden alone. She wanted, no, *needed* someone to lean on. With a small, wounded cry, she flew into his arms, and the security enveloping her as they closed around her was the sweetest feeling this side of heaven.

Her arms tightened around his neck, and she covered his face with a string of desperate kisses.

"What a homecoming," he said with a chuckle. Then, as he slowly realized her desperation, he lowered her feet to the floor and held her away from him. "What's the matter, Amanda? The baby—"

"Is fine," she assured him, forcing her troubled gaze to meet his. "I was just going to call you. It's... Heather."

The happiness in his eyes vanished; fear stood in its stead. "Heather? What's wrong?"

"They haven't brought her out of recovery."

"What!"

Amanda explained the situation as best she could and watched as the expression on his face became a twin of Jeff's. "Jeff is afraid you'll blame him," she finished.

The faraway look in Way's eyes vanished. "Blame him? Why?"

Amanda shrugged. "Because he got her pregnant."

"That's crazy!" Way said roughly. "That's like saying we didn't win the game today because I only got a base hit in the top of the sixth."

"I know, but he's—" tears filled her eyes "—he's inconsolable."

Way took her hand and pressed a kiss to her palm. "Come on. Let's go talk to him."

Hand in hand they went back to the waiting room where Jeff stood, watching as the first feeble fingers of daylight poked through the dark curtain of the night.

"Jeff," Amanda said softly.

He turned, the look on his face expressing without words that he was braced for the worst. When he saw Way, his gaze flew to Amanda's and back. "W-when did you get here?"

Way's heart went out to the younger man, who looked as if he'd just finished fighting off the fiends of hell. "Just now," he said, crossing the room and smiling reassuringly. "I decided I couldn't wait to see my new granddaughter, so I caught the red-eye flight back."

A faint, answering smile lit Jeff's eyes for a second. "She's pretty, Mr. Dalton. Real pretty. She looks like Hea—" his voice broke "—Heather."

Way went to him then and put his arms around him, the first masculine embrace Jeff had ever known except his grandfather's. The tears he had been holding back broke free with a heart-wrenching sob. Way let him cry a minute, and then grasped Jeff's upper arms and forced him to look into his eyes. "It's not your fault, Jeff. And it's going to be all right," Way told him gruffly.

"Is everything all right, here?"

Everyone turned at the sound of Dr. Palmer's voice. He stood in the doorway, his aging face tired and lined, though there was a kindly twinkle in his blue eyes.

"I understand that everyone got a little nervous when I went in to see about Heather a little while ago," he said with an apologetic smile. "I'm sorry to upset you. They called me back to deliver another baby, and while I was here, I thought I might as well check in on Heather and see how things were going. She's fine. The uterus is firming up nicely, and I have no reason to think she won't continue to improve. We want to keep an eye on her until she finishes the IV, just to make sure, and then we'll put her in a room."

"She's going to be all right?" Jeff asked, his voice cracking with emotion.

"Of course she's going to be all right."

Jeff's knees gave out with him, and he sank into a green vinyl chair. Way's brown eyes looked suspiciously bright, and Amanda's dropped shut with silent thanks.

"Have you seen the baby?" the doctor asked in a tactful effort to turn everyone's thoughts to a happier channel.

"No, I haven't," Way said. "I just got here."

"Then you'd best go have a look at her," the doctor said with a smile. "She's a dandy."

THE AUTUMN MORNING was crisp and cool, though the sun shone brightly. A capricious wind tossed the fiery locks of the trees and blew Amanda's hair into her face, bringing a blush of rose to her cheeks.

"Heather looks really good, doesn't she?" Way asked as they walked toward the hospital parking lot, their clasped hands swinging between them.

Amanda recalled Heather's beaming face when they'd all filed in to see her thirty minutes before. Jeff's attitude as he'd leaned over the bed and kissed her had been almost worshipful, and Heather had been tired but ecstatic. "Considering the scare she gave us, yes. I'm glad you came on home," she said, turning her head to meet Way's eyes.

"So am I."

"I needed you. I never knew how much until last night."

"Then I'm really glad," he told her, bringing their locked hands up and kissing the back of hers.

"Last night, I realized . . ." Her sentence broke off as she stumbled, so tired she could hardly put one foot in front of the other.

Way stopped and pulled her into his arms, silencing her with a brief kiss. "Last night was an emotional one for us all. You're tired." He rubbed his nose against hers. "Go home and get some sleep. I want to have a long talk later on, and I want you wide awake."

Amanda nodded and hugged him tightly, knowing exactly what he wanted to talk about. When they reached the car, she asked, "Do you want me to drop you off?"

Way unlocked her car door and opened it for her. "I'll get a cab. How about you? Will you fall asleep at the wheel?" he asked.

She covered a mighty yawn with one hand and sank into the car's interior. "I can make it."

"Okay. I'll see you late this afternoon. Maybe we can catch an early dinner and then come up and see Heather and the baby."

"Sounds good," she said, stifling another yawn.

Way laughed. "Go home. You're out on your feet."

She nodded and he slammed the car door shut. Then, blowing him a kiss through the closed window, she pulled out of the parking lot and left him standing there looking after her, a smile on his handsome face.

AT THREE THAT AFTERNOON, Amanda woke up to the fact that she was a grandmother. A quiet joy filled her and the warm, happy sound of her laughter drove the quiet from the room. She was a grandmother and she was in love. What more could anyone want?

The night, filled with both worry and joy, had been a revelation to her. She knew that she needed the security

Way offered her, knew she loved him more than life itself. She realized, too, that even though she'd done her best to give Jeff as much of herself as she could, she'd never filled the place in his life and heart that required a father's love.

The memory of Way holding Jeff while he cried brought a rush of tears to her eyes, and she was thankful that at least now, Jeff had someone. How many other times had Jeff needed a father's touch, a man's understanding and perspective—and he'd only had her feminine understanding and viewpoint? It was only natural that men looked at things differently; they were geared to approach life differently than women. She smiled wryly. The miracle was that Jeff had grown up as well as he had.

So what's your problem, Amanda? If you know that you love him and need him, why do you still have these nagging doubts about making a total commitment?

"It isn't him—it's me," she said aloud, rolling to her back and staring at the ceiling.

It was true. She'd been single for more than sixteen years. And sixteen years of being the backbone of a family, of being the sole provider of monetary and emotional support, translated to a lot of responsibility and a lot of independence. She was set in her ways. She liked to sleep late on Saturdays, and she'd already learned that Way was an early riser. He didn't like breakfast; she wanted something as soon as her feet hit the floor in the morning—and she didn't want a sweet roll. She was into good eating habits, and Way was the original junk-food junkie.

That's small potatoes, Amanda. What's the real problem?

Her concerns were small things, but her mother always said that it was the gradual pileup of little things that finally destroyed a relationship—the proverbial straws that break the camel's back.

And then there was the fact that Way was not just Way, a man she loved. He wasn't just a man. He was Waylon Dalton, baseball star. A man used to dating the most glamorous women in the country. A man who made more money in one year than she could even comprehend, for hitting and catching a little white ball in front of thousands of people.

Amanda sat up in bed and rested her forearms on her raised knees. She'd had no idea that there was so much money in professional sports, and she didn't know how she'd fit into Way's life and life-style, or even if she could.

She did know that she would have to make a decision soon, maybe even that very night.

Her thoughts still churning, she fixed a pot of coffee and had a couple of cups while she took a leisurely bath and did her hair and nails. She pulled on soft leather boots, whose tall tops were partially hidden by her circular cashmere skirt of silver gray. A matching sweater with a cowl neck was accessorized with several silver chains, matching earrings and a silver-and-gold watch. She did her makeup to perfection and her hair curled around her face and onto her shoulders becomingly.

Amanda was putting silver hoops in her ears when the doorbell rang at five. Way was early, she thought, going to the front door while she secured the back on one earring. She couldn't wait to see him, couldn't wait to go and see Heather and the baby.

She flung open the door, a wide smile of welcome on her face.

"Hello, sweetie."

Amanda's smile vanished as quickly as it had come. It wasn't Way who stood there calling her sweetie. It was a man she had seen only twice since he'd walked out of her life. Her former husband and Jeff's father...Deke Farrell.

CHAPTER SIXTEEN

DEKE STOOD in the gathering twilight, smiling a smile that could only be described as oily...which pretty well described him in general. Deke had always had a polished handsomeness. Too late, Amanda had recognized that it was too polished, too slick, just as his lines were too pat, too smooth. As a teenager, his cocky attitude had been a desirable trait to Amanda, a challenge to her fledgling feminine wiles. At almost forty, it was sickening. He was, as Jeff would say, a jerk.

Physically he hadn't changed much since she'd seen him last, a little more than seven years ago. His wavy blond hair was still stylishly cut, his smile just as wide and white. Only someone who was looking—or someone who was as familiar with him as Amanda had once been—would notice the telltale puffiness around his eyes and the unflattering network of red lines that hinted at his long-standing and close acquaintance with the bottle. Only someone who had known him before would note the thickening of his middle that even the excellent cut of his sport coat failed to hide. Despite his attire, Deke looked like what he was: a forty-year-old down-and-out golf pro with a drinking problem.

"Aren't you going to ask me in?" he asked in the husky voice that had once sent her into a frenzy of longing...back before she'd known he used the technique on every willing female under fifty.

Amanda ignored his question and shot back one of her own. "What are you doing here, Deke?"

He shrugged. "I thought I'd stop by and see how you and the kid were doing," he said jovially.

"Why now—after seven years?" she asked, shivering as a chill swept through her.

"Can't I even come check on my kid once in a while?" he asked, his smile still firmly in place. He reached out and ran his hand from her shoulder to her elbow.

Wrenching free, she crossed her arms across her breasts, loathing the thought of him touching her.

"You're cold, baby. Why don't you ask me in for a cup of coffee so we can talk this over like adults?"

She could see that he wasn't going until he got whatever he'd come for, and since she didn't have to worry about Jeff being subjected to his presence, she stepped aside. Deke strolled in, leaving a wake of expensive, masculine cologne behind.

"You've improved the place since I was here last," he said, looking around with interest. "You must be doing okay."

"I'm teaching now," she said, leading the way to the kitchen.

"What grade?"

"Freshman English. College." She poured him a cup of the coffee she'd made earlier, taking a perverse pleasure in the knowledge that by this time it would taste like mud straight from the Mississippi.

Deke pulled out a chair and let out a long, slow whistle. "A college professor. I'm impressed."

Sitting down across from him, Amanda folded her hands together on top of the table. "What about you, Deke? How have you done?"

He held up his arms, displaying an expensive gold watch and the cuffs of a freshly starched shirt. "You can see for yourself. I didn't get these threads at the five and dime. I met this woman, who—''

"I get the picture," Amanda interrupted, pitying the unknown woman already. "Look, Deke, if you haven't come for money, why have you come?"

His features held real surprise. "Money! Now why would you think I'd come for money?"

"Because that's what you've wanted when you've come both times before," she told him with extreme patience.

"What do you mean—both times? I've been here more often than that."

Amanda shook her head, wondering if he really didn't realize the truth or if he'd been deluding himself for so long that he really couldn't tell reality from his flamboyant dreams. "I'm afraid you haven't."

He had the grace to look nonplussed. He cleared his throat. "Time has a way of getting away from you. So where is he?"

"Who?"

"The kid. I've been thinking that I'm not getting any younger, and I'd like to see what he's like . . . see how he turned out."

Amanda's temper flared. How dare he think he could walk out of Jeff's life at three and then sashay back into it and expect to pick up where he'd left off?

"He turned out just fine. And his name is Jeff, Deke . . . Jeff!" she cried in a shaking voice. "Or have you forgotten that the same way you seem to have forgotten that you didn't care enough about 'the kid' to send him one penny in sixteen years?"

An unattractive red crept into Deke Farrell's face. "You haven't changed," he said, his smile losing its veneer of pleasantness. "You're still the same frigid self-righteous bitch you were when I left. You still think you have all the answers."

"Self-righteous!" Amanda cried, pushing herself away from the table and leaping to her feet.

"Self-righteous!" Deke shot back, rising and facing her across the expanse of the small circular table. "You never let me forget that you were working so many jobs, how tired you were. But you didn't mind. Hell, no, you didn't mind. You made yourself out as some kind of martyr."

Amanda's eyes widened, the very foundation of her world shaken by his accusation. Was this the thanks she got for working so hard, or had that really been her attitude?

"I was trying to help us get on our feet," she whispered.

"Like hell. You just wanted to be the boss, to control the marriage. All you ever did was harp on making more money."

"Because we didn't have *any*."

"A man likes a woman to depend on him, Amanda, not try and take his place. You never wanted to have any fun. Never wanted to go to the movies or out to eat."

Because we couldn't afford it. The thought screamed silently through her mind.

"And not only that," he told her, shaking his finger in her face, "but you were damn little comfort in bed, Mandy. Once you had the kid, you might just as well have put on a chastity belt."

"Jeff!" Amanda cried. "Dammit, his name is Jeff! And I never denied you my body. Not until I found out about all those other—"

The sentence was never finished. Deke's hand shot out, his palm hitting Amanda's cheek with a loud crack at the exact moment Jeff burst through the door, a

questioning look on his face and a "Whose car?" on his
lips.

When he saw the stranger's hand connect with his
mother's face, sheer disbelief stopped him dead in his
tracks for a millisecond before the surprise was replaced
by an all-consuming rage.

In that split second, Deke's hand fell to his side and he
stood staring at Jeff, comprehension slowly dawning.
Amanda's hand crept to her stinging cheek, aware that
the moment she had dreaded and tried so hard to keep
from happening was suddenly upon her: Jeff and
Deke—face-to-face.

It was funny, but somehow a part of her mind was
able to function on a level above the emotional one.
She'd always thought that Jeff looked like Deke, but he
didn't. He was taller, broader and actually looked more
like her dad. Their voices were nothing alike, either.
Jeff's was huskier and more robust, unlike Deke's prac-
ticed, silky-smooth tones.

Without a word, as Amanda was comparing the two
men, Jeff barreled into the kitchen and grabbed his father by his coat lapels, shaking him like a terrier with a
hapless rat. All Amanda could do was watch. "Don't
touch her!" Jeff snarled. "Don't you ever touch her
again!"

Deke was many things, but he wasn't stupid—and
he'd no doubt had a lot of practice with irate men.
"Jeff," he said in a reasonable, let's-talk-this-over tone,
"you've got this all wrong."

"Do I?" Jeff asked in a low voice. But he released his
hold on his father's coat.

What was Jeff thinking? Amanda wondered, knowing from past experience how persuasive Deke could be.
Was her son wishing he'd had the opportunity to meet

his father before now? Would he think that she had lied about Deke all these years?

Deke smiled engagingly. "I was just—"

"Hitting my mother," Jeff interrupted coldly.

Deke shrugged and straightened his jacket nonchalantly. When he spoke he looked uneasy and his words sounded forced. "A man's got to keep a woman in line. You remember that when you get one."

"You might be interested to know that I already have one. And a daughter."

Deke slapped Jeff on the shoulder with intimate goodwill. "Well, that's great. Maybe I could come by and meet them while I'm in town."

Amanda switched her gaze to Jeff's face to gauge his reaction.

"I don't think so." Jeff's tone was flat, unrelenting, and Deke's facade slipped another betraying notch.

"Hell, I should have known better than to come back to see you—to try to get to know you. I should have known she'd blow bringing you up the same way she blew our marriage. You're just like her. Holier-than-thou, snobbish and ungrateful."

"You've seen me," Jeff said. "And I have no desire to get to know you. But I'm not ungrateful, believe me. I'm very grateful. Grateful that my mother had enough sense to get rid of you. Grateful that I wasn't brought up by someone like you."

Deke's mouth hung open in surprise at the controlled anger in Jeff's voice. He looked from the son he'd lost and then to Amanda, an ugly light in his eyes.

"Now that we know where we stand, why don't you get in your car and go back to whatever rock you crawled out from under?" Jeff said quietly.

"You—" Deke's face was mottled with rage. Hate gleamed in his eyes. After a few seemingly endless seconds he pivoted on his heel and left the room. Jeff followed to make certain that he did leave.

Amanda sank into the chair, the memories of the past mingling with the scene that had just taken place. Tears filled her eyes as the little bit of self-worth she'd struggled so hard to gain slipped slowly from her grasp.

When Jeff came back, he took her in his arms and held her while a deluge of misery and tears flooded her. She cried because she was tired and the emotional scene with Deke had only added to her weariness after a long night of worry. She cried for the loss of her self-respect, which Deke had snatched from her. She wept for the woman she'd thought she was, the woman she wasn't certain she could ever reconstruct the second time.

MUCH LATER, after she'd gotten herself under control and Deke's visit was gradually becoming an unpleasant memory, she asked, "Why did you come over? I thought you'd be at home sleeping or at the hospital."

Jeff smiled wryly. "I was so excited I wanted someone to talk to, to share it with. I couldn't believe it when I let myself in here and I heard what he was saying to you. I don't know how you stuck with him as long as you did."

Amanda's smile might have been a clone of Jeff's. "To hear Deke tell it, everything was my fault."

"You didn't buy in to that guilt, did you?"

She sighed. "I don't know. Maybe he's right. Maybe I—"

The doorbell rang, shattering the uneasy mood building inside her. Her eyes, still red rimmed from her tears, flew to Jeff's.

"Way," she whispered. "We were going to have dinner and go to the hospital."

"And you still are," Jeff told her firmly.

Amanda shook her head. "I can't."

"Look, Mom," Jeff said, rising and heading for the front door. "You've got to go see Heather. She'll wonder what's wrong."

He was right. She had to hold herself together long enough to get through the evening, and then she could wallow in her failures. Her sorrowful gaze followed Jeff from the room.

In a matter of minutes, Way strode into the kitchen, bringing a breath of autumn with him. He squatted beside her chair and took one of her cold hands in his. With the other, Amanda reached out and smoothed the wind-tousled hair near his temple.

"Jeff told me what happened. Are you all right?"

She nodded.

"Do you want to talk about it?" Way asked.

Her voice was barely above a whisper. "No. Not now."

"Okay, then," Way said with an easy smile. "Let's go have dinner and see our new granddaughter."

Amanda didn't argue; she was too tired. As she'd found out too late, it was nice to have a man take charge. Would things have been different sixteen years ago, if she'd only let Deke handle things?

HEATHER WAS ALREADY claiming cabin fever, and the baby, named Leslie Carol, after Heather's mother, was now wrapped up in her pink blanket and lined up in the nursery window along with the other newborns.

Even though Amanda's heart swelled with pride at the sight of Jeff's daughter, even though she made the right comments about how beautiful she was and whose nose she had, Deke's unannounced visit played through her mind like a recurring nightmare.

She was thankful when Way pulled to a stop in her driveway, thankful that it was only a matter of minutes until she could give in to the depression threatening to tow her under.

Way unlocked the kitchen door and followed her inside. He knew she was hurting and had noticed the faraway look in her eyes. "How about some coffee?" he asked.

Amanda turned, her expression evasive, closed. "I'm really tired, Way. Maybe tomorrow."

Taking her into his arms, even though he knew that was the last thing she wanted, he said, "I'll be playing tomorrow and I haven't held you in days."

Despite the turmoil raging inside her, Amanda couldn't help leaning against him and, feeling the slight relaxing of her body, Way drew her nearer.

"Thanksgiving is getting closer," he said, and immediately he felt her stiffen in his embrace. Way's eyes took on a grim, determined light. As Jeff had warned him, Deke Farrell had done a number on Amanda, but something told him that if he gave her more time now, she would only use it to make up reasons for not building a life together.

He rubbed his chin back and forth against the top of her shining head. "I've tried to be patient, tried to give you some room, but I want an answer, Mandy. And I want it tonight."

For what seemed an eternity, she was still in his arms. He didn't push, didn't force her answer. But he held his breath, praying and hoping. . . .

Finally, she raised her head and tipped it back to look up at him. Her violet eyes were tear spangled and full of misery. "I'm sorry, but I—"

Not wanting to hear what he knew her answer would be, Way's mouth swooped down and took hers in a

bruising kiss, which she answered with a mind-
destroying desire. Even Deke's visit couldn't affect her
response. They broke apart, both trembling and out of
breath. Way supposed that he should at least be thankful for her passion, but when Amanda lifted her eyes to
his, her answer hadn't changed.

Thrusting her from him, Way spun on his heel and
strode the length of the kitchen. She watched as he raked
his hands through his hair and locked his fingers behind
his head. "Why?" he ground out in a husky voice.

"Because I've tried marriage, and I failed...
miserably."

He turned to look at her. "It failed, Mandy, not you.
From what Jeff's told me, which isn't much, your ex
must be a real winner. He had a responsibility to you,
and he didn't live up to it."

"If I hadn't tried to do so much, maybe he would
have...done better."

"And maybe you'd have wound up on the streets."

Amanda didn't hear. She was too wrapped up in her
what-might-have-beens. She stood near the sink, her
arms crossed over her breasts, her eyes filled with doubts
and fears and the reflections of her shattered hopes.

"He's a manipulator, Amanda. He knows he was
wrong, and he's trying to shift the blame to you, because he knows you'll let him."

She looked at Way then, and shook her head. "It's
never just one person's fault a marriage breaks up. There
are always two sides. I think I must have destroyed
something in him, even though I was only trying to
help."

"Amanda—"

"He said I wanted to be the boss. That I set myself up
to be some k-kind of a...martyr."

Way crossed the room and took her shoulders in his hands. "Amanda. Don't let him do this to you—to us."

"We're too different, Way," she told him. "We come from different worlds."

"Then I'll leave my world and become a part of yours."

"You can't do that. You're Way Dalton, superstar."

"Dammit, I'll become Mr. Amanda Farrell, if that's what it takes."

"It won't work," she said adamantly.

Way released her, his agitation obvious. "Why won't it?"

"It isn't you—it's me. And I'm too afraid of making another mistake to chance it again. I love you so much that if I failed you the way I did him—"

"You didn't fail him, Amanda. He failed himself. *And* you and Jeff," Way pointed out.

She only offered him a sad smile and went on talking as if he hadn't spoken. "I couldn't bear not being what you wanted or needed, and I don't think I have the strength or will to build my life a second time."

"That won't ever happen," he told her.

"Can you guarantee it?" she asked.

The futility of their situation hit Way suddenly. Amanda wasn't going to change her mind. At least not now. His own heartache thickened his voice. "Life doesn't come with guarantees, Amanda. It only comes with hopes and dreams, and the will to keep trying no matter what. If we love each other, that should be enough to give us the will to keep trying."

"I—"

He placed his fingertips over her lips to stop her from saying no again. "Don't. I can't stand to hear it again." He turned to go, and when he got to the back door he stopped. Then, while she waited to see if he would turn and say something else to try to change her mind, Way opened the door and stepped outside. Into the night. Out of her life.

THE NEXT FEW DAYS were the longest Amanda had ever lived through. She watched the two local Royals games on television, having to content herself with seeing Way play ball while her heart taunted her that she could be spending every night in his arms. When Amanda learned from Jeff that the team had gone back to Atlanta, she began to see how long the rest of her life would really be.

Heather and Leslie came home the day Way left, and Amanda had spent the past two days with them while Jeff worked at Wayfarers. Heather knew that her father and Amanda had parted on less than the best of terms, but, afraid that her new relationship with Amanda might be jeopardized if she pursued the topic, she didn't press.

Jeff had no such qualms, and had told his mother without mincing words that she was a fool.

"Deke Farrell is an A-number-one jerk, Mom!" he told her.

"I know."

"You're none of the things he said."

"Then why did he say them?" Amanda countered.

"Because he knows he's screwed his life up, and he's got to blame somebody!" Jeff said, echoing Way's view of the situation. Then, in a gesture that underscored the role reversal their relationship seemed to have taken on since Deke's visit, Jeff forced her to look at him. "You're not selfish, and you've never played the martyr. You're not bossy and you don't want to take a man's place."

"How do you know?" she asked, her troubled eyes probing his.

"Because I've lived with you for almost twenty years. You're the most giving person I've ever known. You're a hard worker and you set high standards for yourself and everyone around you, but that doesn't make you the things Deke said you were. If you hadn't done what you did back then, we'd have probably starved to death."

"And then again," she said, obliged to play devil's advocate, "maybe if I hadn't taken the load, he would have. Maybe I damaged his masculine pride, because by taking more and more on myself, I insinuated—on a subconscious level—that he couldn't take care of us."

Jeff shook his head. "He doesn't have pride, Mom. He has ego. And look what he's done with himself all these years he hasn't had you to blame. Has he gone out and made something of himself? No. You said that he was on top this time because he'd met a woman. She's taking care of *him*, I guarantee—not the other way around."

During the next couple of days, Amanda had pondered Jeff's assessment of the situation and come to the unsettling conclusion that he was probably right, at least to a point. She wondered how her son had gained so much wisdom in such a short time. It never occurred to her that she'd had anything to do with it. What did occur to her was that she'd let her old doubts and fears play havoc with her happiness. And, while she still wasn't certain that she could make a go of things with Way, she did accept her part of the blame for her first marriage failing. Her part, but no more.

IT WAS THE SIXTH GAME of the Series, and Amanda was watching it in the sanctuary of her living room. It was beginning to look as if the play would go into the seventh and final game. According to the sportscasters, it had been an exciting series, two strong teams eking out each run by hard work and strategy.

Amanda watched Way step up to the plate, watched as he and the pitcher sized each other up, watched the pitch and Way's swing, which contacted with the ball and sent it up and out toward the spectators. But this time, instead of going over, it hit the wall and bounced back, throwing the outfielder—whose calculations had told him the ball was headed out of the stadium—out of step.

Amanda was on her feet, yelling along with the crowd in the packed Atlanta stadium. Way was almost to third by the time the chagrined outfielder got hold of the ball and fired it to the second baseman, who threw it home. It was a race between Way and the ball, and Way made the slide to home plate among cries of jubilation and a cloud of dust, somehow sending the catcher for a tumble in the process. The umpire pronounced him safe, and the catcher, who had landed on Way, struggled to his feet to offer Way a hand up.

The cameras zeroed in, and Amanda saw Way reach for his knee and shake his head. The commentators tossed theories about what had happened back and forth, but Amanda didn't hear them. Several men came out of the dugout. Someone said that one of them was a doctor. The next thing she saw was a stretcher being brought out and Way being helped onto it.

The last thing she heard before she ran to the telephone were the words, "Dalton has a history of knee problems. I hope this doesn't put him out of the Series."

CHAPTER SEVENTEEN

"JEFF!" AMANDA CRIED into the receiver as soon as he picked up the phone.

"I saw it," he said, bypassing his hello and getting straight to the point.

"What can we do?"

Jeff heard the panic in his mother's voice and tried to temper it with his own calmness. He could hear Heather's laments from the living room. "Right now, let's hang up and listen to what the announcers have to say. This may not be as serious as it looked, once the doctor checks him out."

Jeff's matter-of-fact tone did do a lot to settle Amanda down. He was right. She was overreacting again. It seemed to be a trend these days. "Okay, Jeff. I'll call you after we hear something."

"No. You let me call you."

As Jeff predicted, shortly before the game ended, the announcers let the world know what had happened. Somehow, when Way had slid into home and knocked the catcher over, he had twisted his knee, which the catcher had then fallen on. The consensus was that he would definitely be out of the Series.

"I talked to the manager and Jose," Jeff told her when he called Amanda thirty minutes later.

"How's Way?"

"In a lot of pain. Jose says the doctor is talking operation, even though they haven't even X-rayed the knee yet."

"Operation? But hasn't he had it operated on before?"

"Yeah. A couple of times," Jeff told her.

"It can't be good to have so much surgery, can it?" she asked, unease settling inside her like the throbbing of a bad tooth.

"I'll be honest with you, Mom. Jose says that if they operate this time, Way can hang it up."

"Hang it up?"

"Yeah. His career in baseball will be over."

OVER. His career will be over. The words became a refrain in Amanda's brain. Late on the night of his injury, Way was flown back to Kansas City by private jet so that the team's orthopedic man could perform the surgery, which had been deemed necessary, after all. The problem was extensive, and even though Jeff tried to explain it, all Amanda knew was that Way wouldn't be on first base for the Royals the next spring...or ever.

She cared for the baby while Heather and Jeff sat at the hospital during the surgery. She called to check on him. She prayed for another chance. Then, on the second day after the operation, she gathered up her courage and went to see him.

They had just moved Way from the wheelchair back into bed when she arrived, and she could hear his curses from outside the door. The two nurses, who were just leaving, gave her an encouraging smile and told her to go on in. Pushing the door open on silent hinges, Amanda stepped inside. Way lay on his back, his leg—in a cast from his toes to the top of his thigh—elevated on some pillows. His eyes were closed and so were his hands, closed over fistfuls of sheets and blankets in an effort to will the pain away. A fine film of perspiration glistened on his cheeks, which were devoid of their usual, healthy color.

As if he felt her scrutiny, Way opened his eyes and saw her standing near the door. "What are you doing here?" he asked, raising his head and glaring at her.

Amanda took two hesitant steps toward the bed. "I . . . wanted to come and see how you were doing."

"Well, you've seen," he said, his tone gruff and angry. "Now why don't you go back to your safe little world?"

Amanda couldn't help the pain that knifed through her at his unexpected sarcasm, just as Way didn't miss the pain he'd inflicted reflected in her eyes. His head fell heavily back onto the pillow, and he spoke to the ceiling. "I hurt like hell, okay?"

"I'm sorry. How long will you be in the cast?"

"Too long," he snarled, shifting slightly and letting loose another round of curses.

Amanda closed the distance to the bed and covered his hand with hers.

"I don't need your pity, Amanda," he told her, his smile nothing but a bitter twist of his lips. "And I don't want you—"

"Time for your shot, Mr. Dalton," the nurse said, blissfully unaware of the tension in the room.

"Go home, Amanda," Way said, targeting her with his relentless gaze. "Go home and leave me alone."

ALONE. Two weeks after the Series, and almost that long
at home, made Way aware of just how alone he was.
October had eased into November with wonderful fall
weather—cold nights and sunny days that were chilly but
still hadn't flexed their wintery muscles.

The Royals had won the World Series, and he'd cele-
brated with a glass of grape juice alone in a hospital
room while the rest of the team and the city partied for
at least a week. Loyally, his teammates had stopped by
to see him when everything was over—all of them.
Without fail they were cheerful, optimistic and full of
plans for the next season when Way would break Aaron's record.

Without exception, each had known he was lying.

There would be no season for him next spring, or any
other. Aaron's record would stand—at least until someone else came along to challenge it. Waylon Dalton
hadn't and wouldn't take it down. His career was over.
Finished.

Feeling a fresh surge of the futile anger that seemed to
be his constant companion, Way slammed his fist on the
arm of the sofa and cursed the fates for striking him
down at such a crucial time. All he'd needed was one
more year. One more good year and he would have gone
down in baseball history.

He felt lost, adrift. Always before when he'd ended a
season, he'd known that in a few months he would be
back at practice. He'd had a purpose. A goal. Now all
he had was time on his hands and a pocketful of memories to take out and reminisce over as he grew old.

Alone.

Alone and afraid.

Carol was gone. Heather was gone. And Amanda was
gone. Like a fool he'd sent her away, because he didn't
want her to see him at his lowest or allow her to change

her mind out of pity. The truth was that he'd spouted a lot of stuff to Amanda that he wasn't certain was valid anymore. Being vulnerable himself, and being plagued with different versions of the insecurity she faced, gave him a new perspective, and he saw how easy it was to get down on yourself. He saw it, but right now, he didn't care.

He stared out the window at the shedding trees, rubbing his mustache absently with his forefinger. Everything he'd ever wanted had been taken from him or denied him. He was a forty-year-old man with nowhere to go and no one to go with.

He was alone, angry and afraid.

"WHAT ARE WE GOING to do with them?" Heather asked Jeff a few days later.

Jeff laid baby Leslie in her cradle and planted his hands on his hips. "I swear, I don't know."

"Muffy says Daddy is driving her crazy since he's been home."

"I know. Every time I go over, he's hardly civil."

"He loves her, Jeff."

"I know that, and so do you, but I think he's forgotten it. Mom went to see him in the hospital, and he told her not to pity him. That he didn't want her."

"Well, Thanksgiving is next week, and I'm not sure I can manage the two of them in the same house with all this—" she gestured vaguely with both hands "—going on."

"Do you think he'll come over?" Jeff asked, surprised that Heather thought Way would.

"Of course he will—it's been planned forever. He's not crazy. He loves her and he'll want to see her, even if they don't say a dozen words." Her brow furrowed.

"You don't think your mom will renege on the invitation, do you?"

Jeff smiled. "Not a chance. For the same reasons."

AMANDA HAD JUST taken the turkey from the freezer when the doorbell rang. Wiping her hands on her apron, she called, "Come on in, Steve. It's open!"

Steve Harris came in, accompanied by a blast of cold air. The weather had finally given in to the not-so-gentle urgings of winter. The temperatures had dipped well below freezing the previous two nights. Kansas City residents had sighed and turned up their thermostats, knowing that despite the date on the calendar, winter had officially arrived.

"Wow!" Steve said. "It's cold out there."

Amanda nodded. The weather was the least of her worries.

"I really appreciate your help, Ms Farrell," he told her, the sincerity in his blue eyes genuine and undeniable. "I know you're busy this week, but the test tomorrow is a really tough one."

"No problem," she assured him as he pulled off his coat and sat down at the kitchen table. "How about some hot chocolate?"

"Sounds great!"

Amanda opened the prepackaged mix, added water to the waiting mugs and popped them into the microwave. "Where are you spending Thanksgiving?"

"I'm going to one of the guys on the football team's house. How about you?"

"I'm having Jeff, Heather and the baby over. And Heather's father," she added.

Steve grinned. "I still can't believe it. You don't look like a grandmother."

"Thanks."

"So how's Dalton doing since his surgery?" Steve asked.

The question threw Amanda momentarily. "I, uh . . . Jeff says that he won't get the cast off until after Thanksgiving."

"I imagine he's really down."

The microwave signaled that the chocolate was hot, and Amanda retrieved the steaming mugs and set them on the table. "Down? What do you mean?"

"Depressed," Steve explained. "I know I'd be lower than a snake's belly. He's been playing since he was nineteen, and suddenly his career is over, man. Over."

Amanda let Steve's observation soak into her mind.

"He'd probably be mad about it, and then, if he hasn't already, he'll get to feeling sorry for himself."

Amanda's forehead puckered in a frown. "How do you know how he's feeling?"

Steve smiled. "I was laid up with mono part of the season my junior year in high school. I was mad at the world in general. It just didn't seem fair. I hated the rest of the team for being healthy and the cheerleaders for being so damned cheerful when they came to see me. I had a chip on my shoulder as big as Texas." He chuckled. "I remember that one of the guys came by to ask me about a play and I thought he was patronizing me or something. Man, I was furious. It was a really bad time for me, but it wasn't until after I got better that I realized what was really wrong."

"What was that?" Amanda asked.

"I was scared. Scared that I'd never get to play again. And I didn't know what I'd do without the game. I imagine that's about where Mr. Dalton is—thinking that he doesn't have anything to look forward to. It'll take him a while to adjust."

Steve pulled out his books and got out his notes, but Amanda's mind was working, thinking, trying to match up what Steve had told her with Way's recent actions.

When Thanksgiving morning arrived she had decided that Steve Harris was one sharp kid. By giving her a glimpse into the thought process of an athlete, he'd more than paid her back for all the tutoring. He might have saved both her and Way—from themselves.

By the time Way, Jeff, Heather and Leslie arrived, the tantalizing aroma of dressing had found its way into the living room. Amanda rushed them inside, directing Heather and Jeff to the bedroom with the sleeping baby and holding the door open for Way, who, even on crutches, looked devastatingly handsome in one-legged Levi's, a bulky sweater and a sheepskin-lined, hip-length coat of tan suede.

"Let me take your coat," she told him, closing the door.

Way's eyes, unguarded for a brief second, met hers, and without warning came the thought she'd tried so hard to hold at bay since she'd risen at five that morning. If she hadn't been so hardheaded, if Way had been granted his wish, they'd be celebrating Thanksgiving as husband and wife. Then her defenses were quickly erected again and there was cool politeness where the vulnerability had existed only a heartbeat before.

"Thanks," he said, "but I'll have to sit down first."

Amanda smiled. "Of course. I wasn't thinking."

He made his way to the sofa and propped his crutches nearby. He sat down, and shrugging out of the coat, handed it to her. Amanda carried it to the hall closet, unable to resist burying her face in the fleecy lining that still carried Way's warmth and the familiar scent of him. She closed her eyes and held the coat to her, hugging it and breathing in a thousand memories.

"Amanda?"

Heather's voice brought Amanda's eyes open and her thoughts back to the present with a jolt. "Yes?" she queried, guiltily reaching for a hanger and slipping the heavy coat over it.

"Is there anything I can help you with while Leslie is sleeping?" Heather asked, giving no sign that she'd witnessed Amanda's temporary weakness.

"Sure," Amanda said with a smile. "We'll give Jeff a break and you can make the salad."

Heather smiled back. "Sounds good to me." She looked uncomfortable for a moment, and then, as if she'd made up her mind, she plunged ahead. "I just wanted to say that I'm thankful today because Leslie has you for a grandmother and I have you for a mother."

Amanda's heart stopped for an instant. Tears stung beneath her eyelids. She couldn't have asked for a better Thanksgiving gift. Moving nearer, she gathered Heather into a close embrace. "Oh, Heather. Thank you."

When they drew apart, they were both a little misty-eyed. Heather's smile was shaky, but her voice held determination as she said, "Now, if we can only make Daddy see what an ass he's being, we'll have it made." At the surprised look on Amanda's face, she added, "He loves you, Amanda. Just be patient."

Two hours later the traditional dinner was over, and the dishes, with Jeff and Heather's help, were cleaned up. To everyone's surprise the meal hadn't been the ordeal they'd expected, because they had all gone out of their way to be pleasant and obliging. Jeff and Heather had bundled up and gone for a walk around the block, and Way was watching the sleeping Leslie while Amanda finished putting away her good china and silver.

A loud squall from the living room sent a pan crashing to the floor and Amanda racing toward the noise. Way—red-faced and beginning to sweat—was halfway through changing Leslie's diaper, and from the sound of things, she wasn't happy about the way he was doing it.

Without stopping to think, without asking, Amanda knelt by the sofa and, literally moving his hands out of the way, fastened the tapes of the disposable diaper.

Her back brushed Way's good leg, and the scent of her perfume drifted up toward his nostrils. He closed his eyes, as if by closing them he could block out the memories that were haunting him. Memories of her body bare and beautiful, memories of her hands moving over him, driving him to distraction. He wanted to reach out and touch her hair, wanted to ask her if she was as tired as she looked. Instead, he watched as she closed the fasteners on the stretch outfit the baby wore and picked her up. Leslie quieted almost instantly, and holding their granddaughter close, Amanda sat down beside him.

"You must have lost your touch, Dalton."

"Obviously," Way said, wondering how he was going to sit there and make idle conversation with her until Jeff and Heather got back. Thankfully, he was spared further torture when the newlyweds burst through the front door, breathing heavily from the icy wind.

"You're back pretty quick," Amanda said.

"We only made one turn around the block," Jeff said. "It's too cold to be out there."

"Has she been crying?" Heather asked.

"Only for a moment," Amanda assured her. "Your dad and I are out of practice. It took us both to get her diaper changed."

Heather laughed and reached for her daughter. "She's probably hungry. It's time for her to nurse."

"You do that, and I'll take a nap," Jeff said.

"Let me get you an afghan to cover up with," Amanda said, rising and following the younger couple from the room.

Way watched them go and envied the closeness he could feel among the trio. Heather and Amanda had become good friends. He was glad, but it only added to his own misery. He was the odd man out—all the way around. He slid to the opposite end of the sofa and reached for the telephone, knowing suddenly that there was no way that he could spend the next few hours alone with Amanda. Not if he wanted to keep his sanity.

When Amanda reentered the room a few moments later, Way had somehow managed not only to get his coat out of the closet, but to put it on. He was standing at the front door, watching for a cab.

"Where are you going?" she asked.

"The weather is killing my knee," he lied. "I think I'll call it a day."

Amanda laced her hands together and stared at a spot on the tiled entryway. "I know you don't want to hear this, but I'm going to say it anyway." She lifted her gaze to his. "I'm thankful this Thanksgiving for having known you. You made me grow as a person, you gave me a sense of self-worth I hadn't had in years."

Way watched the determination in her eyes change to softness.

"And I'm thankful that only your knee was hurt and that you won't have to spend the rest of your life in a wheelchair, like some other people do."

Surprise rendered Way speechless.

Amanda moved to within a few inches of him. "And I'm thankful that you were right about Jeff and Heather—you were right about love."

"What are you talking about?" he managed to get out around the lump forming in his throat.

"You said that life didn't come with any guarantees, and that no matter what the problems were, if our children really loved each other, their love would be enough to make things right. You said the same thing about us, but I couldn't see it until now. I was a fool."

A car horn sounded outside the house. Way didn't speak—didn't move.

She lifted her palm to his cheek. "I love you, Way Dalton. More than anything. More than anyone. And I'm still scared to death to try to make a marriage work. But the difference is that now I'm willing to try."

He looked as if he wanted to say something, but the cabbie honked again, an impatient sound that drew his head toward the door. Amanda lowered her hand and stepped aside. Way looked at her for a moment, and then, at the sound of another grating honk, he turned and opened the door, leaving her without a word and without a backward glance.

Amanda watched with a soul-deep sorrow as the driver helped Way get in the cab. But she didn't cry.

Not until they pulled away from the curb and disappeared around the corner.

AFTER A NIGHT spent mostly tossing and turning and wondering if anything she'd said to Way had penetrated the barriers he'd put up between himself and the world after his accident, Amanda finally drifted off to sleep. She woke up at two the following afternoon to find that, as the weatherman had predicted, the cold winds had brought along the first winter snow. Sick at heart, the beauty of the blinding white blanket escaped her. All she knew was that it was cold. As cold as the lump of pain that nestled like a frozen snowball inside her.

Not bothering with makeup, she put on a sweat suit and tennis shoes and fixed herself a bowl of tomato soup and some hot tea. She tried to read a book, but it didn't hold her interest. At five, in desperation, she turned on the television, only to find that its offerings weren't much more interesting than the discarded book. She had her choice among two game shows and a local sports show. Amanda was reaching to turn it off when the camera pulled back and the host announced that their celebrity sports star for the week was Waylon Dalton of the Kansas City Royals.

Amanda sank back onto the sofa and curled her feet beneath her, drinking in the sight of him.

"So how's the leg?" the host asked, gesturing toward the crutches leaning against the chair.

"As good as can be expected," Way said, flashing the grin that had accelerated the pulses of several million American women. "The cast comes off today."

"There's been a rumor floating around town that the injury might put an end to your career. Is there any truth to that?"

"Yes, Bob, I'm afraid it is true. That's why I wanted to come on the show. I'm officially announcing my retirement from baseball."

Amanda's heart dropped to the pit of her stomach.

"There's no chance it'll be better in time?"

"Maybe if I was younger, it would be worth the time. But at my age, taking a year off and trying to make a comeback is just too hard." The smile returned and he said, "I'll leave it to the youngsters coming along."

"So what are your plans for the future?" Bob Downes asked, leaning across the desk with real interest on his face. "What do you do with yourself after playing ball for twenty years?"

"Well, as most everyone knows, I own a couple of restaurants. I want to make a go of them, and spend some time with my new granddaughter."

"I heard about that. Congratulations. She was born during the Series, wasn't she?"

"That's right."

"Anything else? Fishing? Hunting?"

"Well, maybe something else," Way admitted.

"What's that?"

"I hope to be getting married soon. By Christmas."

Married? Amanda's heart began a slow, expectant thumping in her breast.

"Hope to?" Bob asked with raised eyebrows.

"Yeah," Way said, laughing self-consciously. "I haven't asked her yet."

Bob laughed. "Well . . . no time like the present. Ask. It'll be a first for the show."

Serious, almost intense, Way looked directly into the camera and said, "Are you watching, Mandy? If so— how 'bout it? Will you marry me?"

Tears welled in Amanda's eyes, and before she could do more than whisper a fervent yes, the doorbell rang. The screen was filled with a commercial. Angry that she'd have to wait to hear the rest of the program, she rose and went to the door. Hardly masking her irritation, she flung it open. Way—minus his cast—stood there with a cane in one hand and cradling a sheaf of red roses in the crook of his arm.

Amanda looked from him back to the television where he once again sat, chatting with Bob Downes.

"How . . . ?"

"We taped this morning." When she didn't say anything, he asked testily, "Are you going to let me in or not?"

Amanda stepped aside and, leaning heavily on the cane and grimacing in pain, Way came through the door.

"You're hurting!" she cried, going to him and taking the roses he thrust at her. She put her arm around him and let him lean on her as they made their way slowly to the living room.

He tried to smile, a pitiful effort that was a total failure. "Yeah. It hurts like Hades. They wanted me to keep my crutches, but I nixed that."

"Why?" she demanded as he lowered himself into the corner of the sofa.

"A man can't propose marriage on crutches," Way said, stretching his leg out in front of him.

Amanda felt a lightness start to replace the heaviness in her heart. "But a man just did—on television," she said, rubbing her lips against the softness of the flower petals.

This time his attempt to smile was successful. "So he did."

"Did he mean it?" Amanda asked, placing the roses on the coffee table and facing him with her heart in her throat and love in her eyes.

"He meant it." Way's voice was husky with emotion, and Amanda thought she saw the glimmer of tears in his eyes.

"Why now?" she asked, perching on the edge of the sofa.

"Because I have a new lifetime goal." Way reached out and slid his hand beneath the silky curtain of her hair. "And that's to make you my wife. To make up for all the hurt you've been through. To love you so much that you'll forget it . . . all of it."

Amanda's throat tightened with tears. "I've already forgotten it."

"Are you sure you want to marry a forty-year-old, washed-up ball player?"

"Yes," she said, leaning closer to kiss him.

"With a bad knee?"

She nodded. Their lips were a breath away from touching when he pulled back. "One more thing I need to tell you."

"Which is?"

"I'm also a grandfather."

Amanda nodded soberly. "That's a pretty big problem."

"Insurmountable?" he asked with a smile.

"That depends. Do you love me?"

"More than life," he told her.

"Then that's enough."

"Are you sure?"

"I have it on very good authority that it's more than enough," she whispered as his lips covered hers.

EPILOGUE

A LUSTY CRY rent the dark quiet of the night.

Amanda poked Way in the ribs with her elbow. "It's your turn to get up with the baby," she mumbled.

Way sighed deeply and flipped over onto his back. "It's your turn."

"Way..." she groaned, fumbling in the dark for the bedside light. "I told you this wasn't a good idea."

"Okay, okay," he muttered, throwing his legs over the edge of the bed and standing up. "But Leslie will probably always remember me as the nice grandparent."

"You are," Amanda said with a sleepy smile. "You're very nice." She crossed her arms behind her head and watched him leave the room, thinking how handsome he was, how sexy he looked in his low-cut underwear and how much she liked being married to him in spite of the fact that he wanted her to roll out of bed at seven on Saturday mornings.

"And you're a con artist," he grumbled over his shoulder.

"Dalton!" she called as he reached the door.

He turned and quirked one eyebrow in question.

"Did anyone ever tell you you've got a cute butt?"

"Flattery will get you a quick roll in the hay, lady," he threatened.

"Promises, promises."

She heard him chuckling as he went down the hall. Turning onto her side, Amanda listened to his deep voice as he changed and fed Leslie. Jeff and Heather had gone away for the weekend—miraculously there was a group who *did* like one of Jeff's songs—and considering that the couple hadn't had a honeymoon, Way and Amanda felt they couldn't say no when they were asked to keep Leslie, despite Amanda's doubts about an entire weekend with a baby.

Spring training had begun, and so far Way didn't seem too despondent. He'd gone out to watch the first practice and come back more quiet than she'd seen him in a long time. But soon he'd bounced back and started telling her of his plans to expand Wayfarers to Saint Louis. Life as Mrs. Waylon Dalton was good, she thought. Very good....

Some time later, the feel of the bed giving and Way's arms closing around her roused her from her light doze.

"Is Leslie okay?" she asked, moving her head to accommodate his lips, which were searching for the sensitive place behind her ear.

"Sleeping like a baby," he said, chuckling. Pulling her back against him, he captured Amanda's breasts in his hands and whispered, "Are you sure there's no way I can talk you into having one of our own?"

Amanda turned in his arms and pressed her lips to his neck. "I think I'm too old for this on a permanent basis." She raked her nails lightly up his hair-dusted thigh. "But..." she said softly, encouragingly, "don't let that stop you from trying."

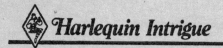

Harlequin Intrigue

Two exciting new stories each month.

Each title mixes a contemporary, sophisticated romance with the surprising twists and turns of a puzzler... romance with "something more."

Because romance can be quite an adventure.

Romance, Suspense and Adventure

Step into a world of pulsing adventure, gripping
emotion and lush sensuality with these evocative
love stories penned by today's best-selling authors
in the highest romantic tradition. Pursuing their
passionate dreams against a backdrop of the past's
most colorful and dramatic moments, our vibrant
heroines and dashing heroes will make history
come alive for you.

Watch for two new Harlequin Historicals each
month, available wherever Harlequin books are
sold. History was never so much fun—you won't
want to miss a single moment!

Harlequin Superromance

COMING NEXT MONTH